Destiny's Game
"Love or Honour"
Book 1

Marcus Dizon

DESTINY'S GAME "LOVE OR HONOUR" BOOK 1

Contents

v

To my beloved mother, finding the right words to convey my gratitude for having you as my mother is a challenge. May this book serve as a token of my heartfelt thanks from the very first day I stepped into this world. And here we go, I made it that filled with immense feeling of being grateful to the universe and back to everyone who really matters to me and to the rest of people who have been part of this journey of mine, thanks for being there as a witness to this kind of odyssey. And to my mentor, my gratitude is eternal for everything. Believe it or not, I could still remember everything how we started, and it was such a remarkable event about the profound exchange of words between us before we started, even though I may took long but nevertheless, you provided the finest and best way of teaching, so l played my part as a protégé to this first novel of mine.

Disclaimer:

This is a work of fiction. Names, characters, businesses, places, events, and incidents are either the products of the author's imagination or used in a fictitious manner. Any resemblance to actual persons, living or dead, or actual events is purely coincidental. Copyright © 2024. All rights reserved. It is prohibited to copy, duplicate, or reproduce any part of the story without the author's permission.

One

PROLOGUE

It was quarter to six in the evening and the grand hall was all set in detail. The grand hall itself was within a huge building isolated from the prying eyes of commoners even far from the suburbs, exuding exclusivity and wealth. The interior walls were accented with off-white colour and minimal floral design. The round banquet tables and chairs adorned with golden satin fabric with velvet red table runners in the middle. The grand gesture was the centrepiece atop the table runners. Costing an average employee's daily wage tax, it was an eye-catcher that was adorned by carnations, oriental lilies, red roses, snapdragons, thryptomenes, and silver suede that were accented by a single bloom of phalaenopsis for each set. Smaller and taller cocktail tables, where the guests could stand by as they wait for the main event and entrees to be served, with a similar theme as the banquet tables were set by the external side areas of the hall. The beige coloured ceiling had three elegant spiral crystal chandeliers, emanating a subtle warm yellow glow that gave an ostentatious ambiance to every area of the hall. A euphonious overture played by the orchestra in the far corner of the hall was being drowned by the idle talk of guests in their nightgowns and suits who were also served by the well-uniformed bussers in black with aperitifs and a variety of food canapés. Among the guests, two men in black tuxedos and bow ties were standing by the cocktail table in the front area of the grand hall and silently observing their surroundings.

"They are all insignificant to me," one of the two men said in an almost indescribable tone. His hair was dark and clean cut with facial features that could be compared to classic Hollywood era like James Dean and Marlon Brando. They were in the back side area of the hall by one of the cocktail tables. He even didn't bother to glance at his companion as he held his dry wine with his right hand. He gently sipped while his left hand rested inside the left pocket of his dress pants, biding his time to scrutinise whoever caught his eye in front of them by glancing around the hall.

"I have no objection to that, sir," replied the other man who seemed to be a subordinate of the first man. His hair was blond and set by pomade.

"I can't wait for the inevitable main event," a ghastly smile formed on the first man's lips as he looked at his trusted man. He then grabbed a piece of peat-smoked salmon with daikon horseradish butter caviar on rye from a passing banquet server. He downed the appetiser with a sip of his drink. He then became jovial as he looked at his companion.

"That's why I personally chose you. You are able to make this grand event possible," he uttered as he grabbed a piece of white napkin from the cocktail table and gently wiped his lips. His face returned to its nonchalant gaze towards the guests.

"It's my honour to work for you, sir," the blond replied. "My group informed me that all of them will be here tonight, a hundred and ten to be exact. I have also made sure this venue has been soundproofed," he added as a man in white suit approached them.

"Hi! You look familiar, but I can't seem to remember your name. Care to remind me?" The man in the white suit playfully directed towards the black-haired man who casually smiled at the newcomer and motioned to his companion to keep quiet.

"Oh, I am just nobody," he simply replied nonchalantly as his gaze remained on the newcomer's ungraceful gesture towards them.

"Fair enough. If you say you're a nobody, still, I have no doubt you would be worth my attention," he showed a naughty and playful smirk, "anyway, see you around boys," he added before leaving and greeting every person he passed by as he went towards the middle main part of the hall, unbeknownst of the fiendish smiles of the two men when he left.

"For now, you may not know my name. But when the show starts, everyone in this room shall know and remember me. It is your destiny to be here and meet your fate," the black-haired said under his breath that the man who left missed it and his companion could barely hear. He started to tap the oakwood cocktail table before he continued in the similar tone, "I started from nothing to have everything, and nobody can stop me."

"Such a nuisance, sir," said the blond pertaining to the man who just left.

"Nevermind him. On the contrary, I was actually amused by his advances," contradicted by the jet-black haired man, "for now, don't mind him and await my command."

"Of course, sir," the man replied and resumed observing their surroundings silently. The silence started to be deafening between the two amidst the noisy chuntering of the guests and the symphonious melody of the quartet in the far corner of the room.

The opening of the event was cued by the sound of a bell as a woman in an all-black corporate attire walked up the platform. The golden badge on the left side of her uniform shimmered against the light shone by the chandeliers above.

The raven-haired man paid no attention to the bell nor the woman walking up the platform. He wanted for him and his companion to be the last to proceed to the main area of the hall.

As he waited for every guest to proceed to the main area of the hall, he discreetly signalled the blond guy to approach him. He whispered covertly to him to gather his team to thoroughly inspect the venue, inside and out, ensuring every necessary detail was in place and ready. The blond man nodded to signal his comprehension of the superior's command and left the table leaving his boss alone momentarily.

The black-haired man, alone, decided to inspect the area and how his trusted man prepared the plan. He briskly walked towards the vestibule while observing how the blond man was gesturing to his team to start the preparations. He noticed the bussers started to clear the cocktail tables while some started preparing the banquet tables. He saw the blond man then engaged in conversation with an asian waiter, who was gathering the used stemware and mingling plates. After a few unnoticeable signals, both made their way towards the main area of the hall.

A couple minutes later, outside the vestibule and in the corridor, the black-haired man crossed paths with a uniformed staff from the audio-visual team. With some inconspicuous nods, the uniformed staff headed towards another man wearing the same uniform. The two men from the audio-visual team whispered to each other as he watched from afar. The two men, then, went to their respective consoles seemingly getting ready. A smile formed as he felt satisfaction with how his team was efficiently preparing. In his thoughts, he would not allow any miscalculations and he was determined to put his plans into action. He retraced his steps towards the main hall. He was met by two security guards who greeted him with polite smiles to which he casually nodded in return.

As the black-haired man entered the main hall, he saw the table in the middlemost part ready. The table was specially reserved for him. There were already a male and a female staff who were waiting for him to be seated so they could start serving the entrees and drinks. He stared at a particular table that was two tables in front of his reserved table. Satisfied with every detail he strictly commanded to the blond man, he started to make his way to his reserved table.

He once again glanced at the entirety of the main hall as he was reverently greeted by the two-wait staff. As he was seated by the male staff, the female staff served him the main entrée. Except for the table reserved for him, the other banquet tables could seat ten persons who were also being served with their food. The first entrée was asparagus and crème fraiche vol-au-vents, while its alternative for the other guests was kingfish crudo with parsley and preserved lemon dressing which was part of a three course meal. He felt several eyes bore on him being in the middle of the hall but was not bothered or he did not really care at all. Within his earshot and at the table besides his, he heard two women talking with each other and within his peripheral vision.

"Ugh, she looks awful in that dress," the woman in the dirty-white vintage evening dress with short and curly locks said pertaining to the middle-aged woman in front of them.

"I agree! And look at her purse, it seems fake!" The other woman in the orange dress and hair styled in a bun replied as both giggled like two junior high school girls bullying a helpless nerd.

"Wait, are these cutleries made of real gold?" The woman with curly hair exclaimed with excitement in her voice.

"Oh my god, you might be correct! I'm not really sure, though," the woman in the orange dress replied while rolling her eyes and took a sip of her wine. She glanced at her companion and just shook her head with her companion's callousness.

The black-hair man simply shook his head in disapproval, thinking to himself how pathetic the two women were like the rest of the guests.

"This will be mine later," continued the curly haired woman, "if I were you, make space already inside your purse to hide yours." She then motioned to the waiter to request for a Lemon, Lime, and bitters.

"Absolutely ma'am," the waiter replied curtly, "I will be back shortly with your request."

The black-haired man turned his gaze towards the other way to pay no more attention to the two women. He continued to drink his Saint Henri Shiraz fully confident that no guest could recognise him.

He even put a synthetic mole on his left cheek to make sure of it. He then saw his assistant, the blond hair man, beelining towards him.

"Sir, everything is ready," the blond haired man said as he reached the table, "the team is just waiting for your signal."

"Well done," replied the man without looking at his assistant while he continued drinking his Shiraz. He was intently observing several tables around him, the guests relishing the served entrées and drinks.

In one of the tables situated on the right side of the main hall and just by the stage, an elderly man in his mid-50s was deep in thought while holding a bottle of beer. His silence was broken by one of his companions.

"Hey, are you alright?" A man who was smoking his tobacco asked, "the night is still young! Why so gloomy? I know we still have to go to the office tomorrow morning, but we cannot pass up this opportunity to enjoy this Crown Ambassador!" He laughed as he took a sip of the beer they were sharing at their table. The man in his mid-50s just looked at him with a sigh and spoke his thoughts.

"I am good, mate," he said, "but there is something odd with this event. The location and everything seemed all coincidental."

"Fuck, mate," the companion scoffed, "what are you trying to imply? This is just a reunion. Although, I kinda agree with you. I hardly know half of the people here," the companion continued, "but, who cares? Look at these free expensive food and booze served!"

"I know. But I have this gut feeling that something bad is going to happen," said the man in his mid-50s, "good thing I left the missus at home. Let's just try to leave immediately after the main event."

"Stop being a worrywart! Just enjoy this expensive meal and let's get these free meals," said the companion as he tapped the older man's right shoulder and showed the silver menu card containing several expensive a'la cartes of the three-course meal.

"Arc de Triomphe appeared during the time of gods and goddesses. However, the arrival of prepossessing and unprepossessing of five letters are about to happen."

A saying written in gold lettering on the bottom most part of the menu card which had been bothering the older man since they found this menu card on their table earlier.

The older man dismissed his thoughts. He slowly smiled and drank his own Crown Ambassador and replied, "I guess you are right, mate!"

"That's the spirit, mate! Cheers!" His companion said. They both started to enjoy the beer and the meal that they ordered. It was then that they noticed a dignified man with a mole on his left cheek wearing a three-piece black suit walking his way towards the stage and began to address the public on the microphone.

"Good evening, ladies and gentlemen," the man with a mole on his left cheek started, "I would like to express my sincerest gratitude to all of you. Your cooperation was the reason for tonight's success.

You, all, might be wondering about the real reason for tonight's festivities. Worry not, later on, our benefactor will reveal himself to us, his reason, and for the cause of this event," he paused to adjust his tie, "For now, please enjoy his generosity with top notch drinks from around the world, lavish plat du jours prepared for us by our Michelin star chefs, and the festivities as we welcome the Melbourne Chamber Orchestra!"

The orchestra began playing their lively overture as they were introduced that started a thunderous applause from the guest. The man on stage turned his back from the guest to proceed to the backstage and to hide his devilish smirk as he felt the crescendo about to peak soon.

Some of the guests decided to dance as the orchestra started to accompany Danielle De Niese with the aria to the delight of the other guests.

"Remember to take the target in my library," the dark-haired man said to his assistant, "and oh, take the annoying man as well in the white suit that approached us earlier. He may also be of some use to me," he added as he watched the crowd dancing to sonata-allegro and turning into minuet and trio. The blond man simply nodded and alerted his team with a simple wave of his hand to get ready.

The black-haired man, using his dessert fork, gently took a bite of the devil's cake into his mouth followed by a sip of his chamomile tea. It was quarter past ten in the evening according to his pocket watch. He put his pocket watch back inside his pants pocket and stood up. He had a decisive stance and demeanour as he turned his gaze to his assistant. With a firm nod, he signalled the blond man that it was time. He made way out of the main hall towards a sound-proof and gas-proof panic room built inside the building, while his assistant went the other way towards the control room.

Inconspicuous white gas mixed with the smoke effect coming from the fog machine started to slowly emit from the walls and crept all over the floor of the hall. In the centre of the room, the guest was still unmindful of what was about to happen. They continued their revelry with booze, food, and pre-recorded music. They were not even aware how the entire wait staff, servers, and even the orchestra discreetly left the main room.

After a few minutes, several guests had already felt the effects of the gas and either sat on their seats or slumped down on the tables. Except for an older man in his mid-50s who started to realise what was happening as he looked around the room. He initially searched for his companion, who by now, was nowhere to be seen.

An incapacitating gas agent! The older man thought to himself. He grabbed the silver menu card with gold letterings and he suddenly was able to process the saying written on it. However, it was too late. He started to fall down the floor.

Meanwhile, inside the panic room, the black-haired man was approached by the blond man.

"Sir, the room is now clear and all of the guests are immobilised," said the blond-haired man, "the hall has been cleared of the gas and the team are waiting there for your next command."

"Great! I am already tired with all this farce as it is. I want to rest as soon as we finish this," he replied as started to get out of the panic room and headed straight towards the hall.

In the hall, the black-haired man saw his assistant's team had already removed their gas masks and they were alert to cover all sides of the hall. The guests either lay on the floor or slumped on their seats. Moans and muffled calls for help can be heard from the hall as the guests were caught by surprise and were not able to move.

"Good evening, once again, ladies and gentlemen," the black-haired man broadcasted over the microphone handed to him by his assistant, "my apologies, but I would rather have you immobilised so all of you can listen to me very carefully as I share important realisation I had achieving all that I am right now."

"Knowledge and wisdom are essential but are useless against purpose and reason when the situation calls for it," he continued, "tonight is a perfect example. You all have what it takes to be on top, but my purpose and reason is much stronger!"

"Who are you?" A man lying on his back, a few feet away from the stage asked the black-haired man.

"I don't even know who you are. Why are you doing this to us?" Said a lady who was debilitated on her seat with her head turned sideways.

"I was nobody. But the half of you here, treated me like nothing when you have everything," the black-haired man with a mole on his left cheek replied, "But this time, I won't hide anymore because I am not as greedy as you all are."

"That is your downfall and sin," he continued with conviction, "greed!"

"And to the rest of half here, my apology but all of you owed me a lot, it was about my everything!"

He, then, slowly removed the synthetic mole on his left cheek. Gasps of surprise replaced the moans across the hall. The blond-haired assistant looked at his boss with admiration for his capability to make things happen.

"You," the man in his mid-50s weakly exclaimed, "how come you are still alive?"

The older man tried shifting his body from the floor but failed as he was still under the effect of the incapacitating gas agent. He just continued to at least give a piece of his mind towards the mastermind of this all incident.

"If I only knew, I should have personally made sure to rid and to finish you!" The older man said as he was coughing and having a hard time breathing, mocking the black-haired man.

"You are an imbecile for not doing that!" The black-haired man shouted with a devilish laughter, "and now, let me show you how I execute my plans personally! Hahaha!"

He signalled his assistant for the next phase of their plan. Everyone in the room heard a whirring sound from the ceiling of the hall. The assistant's team started to vacate the room, except for a few staff who still have a job to do. The guests shuddered as they tried to turn their heads towards the ceiling and saw that the huge chandeliers were mechanically replaced by huge kerosene heaters.

"As the old saying goes: what you see is what you get," the black-haired man said hoarsely as paid no attention to his aching throat due to the shouting and speaking he had been doing, "but I do not want to deprive you of feeling my rage. As the effects of the gas are slowly fleeting, I want all of you to still feel the heat of my rage!"

"I am begging you, please, forgive me," the man in his mid-50s pleaded in the last effort to save his life.

"Can you now see the big difference at how I personally get the job done with how you do yours?" He replied, "the words mercy and forgiveness don't exist in my dictionary!"

"You are the fucking devil incarnate!" The older man yelled as he tried to get up but to no avail. He was able to feel the heat from the kerosene heaters but was still immobilised by the gas.

"The devil? A handsome devil!" The black-haired man scoffed then maniacally laughed, "men, it's time!" He exclaimed as he started to leave the room with his assistant and the rest of the team, then he nodded to the last two men standing which was the security at the main entrance while opening the door for them and simply smiled as he already instucted them as well before the event started, his plan for that night was flawless and once the right time has come, a total surprising for everyone!

"This is just the beginning of me getting everything!" He continued with a demented laugh.From the outside of the building, screams and moans of pain were heard.

Two

Genuine Friendship is Like a Treasure

With conflicted emotions, Margarette Alexandria had the urge to command the pilot to return to Europe or stay here in Australia as the Gulfstream G700 private jet landed at Tullamarine Airport in Melbourne. Although, she knew she had to stay. It was eight in the morning and the private jet was being taxied towards the bay. As the seatbelt sign was still on, she continued browsing at the wall mounted screen until she came across an international news feed.

"...the famous French heiress had an altercation with who appeared to be Australian sole heiress at a high-end bar in Madrid, whom we are waiting for.." the newscaster reported as a blurred picture of the two involved ladies with the alleged bar was shown in the background. Margarette Alexandria just smirked at the memory of what happened almost twenty-four-hours ago. A memory she left in Europe and the incident that revealed who she really was not only to the entire news and social media but to the entire world.

She stopped browsing as she heard the 'ding' from the intercom signalling that the seatbelt light was turned off. She started to unfasten her seatbelt when her left elbow accidentally nudged the approaching flight attendant who brought the cappuccino she ordered earlier for when the plane touched down.

"What the hell did you do!" She yelled as the flight attendant un-intentionally spilled the drink on her. Luckily, the coffee was not hot enough to scald her else she would have done worse than just yell at the attendant.

"Oh my god! I am so sorry, Ms. Alex," the flight attendant said apologetically. She started to remove her scarf to wipe the spilled liquid on the black trench coat, more worried about Alex's wrath than the stain on her scarf.

Alex stared at the attendant and raised her hand, "just stop! You better leave my sight as you made my day worse than it could have been! And get me my coffee!"

The scared woman quickly walked towards the galley, knowing fully Alex can do worse than just shout at her. Alex, then, stood up and removed her pewter trench coat and threw it on the other side. She opened her luggage to grab another coat to wear. She chose a black coat. She sat back and looked at the sun slowly rising in the horizon from the window.

"My god, Alex! I can hear your yelping even from the toilet," said the lady, in lavender dress and purple coat, who just came out of the toilet and headed towards the seat opposite Alex. "Chill, OK?" She continued as she grabbed the coat Alex threw and tossed it behind her seat. She started rummaging in her violet Hermes Birkin bag. She felt Alex's death glare and as if to mock, she returned it with a wide grin. She stopped rummaging and sat down besides Alex.

"C'mon, Alex, you knew the consequences when we left Madrid," she reminded Alex, "we are already here and there's nothing much we can do!" As she continued scouring through her bag.

"Ugh, I don't care Elissandra," Alex replied, "what the hell are you looking for?" She continued to dismiss her annoyance towards her best friend.

"When did you last see my ring?"

"Oh, the ring!" Alex replied as she got concerned as she knew how Elissandra valued that particular ring from her vast collections of jewellery. It was her best friend's family heirloom which was handed down by Elissandra's mother, "I think you were wearing it couple of days ago when we had coffee at Brunchit."

Alex saw the worry on Elissandra's eyes that she stood up from her seat to grab her best friend's other luggage to help her look for it. After a couple of minutes, several clothes strewn all over, a few unwanted collections of jewellery found, and upturned luggages, the two friends did not find the ring. Alex now saw the worry turned to despair in her best friend.

"Don't worry, I will contact my butler in London to go to Madrid and look for it in the flat," she assured Elissandra. Elissandra knew they could trust Alex's personal assistant in London to make things possible and find her ring. Since they also stayed at the same flat when they stayed in Madrid to celebrate their graduation from college. Alex graduated with a Master in Business Administration from Saïd Business School of Oxford University, while Elissandra finished hers as Master of Fine Arts in Communication in the Royal College of Art as she practised her first love which was modelling.

Elissandra, though worried about her heirloom, felt a surge of relief. If there was a person she could trust her life with, it was Alex. They had been together for more than two decades. They had been together since grade school to senior high school; and, although they had different paths and choices in college, they both decided to study in the United Kingdom so they would not be too far apart.

"Thanks a bunch! It is such a relief that you have my back," Elissandra exclaimed then gave Alex a huge embrace.

"Don't mention it. And if it is not here, I'll instruct the cabin crew to look for it." Alex replied. Their eyes met and for a moment Alex saw the gratitude in Elissandra's eyes turn into worry. She understood what it meant and before her best friend could voice out her concern, she cut her off, "I am fine. No need to worry about me, I can take care of myself."

"Are you sure? I can explain to your parents that it was my fault not yours," Elissandra said pertaining to the debacle in Madrid that circulated Alex's identity.

"Thanks, but as I have said, I can perfectly handle it. Plus, I guess it's about time the world knew about me."

"Alright. But if you need a wingwoman, I got your back!"

"Oh, that's sweet! We may never agree on several things, but you never left my side. And I love you for that!"

"I know, right! Birds of the same feather flock together! Ha ha!" Elissandra chuckled and they both giggled while holding each other's hand and hugged once again.

Alex couldn't help but reflect on what happened. Her laugh began to simmer down as she looked at her best friend and thought she would do it again if she had to. She felt a sudden conviction that made her giggle, once again.

"Although I love that you are taking things lightly, aren't you taking things too lightly?" Elissandra asked. But Alex just caressed Elissandra's left cheek to signal her that there's nothing to worry about.

"You know what, that guy deserves it! I don't care even if he is engaged to that French heiress," Alex retorted. "In fact, it made him more of an asshole. Being engaged and yet still harassing other women at a club?"

"Not that I can blame him. I mean, you are Ms. Elissandra Davis! But no one can assault you, especially when I am around!" She continued, "I bet his cheeks will bruise for a week from our slaps! Ha ha! The two of them deserve each other. Imagine that girl even defending that pervert fiancé of hers!"

"Absolutely! Thanks again. You're the best!" Elissandra gratefully said but her mood suddenly shifted to apologetic, "but the situation brought your family's name in a bad light."

"And I told you not to worry. I can manage this okay?" Alex reassured her. "Now, how about we visit some boutiques in Collins Street?" She continued with a wink.

"Oh no, but thanks! We had enough of shopping in Europe," Elissandra replied, "plus, you are on the hot seat, remember? Maybe one of these days when the dust settles."

"But it's still early and my parents will not be home until five or six in the evening," Alex insisted.

"Well, apparently, I haven't got anything in mind that I want to get. So, let's just you home and get us some rest," Elissandra replied and smiled at her.

"Alright, you win," Alex said as the flight attendant returned them with her coffee and informed them they had taxied in the Fixed-Base Operator.

"Actually, I don't want that coffee anymore. So, you can have it," Alex snapped, which made the staff hesitate, "I don't care if you wanna drink it or not. But I want you to gather all our belongings, but please be careful."

"Sure, Ms. Alex. And my apologies again for earlier," the attendant replied.

"Thanks." She replied, then looked at Elissandra and they both smiled.

"Shall we?" Elissandra asked and motioned Alex for them to leave.

"This is it!" Alex said defeatingly, "I can't wait to leave this place, even though we have just arrived."

"I don't think so. You can't do that without me. Remember, I have to stay here for a few months?" Elissandra winked at her.

"Wow, really? Was that a threat?" She sarcastically replied.

"Nope. Not really. I was just stating a fact, don't you agree? Ha ha!" Elissandra said jokingly.

Alex didn't even reply but she smiled and rolled her eyes at Elissandra.

"Ms. Margarette Alexandria de Ayala, Ms. Elissandra Davis, I hope you enjoyed the flight with and I'm looking forward to being your personal flight attendant again," the same attendant said with a pleasant smile.

"Yes, I did. Thanks!" Elissandra said.

"Oh, not entirely for me. Alex said with annoyance. Then saw the great desire in the flight attendant's eyes. Desire to be her. She cannot blame the staff, almost every woman she met wanted to be her. Having not only everything as the sole heiress of her family's wealth, but also their genes. Her mother was Australian and her father was of mixed Spanish-Filipino descent. She also became one of the most sought after elite bachelorettes in the world after the news about her began to spread like wildfire, but to be honest will she still wanting to be like her once she finally see the depth of her frustrations?

"Although, there is actually something you can do for me. Please try to look the emerald ring in the belly cargo later after you put our bags in the car. Because it means so much to my best friend." Alex added.

"Of course, Ms. Alex," the attendant gladly replied.

"Thank you." Then she glanced to Elissandra and the attendant quickly carried their belongings and followed them behind.

She beelined to the private jet's opened door followed by her best friend and the attendant not far behind. She put on her Chopard sunglasses as the sun was high in the sky, while Elissandra wore her Gouverneur Audigier. Alex descended the jet's steps with such grace and sophistication that everyone in the Fixed-Base Operator turned their heads towards them. She smiled as she saw the car that would pick them up. It was a black Rolls-Royce Wraith.

By the car, two uniformed men in black and dark sun visors awaited them. Alex also noticed two airport staff who accompanied her bodyguards to stamp their passports to avoid any potential media reporters.

Alex and Elissandra went to the car with the attendant handling their carry-ons behind. The driver opened the backseat door for them.

"Welcome back, Ms. Alex and Ms. Elissandra! Your bodyguard will be back shortly as soon as everything is sorted inside," the driver in black uniform mentioned, referring to one of her bodyguards with their passports.

"Thank you," Alex simply answered as they both entered the tinted vehicle.

"Hi there! It was fine, thanks!" Elissandra cheerfully followed up with a wink. The attendant gave the carry-ons to the driver who gladly accepted them.

All of their family staff knew and respected how Alex was reserved in speaking to them. She was not rude but she made them aware that she's always considering her thought unless she knows you well.

The driver returned to his post and sat down as soon as her bodyguard returned with their passports and gave it to Alex and Elissandra. The bodyguard, then, sat on the passenger seat beside the driver.

Alex leaned on her seat and glanced at her watch to see that it was almost half past nine in the morning. She closed the power window that gave them privacy from the driver and the bodyguard since she can use the intercom if she needed from the two in front.

She grabbed a bottle of sparkling water from the coolbox right next to them and spoke on the intercom.

"Kindly please stop in any safe place. I want to smoke and get two normal sizes of flat white," Alex requested.

"Oh, me too!" Elissandra said as she was retouching her makeup.

"Right away, Ms. Alex," replied the driver.

Few moments later, she noticed they turned right and parked. She quickly took her Hermes Himalayan Kelly where her mobile phone, cigarette, and lighter were while Elissandra took her Sophia Shisha Sticks. The bodyguard opened the door for them while the driver went straight inside the café to order for the two of them. Alex need not give him money as they were given a platinum card to spend for her in cases like this.

Alex and Elissandra felt all the stare towards them as they entered the café. Their mere presence commanded the attention of the whole place. Alex realised that everyone recognised her as she was outed from the news. She gathered that the crowd's awe was the fact that an international model with the sole-heiress of the biggest company in Australia would be in the same place at a simple café. She noticed how the customers and the staff whispered and stole glimpses of them, but she casually ignored this. It didn't bother her at all. She let them talk about her or both of them.

"You really are a total complete package," Elissandra mockingly whispered, "the sole-heiress, one of the most elite bachelorette, and now, a worldwide fame," she continued only to have Alex roll her eyes at her with a smile.

They found a table at the al fresco and situated themselves there. Alex's bodyguard stood nearby by the café's door. After a while, her driver approached them with their drinks.

"Thank you."

"You're welcome, Ms. Alex. Just tell me if you need anything else," her driver replied and went back to his post by the car.

Alex took a sip from her cup after smiling to the driver as Elissandra started to scroll on her phone before drinking her coffee. It was then that Alex thought of calling her mother.

"I'll just call mom," she said to her best friend who looked up from her phone to nod affirmation and went back to her scrolling.

"Hello, dear," Alex's mom said over the phone after she answered, "welcome back! I'm sorry I wasn't able to pick you up. Since the online board meeting with Japanese business partners extended to discuss some matters with them.

"But don't worry dear, I will be cooking your favourite dishes later to make it up to you," her mother continued frantically.

"It's okay mom, no worries. I'm all good. I'll see you later then," Alex replied before ending the call dejectedly, she tried to be the good daughter they expected her to be. Although she kept herself from saying something disappointing to her mother, she kept it to herself. She even recalled how her mother did not mention anything about the controversy about her.

She lit a cigarette to collect herself, only to realise how almost everyone in the café was still staring at them. Judging them, her. Looking for something against her. A fault, a chink in her armour she personally built around her. It irked her. Albeit Elissandra being the only one who knew the crack she was hiding so well.

She stubbed her cigarette out in the ashtray and signalled her best friend it was time for them to leave. Elissandra took a last sip of her coffee and gathered her things. They both stood and decided to return to the car. They badly needed sleep and rest after the long flight as jet lag started to affect them.

As they were about to leave the al fresco, they heard a group of young men talking about them.

"Bro, it's the international model, Elissandra Davis."

"And isn't the one with her the controversial heiress from the news?"

"Oh shit! You're correct! Margarette Alexandria!"

"Man! They are so hot!"

"But they seem elitist and snobbish…"

Alex threw them a side glance when she heard their derogatory remarks and was about to say something when Elissandra, understanding her best friend's emotions, nudged her. Alex immediately knew what her best friend meant by the simple gesture for her not to stoop at their level. So, they went straight to the car.

"Is there any place you want to stop by, Ms. Alex?" Asked her driver through the power window.

Alex looked at Elissandra and saw she was as tired as she was before answering, "none. Let's just go home."

"Got it, Ms. Alex."

As they were traversing the boulevard towards Toorak, an inner suburb and residential area known for its gated cul-de-sacs and tree-lined streets where elite personalities resided, Alex caught a glimpse at the shopping centre they family owned. She drew a deep breath that did not escape Elissandra's attention. Alex realised that several establishments they own can be seen in the whole metro. Elissandra looked at her with concern only for her to return with a weak smile. Their exchange was interrupted as the vehicle came to a halt at a red light.

"Barron please do look for an alternative route, we are in dire need of rest and just want to arrive as quickly as possible," she commanded her driver via the intercom while she noticed her best friend in her peripheral vision busy with her phone.

"Sure, no worries Ms. Alex."

Alex saw how Barron took a different route then she closed her eyes and several moments passed, she finally saw a familiar place, the Toorak area.

As they arrived at the mansion, the driver parked the car in front of driveway. The bodyguard opened the door for Alex, while the driver opened the other side for Elissandra. Alex gave them a smile and saw their staff led by the house butler to welcome their arrival, then another realisation came to her mind.

"Welcome back, Ms. Alex and Ms. Elissandra!" The butler courteously said to them, then directly spoke to Alex, "Your mom and dad are currently not here but your mom called to inform us that they will be coming home as soon as their meetings are done."

"Please take care of our belongings in the trunk. And get rid of all the newspapers, I don't want to see any of them." Alex commanded and led Elissandra directly on the second floor where her room was.

Once they entered Alex's spacious and elegant room, they both plopped on the bed; they both let out a huge sigh of relief and giggled. Elissandra turned on her side to face Alex and held her hand.

"So, are you ready for when they come home later?" Elissandra said breaking the silence pertaining to Alex's parents.

"Of course. Always am," Alex replied casually.

"Alright, I believe you. Anyways, I'm gonna make a call so just do your thing," Elissandra said as she stood and went to the balcony of Alex's bedroom for a better reception.

"Sure, take your time. I'll just soak in the bathtub."

Alex went the opposite way towards her walk-in closet to choose a more comfortable outfit. While waiting for the bathtub to be filled, she faced the full-length mirror in the bathroom to see her own reflection. She smiled as she was pleased to see the beauty in front of her as she was sculpted by a Renaissance artist. Taking care of herself like cardio and yoga with her best friend, her body was well-proportioned from her supple bosoms to her well-defined waist to her buttocks. She even turned around just to appreciate her body more.

After settling herself in tub, Alex smiled while glancing at the scented candles. *"He even knew my favourite scent,"* she thankfully thought to herself about the butler. She appreciated the warmth of the water embracing her nudity and the soothing scent that filled the room. The ambiance of her bathroom was comforting that it made her close her eyes.

As she stirred, she realised that she was able to nap for a while. She stood up and went directly under the shower area to finish off her bath. She, then after, dried herself with a white towel and wore a casaual dress and thinking of asking Elissandra if she wanted to freshen up. Alex found herself surprised not finding her best friend in the bedroom or on the balcony. She checked her phone on the bedside table and saw that Elissandra left her a text message.

"I am so sorry honey, but my livid dad fetched me. Oh, I'm on fire too! So, please pray for me! XOXO"

She replied with a short reassuring message that if Elissandra needed support just tell her. After sending her text message, Alex lay down on the bed and stared at the cream-coloured ceiling. A thought bothered her. She wondered of the possibilities that could have happened if they were just ordinary citizens of the state. Would they be a happy family? Would they be together constantly? She was grateful that Elissandra was always there for her, to keep her company, to make her feel she was not alone. But now, she was alone in her room, she felt the emptiness from her parents not welcoming her home. She barely noticed as a tear escaped from her eye. Until all frustrations and disappointment lulled the beautiful yet pained woman to sleep.

Three

The Secret Agent

The sun was already up over the City of Sydney and Osmond felt its warmth on his face as he sat in the outdoor seating area of The Rocks café. He just finished his laps at the First Fleet Park when he decided to get his morning coffee. The morning sun was welcoming him as a great day to have while he was waiting for his order, he was wearing a red hoodie jacket and a plain white shirt under of it then a black track pants, and a white running shoes. The paved way was lined with a variety of trees with leaves swaying with the soft morning breeze along George Street. Assorted flowers were in full bloom in white flower boxes in front of the café. The sidewalk was getting crowded while the main road was starting to get busy as the sound of their engines can be heard, an indication that they were in hurry but the chirping of the morning birds mixed with the scent of the blooming flowers and morning view that made Osmond stop reading and enjoy the atmosphere instead. His contemplation was disrupted when he felt a presence approaching him and he glanced to his right.

"Your white medium flat with one sugar," said the blonde woman in white uniform with a warm smile on her face as she put Osmond's coffee on the table in front of him.

"Thanks! Have a lovely day ahead," he replied and reciprocated her gesture. As he took a sip, he saw in his peripheral vision the old woman with salt-and-pepper hair feeding the seagulls by the board-walk.

As he set down the cup, he remembered his full schedule later after lunch. He inhaled deeply, smelling the morning bloom of the flowers near him, and exhaled slowly. But for now, he intended to enjoy the morning view.

He sipped, once again, from his cup. As he placed the cup back, he decided to check his phone for any other new urgent emails related to his work, then so far none for now and as he was about to lock his phone, it pinged for a news notification with its headline showing about a particular heiress who was involved in a prevalent contro-versy in Madrid, Spain. He nonchalantly locked his phone and re-turned it in his pocket. He didn't bother to read further as it was all over the news this morning as it only happened within twenty four hours, so it was not new to him. He even thought that it only made the news because it involved plutocrats. Had it been a debacle between average wage workers, it would not make the news.

With these thoughts in mind, he sipped the remaining coffee in his cup, put his hands inside of jacket and casually left the coffee shop as he decided to shop at the supermarket.

He was at the intersection waiting for the pedestrian light to turn green. Across from him was a man in his black jumper and white jog-ging pants also waiting for the walk signal, until they both heard the go signal.

"Morning mate!" The man said with a cordial smile.

"Morning too, mate!" Osmond replied, returning the smile and greeting as his guts did not sense any hostility from the other man. They both continued their way with opposite directions.

Osmond made way to the entrance of the grocery when he saw a busy woman who seemed to be a mother at the checkout lane carrying her shopping bag. She unknowingly dropped a hundred-dollar note as she grabbed her phone from her pocket.

Osmond quickly picked the money and handed it to the woman, "ma'am , you dropped this."

"Oh! Thank you, young man!" Said the woman who was visibly grateful to his demeanour, "I am sure your parents raised you well."

"Oh, thanks for the kind word ma'am, you're welcome and have a lovely day ahead." He gently replied with a nod of his head.

"You as well, thanks." Said the woman who went on her way towards the exit of the grocery.

Osmond was smiling at the last comment by the lady. He grabbed a plastic shopping basket from nearby and headed directly to the personal care aisle. There, he started to fill his basket with men's hygiene products from moisturiser, aftershave, and lotion as he was running low in stock. Next, he went to the health and wellness section where he got vitamins and medicines. He glanced at the green colour basket he was holding and surmised that he got what he needed. As he was about to proceed to the self-checkout lane, he passed the confectionery section where he grabbed some dark chocolate lollies. At the self-service checkout, he started to scan the items and put the paper bag in the kiosk's bagging area.

After his purchase, he decided to have an early lunch at Ribs & Burgers; it was now about half past ten. He sat down near the window and scanned the QR code on the table using his phone to order. He selected the Wagyu Royale with sweet potato chips paired with aioli and a bottle of sparkling water. He then entered his debit card details on the payment page of the application. His order arrived after only ten minutes which he consumed heartily as he was a bit hungry. He took a little rest in his seat after eating and browsed the patrons of the restaurant. There was a family in the middle part who were happily dining, laughing earnestly, and spending quality time with each other. They reminded Osmond of his parents and two siblings back in Queensland. He suddenly missed them. It was then he finally stood up after checking the time on his watch before he left immediately as he wanted to rest at home before the meeting.

He was somewhere in Kurraba Point in New South Wales, the place where he preferred to call home. He chose this area even though he can afford to live in an upper-class suburb where there were better places. He favoured living a simple lifestyle even if he was earning exceptionally from his profession with competitive salary and multiple benefits. He then remembered the hardships he experienced when he was young in Cassowary Coast. But then he started to organise his grocery. He systematically arranged the confectioneries in the pantry where he saw he still had some bags of chips. He then went to the bathroom still carrying the shopping bag and sorted his personal care. He put the vitamins and medicines in the medicine cabinet. Satisfied, he started to prepare for their once in a meeting every month by two o'clock. They ended after almost an hour and it was now past three in the afternoon. On his way home, as he was driving his black Toyota Supra, he received a call from the Director-General of Security of Australia. Osmond immediately answered the call using a wireless earphone. He knew that when he got a call from this man, it was an urgent matter or a special mission. It was impossible for him to miss a call from this man as he owed him a lot and he was a nice bloke too.

"Yes, General?" He asked while driving in Sydney Harbour bridge and less than one kilometre away from him, he saw the iconic Sydney Opera House from his peripheral vision.

"Agent Gomez, check your email since there is a sudden and urgent tough mission," he heard the General in an authoritative but calm tone from the other line.

"Sure, General. I will, I am on my way home as of the moment," he answered. With that, the line was cut by the General.

As usual, that man would hang-up the call after saying his intent, it was not new for Osmond and he continued driving on his way to his apartment. Upon arriving back in what he could call home, he put his keys in the entryway key bowl. He proceeded to the lounge area and decided to turn on the TV. He was just getting comfortable on his seat when he caught the tragic news between anchor and a field reporter were talking about. It was about the kidnapping of a six-years old girl in another part of the country. According to the reporter, it was the only child of the couple that being interviewed by the field reporter.

A surge of emotions from anger to sadness then frustration suddenly flooded Osmond. Anger for the heartless criminal, sadness for the missing little girl, and frustration that he cannot do anything much about it. A mixture of emotions he first felt when was fourteen years old and now he was reminded because of the recent news. A scar in his memory that was etched in his heart and mind for the rest of his life. He tried so hard to cover this scar only to be unveiled by the recent tragedy. He remembered his childhood best friend, Isabelle. He quickly turned off the television and took a deep breath to suppress his emotions. He stood and went to his bedroom. Inside his bedroom, he took off his Tag Heuer Connected chronograph watch and gently placed it on the brown medium-sized table right next to his king-sized bed covered in all white colour.

However, he cannot shake off the feeling he had because of the recent news. He pondered on an agonising reminiscence that made who he was now.

He was Osmond Gomez, twenty-eight years old and Australia's top secret-agent. He was half-Australian, half-Mexican who was born and raised in the Cassowary Coast Region, a rural area in Queensland, Australia. He stood at five and ten inches tall, well-built, proportioned body, and olive skin complexion. He took his severe and harsh training at United Kingdom's special security service, MI5, before he became the country's best. He knew the profession he chose was dangerous but he accepted it full-heartedly because of his experience when he was young. He can even remember how he and his best friend would watch Sean Connery's old movie, Agent 007. They would talk about it for hours, how someday he would be a good agent like James Bond to prevent bad humans hurting innocent people and how his best friend would be voicing her support for his dreams. Their dreams, her admiration for his aspirations.

He recollected these memories of how he met Isabelle while he started to take off his black suit as he was sitting on his bed close to the lampshade.

When his dad was terminated from his former employment, Isabelle's dad hired him since they knew each other from quite some time. During payday, his parents were regular patrons of Isabelle's dad's assorted freshly harvested produce from their family farm. His dad, then, became the head of the farm owned by Isabelle's parents.

As clear as daylight, the memory of how he and Isabelle first met.

It was one sunny morning and he woke up earlier than his siblings. After he had breakfast and as he was drinking his milk, his father was drinking his coffee across the table.

"Osmond, son, do you wanna come with us?" His father asked him. To which, he happily agreed.

Young Osmond and his parents walked under the warmth of the morning sun for almost twenty minutes until they reached a familiar house. The garage area of the house was open and was set up with a long table. The long table was filled with varieties of vegetables and fruits. Several people were lined up in front of it, either scanning the harvest or buying them, but one blonde girl stood out of the crowd for the young Osmond. The girl was helping her parents assist the customers. He cannot help but smile.

It was not the first time he saw her, but it was the first time she saw him smiling. The girl noticed that he was looking at her. She smiled back. He waved at her and so did she.

It became their routinary greeting every time Osmond would join his parents to buy fruits and vegetables from the girl's family's home store. He would smile and she would smile back. He would wave and she would wave back.

Until one morning when everything changed. It was a facile morning and there were only a few customers. So the girl was not in her usual place helping her parents, as they did not need any. The young Osmond found her reading a book while sitting on a wooden chair beside the long table. Since his parents were preoccupied filling their basket with comestibles, he decided to approach the little girl.

"Wow! I love books, too. And comics!" He exclaimed, "I am Osmond. What's your name?"

"Isabelle," she replied curtly with a smile.

"Hey, maybe we could exchange some of our books?" He offered, "I can bring some of mine when we come back!"

"Isabelle, honey, please clean up the kitchen. Your aunt is coming with your cousins later," Isabelle's mom requested before Isabelle could answer young Osmond.

"Sure, mom!" Isabelle answered as she stood up then glanced back at the young boy, "I would love that. You can bring your books next time and I can show you mine, so you can choose which to borrow. I have to go inside now, bye."

"Sure thing! Thanks!" Young Osmond replied and watched until Isabelle was out of sight as she entered the house.

That agreement started a beautiful friendship between the two. The young boy would even ride his bike alone to go to the young girl's house where they spend afternoons reading and talking about the latest comics or story they've read. Other times, they would join children from a neighbouring farm. They would actively play different children's games like hide and seek, tag, and many more with the two boys and another girl. However, young Osmond and young Isabelle remained the closest of them.

Their closeness became stronger when Isabelle's father hired Osmond's dad as the head of staff in the farm owned by Isabelle's family. The two kids became best friends. Young Osmond believed that they would be forever, but that changed drastically one day.

It was supposed to be a usual afternoon that young Osmond thought that they would be playing hide and seek with the other children, two boys and a girl, from other farms. He arrived at the edge of trees bordering the farm of Isabelle's family where they would play, but he found Isabelle was just sitting on a garden wooden wagon bench while holding her book and was watching their playmates already in the middle of their game. He approached her forthwith, instead of greeting the other children. He immediately saw the sadness in her eyes.

"Isabelle, why are you sad? Come and join us!" He exclaimed.

"I'm okay, Osmond," she replied flippantly, "I want to stay here and watch."

Young Osmond noticed the melancholy in Isabelle's voice. Instead of coaxing her to tell him the truth, which might irk her, he decided to tacitly sit beside her. He saw she was holding on to a book titled 'Vanished' by Danielle Steele. He tried to grab the book to find what it was about but she swiftly kept it away out of his reach.

"I said, I am just fine here!" She retorted. He saw the hesitation in her eyes this time.

"I'm sorry I intruded," he apologetically replied. He was about to leave her to have peace when one of the boys who were playing not far from them called out to him.

"Hey, Osmond! Come here and just leave her alone," one of the boys shouted, "she doesn't want this game, anyway. Besides, she's so clumsy that nobody wants her to be with any team! Hahaha!"

Osmond looked back at Isabelle. It bothered him that, instead of sadness or anger, she did not show any sign of being upset or afflicted. He stood up and went straight to the boy who made the rude remark against his best friend.

"Apologise to Isabelle this instant!" Young Osmond commanded the rude boy.

"I don't want to!" The boy replied defiantly, "I am telling the truth! What will you do about it? Huh!"

"She did not do anything wrong to you for you to be mean to her!" Osmond riposted.

"Why are you even defending her? Are you her boyfriend?" The second boy asked Osmond to support the rude boy.

The two boys laughed. Something within young Osmond was triggered. A sense of justice that he discovered he had. He could not let this needless teasing against his best friend pass. He cannot help but to defend the honour and dignity of his best friend.

Young Osmond pushed the rude boy who retaliated by pushing him back. The two engaged in a brawl. The other girl tried to stop them, but the second boy joined the fight. It was two to one and Osmond was getting overpowered. The other girl stood petrified, while Isabelle ran towards her house as it was nearby.

"Hey boys! Stop that!" A loud voice boomed from behind young Osmond trying to fend off the attacks from the two boys. Isabelle came back with her father to whom the sonorous voice belonged.

The rude boy and the second boy suddenly stopped and ran with the second boy dragging the other girl behind him.

"Are you alright, Osmond, buddy?" Asked Isabelle's father after the three kids ran.

"I'm fine, sir," young Osmond replied, "I could've handled those two just fine."

"I know you can. But remember, violence is never the answer. Even if they say mean things to you or Isabelle. But you also need to know how to protect yourself and your loved ones. You got that, buddy?"

"Yes, sir!"

"Alright, Isabelle and I have to go home now. She has her homework to finish. You get going now, too. Send my regards to your folks, okay?" Isabelle's father said as he led Isabelle towards their house.

"Of course, sir," young Osmond said as he turned to Isabelle, "I'll see you again tomorrow. Bye for now, Isabelle."

It was the last words he said to her and the last time he saw her, waving goodbye to him as they walked in different directions.

Osmond stopped himself from reminiscing about the past. It was dark and painful. Torturing him emotionally. Until now, Isabelle missing without a trace was a case full of mystery. One of the unsolved cases in the country.

He tried multiple times to solve and to gather some information about that incident fourteen years ago. He failed multiple times. Even clues or any names of the criminal or any dark organisation, nothing. However, he had this feeling that one day he would be able to solve this shadowy case. He just needed even small details that would greatly help him punish whoever was responsible for Isabelle missing. He still had hope that his childhood best friend was still alive. Thus, he became the finest agent in the country—to find her.

Osmond took a deep breath before he removed his slacks until almost nothing was left from his body except a white Calvin Klein boxer-brief. He walked towards the kitchen to grab something from the fridge. He took the braised beef Ragu out from the box, put it in the air fryer, and pressed the auto-cook button. He went to the couch in the lounge area to check his email on his laptop. He saw the classified email from the General. He was immensely surprised because the correspondence instructed him to put under surveillance an old, high-profiled philanthropist. There were well-analysed speculations that the old man was involved in human trafficking! After he got all the needed important details, he went back to the kitchen as he heard the air fryer's sound that it was done. He grabbed and put the food in a plate and sat on the bar stool while thinking how maybe his next mission could be connected to the enigmatic incident when he was fourteen at Cassowary, Queensland.

Four

Twisted Events

Alex was roused from sleep by the continuous knock on her bedroom door. She glanced at her digital clock on her bedside table, it was already past five in the afternoon. She never expected to be in a deep slumber as it seemed she overslept.

"Hold on!" She shouted as she heard a knock on her bedroom door. She got out of bed and walked towards her closet to change into more appropriate clothes, a white cotton shirt and cotton shorts and after she headed to open the door and saw her mother in a grey corporate attire after opening it.

"Good afternoon my dear daughter! Welcome back! I'm glad to see you again," Evangeline, her mother, perkily said and hugged her tight.

"Good afternoon, too, mom! I can't breathe," she chuckled, "by the way, why were you so late?" She added huffily while pouting just to conceal what she feels at that moment while looking at her mother's face.

"Your father and I had so much on our plate and had so many ideas during the meeting today and they went straight to a cocktail party at the Westin Hotel to discuss more things; but we decided not to join and just let our trusted associates deal with them," her mother verbosely answered.

"Alright mom," she replied curtly.

Evangeline then gently reached Alex's hand and asked her to go downstairs.

"Mom, where's dad?" Alex asked once they had reached the ground floor of the mansion.

"He's in the dining area, waiting for us," Evangeline answered with a smile, and she saw there was something amiss in the eyes of her daughter but she pretended to ignore it.

"Okay," Alex simply replied while walking. She started to gather her composure and began thinking how she would handle things once they arrived at the dining area. She knew her father was unlike her mother who was always calm at all times.

"Calm down Alex. Just be honest and remember that your dad owes you a lot," she thought to herself to try and control her feelings as she was about to face her father, Enrique de Ayala, the heir of her grandparents that became the major stock owner of the biggest company in Australia.

"Hi dad! How are you?" Alex greeted her father once she and Evangeline reached the kitchen, she saw how her father dismissed one of their house staff with a nod. The staff, who were preparing the dining table, quickly left the area.

"Hello, dear!" Her dad answered in a rather disappointed tone, "I am not good at all because of the uproar you've caused recently. It even made the international evening news!" He continued as he grabbed the glass of whisky and finished it with one gulp as if to reiterate his displeasure.

"Enrique!" Her mother warned her father.

"Evangeline, please stop defending your daughter! She caused us a huge trouble! Not only to the family's reputation, but to our businesses also! For Christ's sake!"

"But it was a very common thing that happens when clubbing right?" Evangeline justified, "how about this, let's just eat dinner first? I have asked the staff to prepare earlier," she continued trying her hardest to diffuse the tension building in the dining area.

Alex saw how her father scoffed at her mother and sneered at them.

"Normal? Do you hear what you are saying, Evangeline? It wasn't just a mere bickering of spoiled brats! It was made known to the whole world!" Her dad exclaimed.

Alex felt her father emitting an overbearing aura in the room. The aura of her father was known for inside and outside of the corporate world that seemed to weaken any human being's will into submission to her father's bidding whenever a serious disappointment occurred.

"It's okay, mom," she uttered while looking at her mother then at her father.

She was not trying to match her father's energy, though trying to show him that she was not afraid and would not back down.

"Dad, let's discuss that later, please?" She continued, "I am aware of what had happened, but I am happy that we are together for dinner. This rarely happens and I've missed you both," she said with a pleasant smile hoping to alleviate the tension between them. She was trying to conceal what she really felt at that moment. She sat down at her father's right side, while her mother was at the left side. She delicately unfolded the table napkin and carefully placed it on her lap. She momentarily glanced at the floor to ceiling window, and behind her mother she had a view of the aspen garden below with a waterfall that led to a small pond turning into hues of the golden sunset.

"Of course, Alex. I missed you, too," Enrique answered calmly, "regardless, we have a more urgent matter to discuss than what happened in Madrid."

Alex did not anticipate her father's sudden change of mood, but somehow, she had an idea of what he would be conferring about with her. Her mother had already given her a heads-up a couple of months ago.

"Dad, I told you, I am not yet ready for that," she said, giving her father a hint that she had an idea of what they would be talking about. She, then, pleadingly looked at her mother for back up.

"Well, dear, your dad and I discussed that matter last month. We both agreed it will be good for you to come with your dad and spend time in the office," Evangeline explained, "plus, I think it's a good way to introduce you to the whole company."

"Evangeline, I don't think introducing her is no longer necessary. The whole world knows her already," Enrique sarcastically added, "I'm certain that this is the right time for Alex to immerse herself in our family's business. Plus, this is a great opportunity for Alex to recompense us with the recent complication she had done in Spain."

"But dad! Please! I know how the corporate world works, so please, spare me the immersion!" Alex exasperatedly said then turned to her mother, "Mom, I thought dad and I have talked about these things? I never said yes to him!"

Even if the world knew who she really was as the sole heiress of their family's business, Alex was not ready to be involved in the world of entrepreneurs. She still wanted to experience things she hadn't done when she was studying. She focused on her studies as she wanted to finish on time and then enjoy her life for a while before taking it seriously. She wanted to experience what normal and average women her age enjoyed and the freedom others have known. She knew that she would not be able to do that now with the situation her parents put her in. She suddenly lost her appetite with all those thoughts bothering her.

"Mom, please, you and dad are dictating my life behind my back. It's not fair! Please understand that I just want to enjoy and have freedom first before you put me in my so-called destined life," she said in a frustrated way.

"My decision is final and non-negotiable!" Enrique firmly answered in a tone that gave his daughter that it was absolute and she cannot do anything about it.

Alex realised that it can be discussed for once more next time, and she was aggravated by her father's words that she wordlessly stood up to walk out from dinner.

"Where are you going? Sit back down! We are not yet done!" Enrique shouted.

Alex paused mid-step and coldly gazed at her father. She shook her head, turned back again and left her parents in the dining area to go to her room.

Evangeline watched as her daughter walked away. She was thinking that Alex might have a point. She realised that it might be too soon for Alex to undertake such a huge responsibility and it might be better to let Alex enjoy for quite sometime, she would convince him by tomorrow to rethink his decision. Tonight was untimely as both her husband and daughter had a heated confrontation.

"Did you see that?" Enrique's reaction to her while shaking his head.

"Oh, what's new? You know how our daughter reacts whenever you don't consider her feelings," Evangeline retorted, "I better go upstairs and get some rest. Let us just continue our discussion about your demands tomorrow," she added as she also left the dining area without a glance back at her husband.

Enrique was in disbelief being left alone and a wry smile appeared on his lips, "like mother, like daughter."

Meanwhile, Alex entered her room, and she quickly sank into her bed; while the thought of preparing herself until she and her father could still compromise. If worse comes to worse and her father would remain unyielding, she would definitely escape the country. She remembered that she needed to update her best friend, so she picked her phone from the bedside table and pressed the call log on the screen and tapped her name. After several rings from the other line, she heard her voice.

"Hey, it's a disaster!" Alex instantly uttered. She wanted to share with her best friend the displeasing situation her parents wanted her in.

"Why? Are you alright there?" Elissandra worriedly asked.

Alex took a deep breath before answering.

"My dad wants me now to start about the family business" she replied in frustration as she massaged her forehead and closed her eyes and trying to calm herself as she was stressed by what happened during dinner.

"Honey, you know I love you. But, this might be for the best. I think you should listen and obey your dad for now," Elissandra slowly said, careful of what she was about to advise her best friend, "think of it as your way to make amends for what had happened in Madrid."

"Really? You gotta be kidding me!" Alex replied as she widely opened her eyes, she was entirely in disbelief of Elissandra's suggestion.

"Think about it, Alex. You really did great with your internship before. Listen, if you cave in with your dad then he might be so happy that he will give you your freedom back. We might get to unwind and party once again!"

"Oh my god!" Alex exclaimed as she stood from her bed with excitement, "I love you so much, bestie! That was such a brilliant plan! "Anyhow, how's things between you and your dad?" She continued as she sat back down in her bed.

"Oh, don't worry about me! As usual, I managed things here," Elissandra giggled.

"You go girl! I'm glad to hear that." Alex said, "so it seems that you have solved your case and I have a plan for mine, I guess we should celebrate!"

"Yeah, we should! As our last hurrah before we temporarily go and settle our dues," Elissandra agreed, "I know your parents would ground you to come here, as my parents have banned me from visiting you. But, I know where we can meet and hangout discreetly and it is completely secure!"

"Sweet! Things will settle soon and will be alright. Thanks, honey! You are the best," Alex replied gratefully as they both ended the call, things may not have gone her way recently, but she appreciated that her best friend was still there for her.

After an hour, Alex realised she was still hungry as she walked out from their dinner earlier. She decided to go to their dining room where she found her mother in her white silk robe and drinking red wine. A staff member asked her if she needed anything.

"I am okay, and could you please give us a moment?" Then the staff nodded at her and left. "Thanks," she replied, "hi, mom," she greeted as she sat by the chair next to her mother.

"Hello, dear," Evangeline replied as she reached over to kiss Alex's forehead. "Everything okay? Aren't you hungry?"

"Yeah, everything's well. I'll just have some light snacks and also a wine please."

"I am having this Chateau Margaux." Her mother responded.

"Sure mom, that would be great."

Then Evangeline started to pour wine in glass after her daughter placing it in front of her. "I am glad that you are home. I missed you."

Alex was about to reply when her mother stood up.

"Hold on, dear, I would just get you a snack."

Alex silently watched her mother after nodding, and a minute after, she came back with a plate and a dessert spoon.

"Here's your fruit platter, dear."

"Thanks, mom," she replied and looked at her with a smile before she started eating the sliced fruits with gusto.

"Alex, I just want to apologise for earlier. I tried to convince you father to think things over..." Evangeline was saying when Alex interrupted her by holding her hand.

"Mom, you don't need to be sorry. I was thinking about it in my room after I left and realised certain things. I think you and dad were right," she said with a smile then she continued to eat her fruit platter.

"So, you mean..." her mother gabbed in disbelief then took a sip of her wine.

"Yes, mom. And you can tell dad that I am finally agreeing to his demand."

"Oh god, Alex, even if I had my doubts of pushing you to agree. But this decision of yours will put everything in place. Your dad will be so happy tomorrow when I tell him about this," her mother reached for her again, this time she hugged her and whispered in her ear, "thanks, dear. I am so proud of your decision. I am the happiest mother on earth right now."

"And I am the happiest daughter in the universe as this moment is rare for us both," she whispered back.

Her mother went back to her seat. They both smiled and enjoyed themselves as they finished their wine before they finally went upstairs to rest for the night. As for Alex, she peacefully slept as there was no reason for her to worry starting tomorrow.

Her eyes were still closed but she could already hear the chirping of the morning birds from outside her room. As she opened her eyes, the rays of the early sun pierced through the huge curtains of her balcony door. She smiled as she stretched her arms wide open and saw that it was almost eight in the morning from the digital clock on her bedside table. She walked towards her bathroom for her morning ritual. After almost an hour, she was done with her self-care and wrapped herself with a white towel and sat in front of her vanity table. As she was brushing her brunette hair, she saw that her phone was ringing and she immediately answered the call as soon as she saw the caller ID.

"Hi! Good morning!" She perkily greeted her best friend while she continued brushing her hair.

"Oh yes! It is a totally good morning for us. My parents left early, so I can go out and meet up with you!" Elissandra excitedly said.

"Actually, I'm not sure if I can go out, but I will DM later if I can be able to," Alex answered as she stood from her vanity table and went to her walk-in wardrobe to get some comfortable home clothes. "Anyway, I had a great conversation with mom last night, I already told her that I am finally agreeing to dad's proposal."

"I'm glad to hear that it went well! I bet she was so happy. At any rate, I'll send you the pin of the location that I mentioned last night. Just send me a message if you will be able to make it later or what time I should prepare."

"Yeah, for sure. She was almost in tears and even hugged me last night."

"Then, that's great to hear! Sorry, I'll go for now, I still have to take a shower."

"Alright! I'll message you once things here are clear to go. Bye! Love you!" Alex ended the call and went downstairs, wearing a pure white floor length robe.

As she reached the ground floor, she saw the butler who greeted her with a nod and a smile.

"A pleasant morning, Ms. Alex! Your breakfast is ready at the al fresco," the butler said as he motioned with his right hand to where her breakfast was prepared.

"Hi, morning! Thanks! Anyway, where are my parents?"

"They left about an hour ago. They said that they have an early meeting," the butler replied and Alex nodded.

She arrived at the al fresco and saw her personal bodyguard waiting by the corner who also greeted her. Alex reciprocated the greeting and sat in front of the breakfast table. She was thinking of how to distract the house staff so she could go out. She grabbed the glass of freshly squeezed orange juice and started to put her food on her plate.

"Ms. Alex, if you need anything else please let the house help know and enjoy your breakfast," the butler said before another staff member came to the table with a pot of freshly brewed coffee.

"Sure, thanks!" She replied shortly as the house help gently placed the hot beverage in front of her, and she picked some fresh fruits from her plate.

"Actually, I can manage for now. Can you guys please leave me for a while?" She said for the house help who was standing across from her and her bodyguard behind her. She saw the hesitation from the bodyguard, "I said, I can manage please and I cannot enjoy my breakfast with both of you near me." She needed to be able to be alone to think of a convincing way how she would be able to go out. As the house help and her bodyguard left, she grabbed the bowl of Greek yoghurt, while assessing her plan. She was about to finish the yoghurt when an idea came to her mind, it was the only sure-fire way that she could think of to get out. She checked her phone for the time, it was almost half past nine then she unlocked it to type a message and send to Elissandra.

'What time can you be ready?'

She eagerly waited and after four minutes, she saw that her message was seen. She saw the typing icon from the other side.

'Around noon, for lunch. I also have some great news for you,' the message read from Elissandra.

Alex's eyebrows raised from curiosity regarding the message of her best friend. She was excited as to what news Elissandra was referring to but decided to wait for them to meet.

'Sure! I'll see you then,' she wrote and after sending her reply, she stood up and went upstairs to her room. She got a notification from her phone and she saw that Elissandra sent her the pin of the location that they would be meeting. After an hour, Alex was ready to get away. She wore a denim jacket under of plain white shirt, acid washed jeans, purple turban, and an aviator to conceal her face. She was now unrecognisable.

As for her plan, she got to her nightstand to use the house's intercom. She dialled for the butler's direct line.

"Ms. Alex, is there anything you need?" Asked the butler from the other line.

"Yes. Elissandra lost her ring yesterday when she was here. It is very important to her as she inherited it from her mother and it is a family heirloom. Please make sure that everyone, including my bodyguard, searches the whole house for it," she commanded firmly.

She remembered earlier that Elissandra's ring was in fact in her purse. Elissandra asked her when they were clubbing in Madrid to keep it for her so she would not lose it even if they got intoxicated. Turned out that they got so preoccupied with the recent events that they both forgot about it. Alex, having been well-rested, was able to remember only that morning when she was eating her breakfast.

She was able to use the ring for her escape plan. She even was able to hide the ring under the carpet in the lounge area half an hour ago, before she changed into her disguise. She would just remind Elissandra later and return the ring when the staff found it.

"Definitely, Ms. Alex. I will let you know once Ms. Elissandra's ring is found," the butler politely answered from the other line.

"Great! Thanks," Alex replied as she returned the phone on the receiver. She opened her door discreetly and walked silently towards the stairs to take a look at the lounge area. She saw the butler assigning the house staff members including her bodyguard areas of the house to look for the ring. Once done, Alex saw all of them proceeding to their assigned places.

Alex smiled to herself as her plan was working. She stealthily descended the stairs until she reached the garage. When she was certain that no one had seen her, she entered the dark silver Bentley Bentayga S. She did not even bother to bring anything with her, except for her phone. She did not want to attract any attention towards her by bringing her expensive stuff.

She only relaxed when she got out of their estate and she was on the road. She input the pin of the location from Elissandra and followed the route shown by the Car Navigation System. She commanded Siri to call Elissandra, but there was no answer from her. She decided to just focus on driving and did not redial her best friend's number.

Meanwhile, Osmond was on his way to meet Agent Cedrick McKain as he was driving towards the agreed venue. Once he reached the place and search for a parking slot so he could park his car. As always, he wanted to be on time.

He was reversing his car to park in an unoccupied space when a dark silver Bentley appeared in his rearview mirror. With his quick reflexes, he was able to step on the brakes and avoid collision.

"That was close," Osmond thought to himself. He opened his door and went down to check for possible damage, then he glance at the woman who was now inspecting her vehicle, she was wearing a denim jacket, with white shirt underneath, acid washed jeans, a purple turban, and dark sunglasses.

"Are you alright?" He politely asked while keeping his senses alert as the woman might be sent to spy on him since she was obviously concealing her face.

"Can you be mindful next time?" Alex, asked in the snarkiest way possible.

Osmond just furrowed his forehead as a reaction.

Alex tried to be defensive since she knew that it was her fault for not slowing down in the parking area. She attempted to save herself from the humiliation just in case the man was pissed off about what happened.

"Let's just move on, since no one was hurt and no damage was done," Osmond casually said as there was not a single scratch on both vehicles. He entered his vehicle and started to reverse, to park on the spot he originally intended to. He stayed alert once he was parked and stepped out of the car to proceed to his expected meeting place.

Alex was about to retort something harsh towards the man in black suit and dark sunglasses, but she decided against it and just kept silent. She realised that the man did not also remove his sunglasses which was unusual during confrontations. The man might also be hiding from someone, like she was. So, she let the situation slide and went inside her car. She carefully manoeuvred around the man's car to search for her own parking spot.

Three blocks away from where the altercation of the two drivers, a hooded man in black was inside of a black BMW sedan observing them.

"Confirmed, Boss. I got a positive subject," the man said on his phone.

"Are you sure?" Said the voice from the other line.

"Yes. I have never failed a single mission," replied the enigmatic hooded man.

Five

The Assassination Attempt

After Alex parked her car, she was still bothered by the incident when she almost collided with another car. She wasn't able to see the man's face clearly as he was wearing sunglasses, there was something inexplicable about him that made her wonder who he was. Something that drew her to him. Her thoughts were cut by the vibrations from her phone since it was on silent mode. The message was from Elissandra telling her that she was inside by the left corner of the cafe. Alex replied about where she was.

'Sweet! I just parked my car. See you!'

She stepped out of her vehicle and turned off her phone. She didn't want anyone to contact her once they finally discovered that she went out without her bodyguard. She put her phone inside her jean's side pocket and walked casually towards the coffee shop. As she entered the cafe, she scanned around to look for her best friend and to see if someone might know her. There were few patrons, but luckily, no one seemed to know her and she knew except for Elissandra who was nonchalantly browsing a magazine. She smiled as she knew that Elissandra might also have turned off her cellphone. She was situated by the arched windows framed by mix-coloured bricks.

Alex's smile quickly waned as she saw a man sitting beside the table that she and Elissandra would be occupying. The same man she almost had a fender-bender with earlier. Alex dismissed her irritation since today was supposed to be chilling with her best friend.

She returned her gaze towards Elissandra who was now looking at her indifferently. Alex smiled and waved at her. Elissandra only looked baffled back at her. Alex removed her sunglasses and raised her eyebrows at her. It was only then that she recognised her and gleefully stood up and approached her.

"Oh my! I hardly recognised you. Well done!" Elissandra whispered while they were hugging.

"Yeah! It took me half an hour just to prepare. I'm glad it worked! Ha ha!" Alex replied as they were sitting at their table, "Good thing my parents went to work early.

"So, spill the tea! What was this about your text message last night?" She continued as she adjusted her sunglasses back.

"Well, the good news is that I've got an official offer from the modelling agency I was talking about!" Elissandra excitedly shared, "a regular modelling career!"

"Oh my gosh! That's so wonderful, honey!" Alex replied with glee.

"But here's the catch, they also wanted me to join next year's national beauty contest!" Elissandra added while holding Alex's hand.

Alex quickly realised that Elissandra would be busy and preoccupied for the next few days.

"Oh, I'm so happy for you! Although I know that you will be preoccupied, this is a great opportunity for you and I know also it will open many more doors for you!" Alex happily said.

"Thanks, honey!" Elissandra exclaimed, "but hey, we will still catch up with each other if we are not busy. Just what I've mentioned last night."

Alex nodded in response when a wait staff approached with two menus for them. They browsed the menus and informed the waitress who gladly wrote their orders before leaving them.

Meanwhile on the other table, Osmond began to relax as he saw that the lady he had a near collision earlier was associated with Elissandra Davis. He was able to deduce that they were close friends and that the lady was not a threat. He ordered a black coffee and an almond croissant, and he checked his phone and realised that Cedrick was running late, again.

Concurrently, Alex told Elissandra that she needed to go to the toilet quickly, while Elissandra decided to stay to wait for their orders as she knew that the place was safe for her best friend to go alone to the toilet.

Alex was heading towards the toilet when she saw in her peripheral vision that the man she encountered earlier left his table and started walking in the same direction as she was. Although her mind was not giving any warning signs for unknown reasons, she decided to get her phone in her side pocket to turn on but in aeroplane mode just in case of any emergency. She thought that the man might be related to the French heiress she had an altercation with in Madrid and the man might wants to mess with her. Granted that it should not be since her family was also associated with influential figures, from politicians to big entrepreneurs, and it would not benefit the French heiress if she would do something against her. With these circumstances, the best she could surmise was to confront the man.

"Are you stalking me?" Alex asked with irritation in her voice.

"Why should I? I don't even know who you are," Osmond replied calmly.

"Then convince me," she retorted.

"I don't have any obligations to," he was now getting curious about the identity of the woman in front of him. She might be a counterintelligence using Elissandra as a decoy.

"So, stay away from us!" She commanded.

"I don't take orders from strangers," he countered with conviction, "and I can assure you that whatever you are thinking about me is totally baseless. So, if you excuse me," he added and walked towards the men's toilet.

Alex was in disbelief with what just happened. If only she could reveal her true identity to the management of the place, she could have requested them to remove that man to remind him of his rightful place. But she decided against it as it would ruin her disguise.

She then decided to not let him ruin her day with her best friend and proceeded to the ladies' room. After she finished using the cubicle, she made sure nobody was inside the toilet before taking off her sunglasses. She looked at her reflection in the mirror as she washed her hand with a thick lather of hand soap. She quickly rinsed her hands and dried them using the hand dryer machine, after she had done her business inside the toilet, she returned to their table.

In the meantime, three blocks away from the coffee shop, it was quotidian for everyone else except for an enigmatic man wearing a black hoodie jumper and a wireless headset on his right ear. The man was ready to execute his plan, to finish his mission without any compromise. He secured his position on the rooftop of a twenty-storey building.

'This might be a game, but it is definitely not an ordinary game," the man thought to himself when he was able to secure his position, he then opened a black duffle bag and grabbed the objects inside, then once he finished, the man looked in the scope of the GIAT FR 2 sniper rifle. As a professional, he was able to drown out any distractions, even the ongoing noises from the busy street, then after securing the target, he pulled the trigger. He meticulously disassembled the rifle and placed it inside the bag, then he nonchalantly left the area and made a call using the wireless headset he was wearing once he was inside his BMW sedan car.

"Mission accomplished," he said as he scanned the area, he turned on the car's engine once he made sure everything was clear and drove off.

"Well done! Your payment is already transferred to your account. I will contact you once I need your services again," replied by his client and ended the call while the man in jacket headed to his place to rest. It took him a week of planning and it paid off very well.

Even farther away from the coffee shop and the street where the sniping incident happened, a well-dressed man in black suit was looking at the great view of the vibrant city from his ceiling to floor glass window. Even the building's location was undisclosed.

"As I've said, what is mine is totally mine. I do not let anyone interfere with it," the well-dressed man said to his loyal right-hand subordinate without removing his stare over the city below, "how's the next part of the plan?"

"It's ready, sir!" The subordinate politely replied.

"Wonderful! Let the show begin! Let's witness chaos unfold!" Said the boss, smiling while still not averting his gaze on the city, "these sudden turn of events might be interesting and eventually, might be entertaining for us to start enjoying the show!" His assistant just nodded in approval for his boss's plans.

Concurrently, back in the cafe, Alex was enjoying her coffee with her best friend when she noticed the man on the other table left after he received a call. She discerned that it was an emergency of some sort as the man walked with haste. Once again, she caught herself affected by that man.

"Hey, I know what's going on? I was hesitant at first, but now, I am certain!" Elissandra suddenly outburst out of the blue, cutting Alex's thoughts.

"What do you mean?" Alex perplexedly asked while composing herself.

"I saw what happened between you and the man in the suit earlier!" Elissandra teased with a mischievous grin on her face.

"Oh, it was just a random encounter," she casually stated.

"Really? With those sneaky glances you've thrown at him? Haha!" Elissandra whispered in her ear, "babe, I'm your best friend. I know what I've seen!"

Alex saw how Elissandra suppressed her laughter. She was cornered by her trusted friend.

"OK, fine! You caught me. It was just that we had a dispute earlier when he was parking and I was in a hurry that we nearly had a collision," Alex explained.

"Wow, that is what I call fate! A rare encounter that resulted in an unusual way," Elissandra said as she caressed Alex's shoulder for assurance.

"I bet this will not be the last encounter between the two of you. You know I have a good intuition with regard to these things," Elissandra added with a beam of smile on her face.

"Hey, don't say that!" Alex replied. She shook her head and voiced out a second thought bothering her, "it won't happen again since it was just a random chance of encounter with a random guy.

"As you say, babe. But since we can't predict anything, I guess I'm just trying to manifest something. Since I like what I saw earlier.'" Elissandra responded.

Instead of entertaining the observations of her best friend, Alex opted to just smile at her and continued eating her food. She kept herself occupied to avoid any more teasing from Elissandra. She listened to the clacking of the keyboard from the next table where the man was sitting earlier. It was now occupied by a seemingly college student, busy typing away in his laptop.

While he was driving, Osmond recalled the General's instruction for him over the call he received earlier at the coffee shop. He stepped on the brake pedal as he saw the orange light signal. He sensed the urgency from the General's voice.

"Agent Gomez, abort the meeting with Agent McKain. I have already informed him. Proceed to the Phantom site. I am now with a person you will know once you get here."

His thoughts were cut when he saw the car in front of him begin to move. His senses were on alert since he left the cafe several minutes ago. He arrived in front of a five-storey building. It looked abandoned and was a few kilometres away from the vicinity of the central business district. He signalled the General by dropping a missed call before entering the building. It was their indication that the place was safe and secured. He then got a text message. He was able to locate the room and knocked on the door. He remembered they used this building before, but they used the room on his left. The door opened and he was greeted by the General himself, and saw the person behind the General. He realised that it was the man the General pertained to in the call earlier. Osmond definitely knew the man, he recollected that he guarded the high-profiled man several times before.

"Mr. de Ayala, how have you been?" Osmond greeted the man with a handshake after his salutations to the General.

"I'm doing well, agent Gomez. But there's a dilemma that needs your expertise," Mr. de Ayala forthright said, "I need you to guard my daughter."

Osmond furrowed his forehead as he glanced at the General. The whereabouts of Mr. de Ayala's daughter was concealed to most, even to their intel. All he knew was she was the only child of the man in front of him. Everything else was purposely hidden to the public and was a mystery until the controversy in Madrid happened that finally the world already knew her. He was now curious about the man's request.

"Mr. de Ayala's daughter is now in Melbourne which she just arrived yesterday. After her altercation in Madrid, she is now totally exposed to the public's eyes," the General said, seemingly reading Osmond's thoughts, "however, we don't know how many syndicates will be targeting her. Mr. de Ayala received an encrypted email this afternoon."

As if on cue, Mr. de Ayala opened his iPad and showed it to Osmond. Osmond read and analysed the email. True to the General's word, it was untraceable and short that made it a threat.

"How's your daughter, Mr. Enrique de Ayala?"

After scrutinising the email, Osmond intently looked towards Mr. de Ayala.

"Agent Gomez, my team tried also to track the source of the email. We couldn't even trace it's IP address," Mr. de Ayala pleadingly looked at Osmond, "you are the country's top-secret agent. I am giving you my full trust that you will be able to ensure the safety of my only daughter and heiress."

"On top of this email, there was an incident earlier. An assassin was killed by another assassin," the General interjected. He also mentioned where the shooting happened to Osmond, who was in disbelief.

He was just three blocks away from the crime scene when it happened! Osmond's innate intelligence started to work as he hypothesised that the incident and email were not a coincidence. They happened purposely. He put his act together in front of the gentlemen after he processed his thoughts.

"It will be an honour to work for you again. I am accepting your request, Mr. de Ayala," he reassuringly said to the well-respected man. Partly, he also has animosity against people with evil intents like those who abducted innocent people like his childhood best friend.

"Thank you so much, Agent Gomez. I'm forever indebted to you!" Mr. de Ayala gratefully said as the patriarch of the de Ayala, he engulfed agent Gomez in an appreciative hug.

"Thus, this," the General interrupted, "is your assignment agent Gomez. This folder contains pertinent information regarding Ms. de Ayala."

Then the General handed the folder to his agent which Osmond opened and it showed him the profile containing a photo of his latest assignment with confidential data about her.

Osmond was initially astonished by what he saw. He quickly regained his composure and was able to hide his initial bedazzlement from the two men in front of him. She was gorgeous, compared to the blurred photos that leaked from the event in Madrid, she was a brunette goddess that went down from the heavenly realm. However, there was something about her that bothered him. Something more enigmatic from what he heard and saw on the news, he hoped his psychoanalysis of her personality was wrong.

"She is Ms. Margarette Alexandria de Ayala. Although, she preferred to be called Ms. Alex. Twenty-two years old. Stubborn. She has a lot of boundaries," the General said professionally even in front of Mr. de Ayala, interrupting agent Gomez's thoughts.

"I have already started monitoring her for you, since Mr. de Ayala reported that she escaped from their mansion this morning. A team tracked her earlier and located her car's registration three blocks aways from the assassination incident," the General continued while showing to the agent about the location.

Osmond nodded gratefully to the General's immediate action in his stead. He started to piece the puzzle together. He was sure that it was Ms. Alex who was in the coffee shop, the lady in purple turban with sunglasses, the companion of Ms. Elissandra Davis. She disguised herself. Osmond furrowed his brows as he realised the gravity of the situation, it was also his first time to handle this kind of mission. He was ready to fulfill the task and starting tomorrow he would be the new personal bodyguard of Ms. Margarette Alexandria de Ayala.

Six

Bound to Happen

Alex was looking out of the SUV's window, her sunglasses reflected the sunlight. She was observing the vehicles and the crowd nearby as the driver slowed down upon seeing the traffic light turned orange to red. They were on their way home, while Elissandra was picked up by her parents. Alex's mother, who was beside her, was on a phone call with the usual corporate operations.

Alex recalled what had happened more than ten minutes earlier at the café, the manager announced that everyone must leave except them. Both of them were perplexed by the demand of the man in black corporate attire until they saw her mother, who was with her best friend's parents, at the main door. Alex and Elissandra became confused after seeing a few armed men in uniform behind their parents including Alex's personal bodyguard. She looked at her best friend and caught her looking back at her.

"How did they find us?" Alex asked Elissandra, shocked by the obvious tone of her question.

"I don't really have an idea, Alex," Elissandra replied as she felt the tension from her best friend's voice.

"I believe you. But I don't like where this is going," she said as she saw their parents and the uniformed men walking towards them.

"Same here," Elissandra whispered as she held Alex's right hand.

They did not let go of each other's hands until the newcomers reached their table.

"Mom, what is this all about? And how did you know where to find us?" Alex asked as she stood up to approach her, and it seemed not angry by the looks of her, it was more of worry that Alex perceived until the two men in uniform closing all the windows of the café while the other two were securing the main entry with her personal bodyguard.

"Honey, we cannot answer any of your questions here. Let's go back home. We need to be there before your father arrives," her mother replied who obviously came from the office as she was still wearing her black corporate attire.

Alex furrowed her eyebrows beneath her sunglasses and glanced at her best friend who was talking with her parents a few metres away from them. And the confusion on Elissandra's face as her parents were explaining something that Alex could not hear.

"Mom, please. I need an answer," Alex pleaded as she felt the heaviness of the tension in the place.

"Dear, I wish I could. Now is not the right time, things are a bit complicated and I cannot divulge anything," Evangeline answered as she hugged her daughter.

Alex hugged her mother back and saw Elissandra approaching them. She disentangled herself from her mother to face her best friend. Elissandra suddenly hugged her silently, but Alex felt the concern and sincerity in it, and hugged her best friend back.

"I wish we could spend more time but it seems that things have drastically changed for both of us. My parents told me that we cannot see each other for quite a while including electronic communication," Elissandra explained as they were now facing each other and holding hands, "don't worry, your parents will explain it to you and once the dust settles we will catch up and hang out once again."

"But why? It's so confusing. I deserve to know what's happening," Alex exasperatedly said to her best friend then shifted her gaze to her mother.

"I'm sorry, dear. Your father sternly instructed me to take you home and that he will be the one to explain it to you," Evangeline replied to her daughter as their gaze met.

Frustratedly, Alex just nodded at her mother. She looked at her best friend again who was ready to leave with her parents. For the last moment, they embraced again as goodbye.

Alex's recollection of the moment earlier was interrupted as she felt the SUV finally halted along their mansion's driveway. Their driver opened the door for her mother and her personal bodyguard opened her side of the door. She glanced back at her mother before getting out of the vehicle. Her mother gave her a concerned smile. Alex took a deep breath knowing that something really had happened. She strengthened her resolve to know what it was and to face her father. Her curiosity was getting the best out of her since they left the coffee shop.

"Why did you leave?" Enrique asked Alex as she and her mother arrived inside her father's study room. Her father was seated behind an oakwood executive desk. She and her mother sat across from him.

"Dad, Elissandra and I both agreed to meet since my immersion will soon start—"

"Which brought you and Elissandra in great danger," her father interrupted her before she could fully explain her side.

She removed her sunglasses and placed on the table. It was then her father picked up his iPad, unlocked it, and handed it to her with an apparent disappointment on his face.

Alex saw what was on the screen.

"How's your daughter, Mr. Enrique de Ayala?"

She glanced at her father then her mother after reading the short email. She realised that the sender was anonymous. Her confusion was still unquenched as she tried to fathom the message. She gently placed the device back on the table.

"Dad, Mom, don't mind that email. Surely, it's from someone looking for attention from us," she nonchalantly said while shaking her head.

"Especially now that the world knows about me. Maybe we should not get ahead of ourselves and worry needlessly," she added and stood up to leave, but she instantly stopped as her father raised the tone of his voice.

"This time, I won't let you walk away and do whatever you want! Sit back down, young lady! There is more to it that you need to know," Enrique exclaimed as he motioned Alex back to her chair.

Alex saw the resolve in her father's eyes that made her obey him. Evangeline, then, stood up and approached her husband to caress his back.

"Enrique, try to calm down. I know how it feels but shouting will not solve anything," Evangeline gently told her husband.

"I know, Evangeline. But she must know what is really happening once and for all," Enrique reassuringly replied to his wife before directing towards Alex, "Approximately three blocks away from that café, there was an assassination. According to the investigations, the target was you. But the mercenary failed. Someone else was watching him and waited for the right opportunity to kill him. You were lucky that the second assassin killed the mercenary who was targeting you before he got to you! It might be a sign of self-interest, but it is still uncertain. The main problem we have right now is that we do not yet know who the real enemy is."

"What? Oh my god! I didn't know..." Alex exclaimed, unable to finish her sentence as she covered her lips with her right hand while her left brushed her hair out of shock. She was totally incredulous at what she had heard.

"For now, I have tightened our security measures." Her father said firmly but with concern, "I already have made plans and will be explaining the details to you tomorrow morning. For now, you need to rest."

Alex wondered about the plans her father mentioned, but he was also correct as she realised that she was tired from the day's events. So, she decided to patiently wait for his explanation tomorrow.

"Is there anything else you'd like to discuss, dad?" She asked.

She saw her father shake his head and, then, smiled at her with great concern.

"None. Let's just continue tomorrow," Enrique replied as he stood up from his executive swivel chair to approach his daughter. Alex also got up from her chair as her father approached her. Enrique gave her a fatherly embrace.

"I am glad you are safe. I was so scared when I got the news from our butler that you went out alone," he added as he expressed his concern while looking intently at his daughter.

"Don't worry dad. I can take care of myself," Alex gratefully answered, "by the way, dad, we should investigate the couple I had an altercation with in Madrid."

"There's no need, dear. My trusted allies have done their protocols and found that they have no reason or connection to what is happening here," Enrique replied.

"One thing is certain, there is someone out there capable and powerful enough to do such things and untraceable," he added then grabbed the iPad to check some updates.

"Your father is right. We should trust his plans," Evangeline added from behind her husband and approached Alex to hold her hands.

Alex simply nodded understanding to her parents' explanations. She tried to avoid thinking further regarding the negative circumstances that had happened to her lately. Their family discussion was interrupted as a gentle knock came from the door.

"Come in," Enrique commanded.

The family butler with one of their staff, a woman in her early thirties, opened the two doors made of oakwood and entered while pushing a silver three-tiered trolley covered by white linen. It was filled with a plethora of food and drinks.

"Thanks! Just in time. I am starting to get hungry," Enrique said as he began to unfasten his tie and took off his black suit which he put on the executive chair's backrest.

Enrique's phone rang but he decided to decline the call. Meanwhile, the butler thoroughly inspected the variety of food and beverages on the trolley. Once satisfied, he nodded and motioned to the patriarch of the house that the food was safe for consumption.

"Sir Enrique, as you requested. Bon appetit. I also informed the rest of the staff about the new mandatory security measures," the butler politely said.

"Thank you!" He replied as the butler and the staff started to leave and closed the door.

Enrique took the bottle of Moët & Chandon Brut Imperial Champagne from the wine cooler. A loud popping sound was heard as he opened the bottle, then, he filled three flutes which he gave the two ladies with him. Evangeline, meanwhile, approached the service trolley.

"Dear, which one do you like?" Evangeline asked Alex while already placing a variety of snacks on the plate.

"It's okay mom. I'll just have a fruit platter," Alex replied. She grabbed a side plate to fill. She smiled at her mom who had handed a plate to her father with his favourite snacks, sweet potato, caramelised onion rolls, vegan rainbow spring rolls, carrot caraway crackers, and several pieces of cheesy baked oysters.

"Thanks, honey!" Enrique said to Evangeline and gave her a quick kiss. Alex saw her parents' sweet gesture and smiled, the memory of the recent events seemed to be blown away slowly as she witnessed the love her parents have.

Evangeline was about to go back to the trolley to get another plate for her, but Enrique stopped her.

"We can share with my plate. There are plenty for the both of us," he said to which his wife lovingly heeded.

He raised his glass of champagne, which Evangeline and Alex followed.

"Cheers!" They all exclaimed, followed by the soft clinks from their flutes.

The next morning, Osmond was sitting in the guest area. He was booted and suited. It was his first day as Ms. Margarette Alexandria's bodyguard. He was earlier than expected as he was to discuss other matters with Mr. Enrique de Ayala. He was told by the butler to wait there until the de Ayala family was done with their breakfast.

As he waited, Osmond recalled how his assignment was altered with high priority. It was last night when he was watching television when his phone rang. He immediately knew who was on the other line when he answered it. It was his most trusted colleague.

"Yes, Agent McKain?" He greeted the caller.

"Agent Gomez! Good luck on your new mission. I've heard she is a high-profiled personality," Cedrick McKain teased.

"Of course, you and your meddling curiosity," Osmond retorted. He immediately knew who Agent McKain was referring to by the tone of his playful voice.

"Haha! Well, nobody told me. But you know me too well, I have my own ways to know things! Good night!" Cedrick abruptly ended the call just to annoy his friend.

"He never change." Osmond thought to himself and smiled. He knew Cedrick was a keen and reliable agent, he was also a devoted person that would stay loyal to their profession.

Osmond, then, remembered how Mr. de Ayala employed him several times in the past. He grew to respect the head of the de Ayala conglomerates, he got to know about the kindness, humility, and amiability of the man.

It was when he received a private text message that night. He initially thought it was Cedrick again to tease him until he saw the name of the sender and how important it was.

Agent Gomez, be vigilant tomorrow from your place until you reached your destination.

The General forewarned him as he himself agreed to be alert at all times. Thus, when he left his apartment this morning, his senses were guarded. He observed his surroundings to ensure nothing's peculiar before entering his vehicle. He was two hours early for the said meeting as he glanced at his wrist watch. He had to secure everything before reaching his destination, even the circumjacent areas. He pulled out his .45 calibre pistol when he entered the vehicle and checked the two holsters on his sides covered by his suit. He also inspected his spare magazines and several daggers. He was ready!

Osmond's recollections were interrupted as he felt a presence and his keen ears heard someone walking towards him. He turned and saw the family's butler on his way to him.

"Mr. de Ayala is ready and expecting you in his study room. Let me lead you there, sir," the butler said, gesturing to him towards the study room.

Upon reaching the aforementioned room, the butler took his leave while Osmond was standing in front of the door. He knocked on it.

"Come in," said the voice from the other side of the door. As Osmond opened the door and entered, he saw several great books stacked neatly on almost all sides of the room. In front of him was an oak executive table, which behind it was the man Osmond was to meet. Mr. de Ayala was seated in a large executive leather black chair. The man put down the newspaper he was reading and directly looked at Osmond.

"Have a seat, agent Gomez," the older man sought him.

Meanwhile, on the other side of the de Ayala estate, Alex just came out of the shower to change her clothes after breakfast with her parents. She knew that her father would continue their discussion from yesterday, thus, she was instructed to proceed to the study room. However, in her mind, she felt that there was another reason.

After arriving in front of the door of the study room, Alex knocked and heard her father telling her to come in. Inside, the first thing or, rather, person that caught her attention was the presence of a man in an all black suit. He was sitting across from her father. Alex had no idea who he was. She wondered who he was, his purpose for being here, and his connection to her father. Until she felt a sensation of déjà vu. She was certain that they had already met before but was unsure when and where and she didn't like what she felt.

She side-glanced at the man to assess him. She knew how her glances could exude power and authority over others. She didn't care if she thought he was a good looking man but she knew that she needed to put up her armour.

At the same moment, Osmond felt the menacing gaze thrown at him by the lady who just came in. He pretended that they have never met before. He matched her intimidation with his indifference, showing her that he was not and would not be affected by her. His assessment of her yesterday was undeniably accurate.

"Anyway, Agent Gomez," both thoughts were cut short as Mr. de Ayala spoke, "this is my daughter, Alex. Alex, this gentleman here is agent Osmond Gomez. He is your new personal bodyguard. As I mentioned last night, this is what I was talking about."

Alex was taken aback and was perturbed from what she heard from her father.

"What? But why dad? Where is my bodyguard?"

"He was let go after you escaped under his watch," her dad replied.

"Fine! But you have to assign one of your bodyguards to me instead of him," she replied and tried to maintain her composure.

"And why not?" Her father curiously asked.

"Dad, I don't exactly know who he is. You know, as a fact, that I don't trust just anyone, let anyone accompany me wherever and whenever I go," she retaliated.

"I know and trust this man very well. That is the reason I chose him. You know what happened, right? So, whether you like it or not, he will be your bodyguard. That's my final decision regarding this matter!" Mr. de Ayala said with finality.

Osmond quietly observed the banter between the father and daughter while trying to hide his amusement as a professional. He knew that he could handle his responsibilities and this mission.

"But dad..." Alex tried but she knew there was no way that her father would change his mind. She was hurt and frustrated but she had to accept his command.

"Fine. As you said, you always have the final say, right?" She added sarcastically. However, she already had a plan brewing in her devious mind.

"Let's see if you will be able to tolerate me," she thought to herself, smiling slyly, as she walked out of the study room, closed the doors behind her, and left the two men inside the room.

Seven

Their Duties

Alex reached her room in a rush. She was so frustrated that tears started to form. She hoped she didn't have to live this life of opulence and desperately desired to live the life like common people do. She was in that state when she heard a soft knock on her door. She quickly composed herself, wiped the almost falling tear. She approached her door to unlock it since it required her thumbprint as it was a biometric door.

"Mom, please talk to dad. Please tell him to give me more time to accept and think about the situation, especially now that I don't even know who I will be with!" She pleadingly asked her mom who was at the door.

"Oh dear, you know your dad well. Once he has his mind set, it can never change. Try to understand him. For now, all we could do is to follow his biddings," answered her mom with concern in her voice.

Alex knew that she couldn't do anything. She also knew that even her mother agrees with her dad's decision.

"Honey, I already arranged your clothes. Please try to be polite to your new bodyguard," Evangeline said.

Alex remained silent. She's not used to this kind of setup. If only she knew this would happen, she would not have gone here and left Europe. The sudden change of her new personal bodyguard annoyed her. She needed to know how to get rid of him as soon as possible. She couldn't not stand his arrogance.

It has been an hour and she was ready to leave soon. She looked at herself in the full-length mirror. She was wearing a black overall sleeveless, accented with a classic pearl choker, and she styled her hair into a simple high-bun. Once satisfied, she grabbed her white trench coat on the bed, put it on, and left her bedroom.

Osmond, who waited patiently in the foyer, tried to hide his amusement as he saw Alex coming down the stairs. He tried to stifle his laughter, trying to be as professional as he could be. He was amused by how he personally thought Alex was overdressed. She was only going to the office yet she was in that attire in high stilettos. He opted to just give a well-mannered smile to make her comfortable around him as her new personal bodyguard.

Alex felt something odd as she saw Osmond smiling at her. It was a strange feeling she couldn't explain, but she immediately disregarded it as quickly as she saw her personal driver come in to inform her and Osmond that their ride was ready.

"Ms. Alex, as you requested, the dark silver Bentley Bentayga S is ready," her driver said warmly with a smile.

"Thank you," she replied and an idea strucked her mind.

"Osmond, hold this please." She handed him her Himalayan Kelly bag.

However, Osmond just stood there without reaching for Alex's bag. He just looked at her. He knew what Alex was trying to do.

"Ms. Alex, I am your personal bodyguard and not your assistant," he monotonously answered.

"Osmond, I wasn't implying anything like that. I am just going back to my room since I forgot something, so no big deal. Right?" She said. She was starting to get annoyed by this arrogant man.

They were just standing there having a staring contest, throwing imaginary daggers through their eyes.

"The nerve of this man!" Alex annoyingly thought to herself. No one has ever dared to decline her command before!

"Ms. Alex, I can hold your bag for you," the driver awkwardly volunteered trying to diffuse the sudden tense atmosphere in the room.

"No, never mind! Let's just go!" Alex said through her gritted teeth, and didn't want to prolong this seemingly futile situation; but she swore to herself that she would do everything just to eliminate that man from her life.

Upon reaching the driveway, her driver opened the metallic silver SUV backdoor. She went in and wore the seatbelt once the door was closed by the driver. The driver quickly went around to get in the driver's side and seat, while Osmond sat beside him. As they exited the electronic gate past the flower garden of the mansion, the gardener smiled to her while the various flowers could be seen and showed great care, from red, white, pink roses, to peach and pink peonies and tulips then she smiled bacck then looked to the front while she got her sunglasses from her bag, hoping to at least to lessen the annoying presence of Osmond. She checked the current weather on her phone, it was about twenty degrees celsius and she liked this temperature in the middle of spring.

She noticed how Osmond became more alert as soon as they left the Toorak area, he was aware and cautious with every car passing, adjacent and behind them. She instantly disregarded it as she thought it was his job and returned her attention to her phone.

"Ms. Alex," Osmond disrupted her browsing on her phone.

"Yes?" She nonchalantly answered.

"From now on, you have to turn off your phone's GPS and you are not allowed to use any social media and communicate with anyone," Osmond said calmly, but with a certain forewarning.

"And why would I do that? To make things clear, I don't have social media," she aggravatedly answered. The nerve of this man to forbid her.

"It was instructed by your father. It is also for your own safety. It is to avoid you being traced," Osmond tried to explain professionally as he could. Mr. de Ayala gave him the authority to do so, particularly there's danger that could come from anywhere knowing that the information of Alex in Australia was compromised. So, Osmond had to make sure that Alex's stubbornness was put in place.

As for Alex, she was mortified. She couldn't accept the sudden change in her security and her father even allowed it to happen. Her father knew how she could handle herself even with regard to technology and how finicky she was communicating with others. She was suddenly stressed and commanded her driver to park in a safe location as she had the urge to smoke. She would throw a fit to the point she was willing to hit him with her luxury bag. She was grateful it didn't happen as the driver parked the car near a pathway under the trees. In a hurry, she exited the vehicle after the driver ran to her side and opened the door for her. She didn't even notice the uneven footpath that caused her to misstep. She closed her eyes expecting a painful fall, plunging face first, which didn't happen. She felt suspended midair. As she opened her eyes and saw that Osmond was quick to hold her left arm which prevented her from falling.

For the first time, their skin touched. Alex once again felt the odd feeling within her; almost the same odd feeling as she was descending the stairs earlier at the mansion, but this time it much stronger. There was a brief moment that they both stared at each other. Alex was able to recover after she heard Osmond.

"Were you hurt, Ms. Alex?" The man asked her.

She saw concern in the man's eyes. She tried to regain composure unsure of what she saw and quickly disregarded it and was grateful that her sunglasses didn't fall, hiding the odd feeling she felt.

"No-nope, thank you," she answered and immediately grabbed a cigarette from her bag and lit it.

"Ms. Alex, you will only have five minutes to smoke here," Osmond seemingly commanded as he was scanning the surroundings.

Alex raised an eyebrow at him.

"Are you for real, Mr. Gomez?" She asked sarcastically, even calling him by his last name. He already forbade her to use GPS and was accused of using social media just a while ago, now he's dictating the duration of her smoking. She was getting fed up with this arrogant man!

"As your personal bodyguard, I have to ensure your safety," Osmond reiterated as he shrugged off the lady's stubbornness. He had to follow protocols of protection.

"Whatever!" Alex said irritatedly while rolling her eyes on Osmond. As she exhaled white smoke, she saw how the man across her was attentively surveying the whole area, observing as a hawk to every passerby and vehicles. Alex realised now how other people would glance at her, to which she shrugged off. She never paid attention to others before, she didn't plan on doing it now, besides it was Osmond's job.

After finishing her cigarette, she approached the nearby rubbish bin to dispose the cigarette. She, then, got a mint in her bag and sprayed a bit of her perfume to alleviate the cigarette's smell. Osmond automatically opened the door for her as soon as she was in front of it. She even purposely avoided thanking him, but instead she just smiled at Osmond.

Osmond checked the surroundings again, once assured that nothing was untoward, he entered the vehicle.

As soon as they entered Collins Street, the busiest area in the central business district of Melbourne, Osmond sent a text message to Mr. de Ayala that they were nearby. After sending the message, he observed the district, alert of the cars and people within the vicinity.

Less than a kilometre from the main office, Alex received a text message from her father.

'My associate will be waiting in front of the building. Her name is Bettina Smith. I'll send her contact info so you will know.'
'OK, dad.' Alex replied then returned her phone in her bag.

After several minutes, the car was parked in front of a high-rise building, which served as the de Ayala's main office. It was the busiest part of the day; thus, many employees and visitors were going to and fro their building.

Alex removed her sunglasses to look up their office from her car window. She let out a sigh, as if trying to prepare herself for a great battle. She, then, put back her sunglasses as her driver opened the car door for her. As she stepped out of the vehicle, she saw how most of the people around stopped to look at her to which she paid no mind.

"Thank you," Alex said to her driver.

"You're welcome, Ms. Alex." The driver replied to her.

She gracefully strode towards the revolving door of the building with Osmond behind her. She saw that he was now wearing a dark aviator, which she thought made him sexier. She quickly cleared that thought.

The moment she entered their building, she felt again the stare of the people in the lobby. She continued walking when she heard her phone notifying her of an incoming call.

"Yes, Ms. Smith?" Alex answered the call.

"Hi, Ms. Alex. I can see you in the lobby. I'm the one waving at you from the concierge," said the woman on the other line.

Alex saw an approaching woman in a grey corporate attire waving at her as she ended the call.

"Nice to personally meet you, Ms. Alex. I'm Bettina Smith, your father's associate," said the woman who Alex thought was around in her late fourties.

"Your dad is in the conference room. He's waiting for you there," Bettina added.

"Alright. Let's go," Alex curtly answered. She doesn't like long discussions, especially as she noticed how the woman in front of her was constantly glancing at Osmond, who was still behind her. The woman lead them towards the elevator. As they approached and waited for the elevator to open, Alex noticed how a number of employees respectfully greeted Ms. Smith. Once again, Alex couldn't help herself but rolled her eyes hidden by her sunnies.

Then the elevator was now opening and Osmond checked the perimeter before allowing Alex to come in. Alex was now situated at the back of Osmond and Ms. Smith.

"Ms. Smith, I hate to be crammed, especially in a confined space," Alex said as several employees attempted to enter the elevator, only for them to be stopped mid-step. Ms. Smith apologetically smiled at the employees, who had no choice but to back away, as she pressed the elevator's close button then the button for the top level of the building. Osmond glanced at Alex and was about to say something but decided to be silent about it, for now. He saw several annoyed stares before the elevator finally closed.

"Oh gosh! I have a deadline to catch!" Shouted a woman in reading glasses.

"What the hell! Who was that? Pretty but snob!" Said by the blonde female employee.

"Hey, she might be a daughter of one of our shareholders in the corporation," answered by the man in black suit.

"Most probably. I saw her when she get off from Bentley Bentayga earlier," said by another man who was still holding his takeaway cup from a nearby coffee shop.

"Oh, shit! Then I would avoid her if I see her again. I don't want to be suspended, or worse, fired!" Nervously uttered by the woman in reading glasses.

Eight

The Mystical Riddle

Alex was introduced to the board of directors, by her father Mr. Enrique de Ayala, inside of the conference room. She sat beside her father while her mother was on the right and seemed satisfied with the current meeting. The oval table allowed her a view of the board, while in front of her was an iPad that contained various files of their company's budget for various operations, from retail, food and beverage, and manufacturing. It was mostly European, as the majority of her father business associates. She browsed another file which contained personnel payroll taxes, costs of purchasing or producing products, sales and marketing, phone, internet and utilities, repairs and maintenance, outside services like accounting and legal, fees and licenses, interest, depreciation, office supplies, company vehicles, travel, and the likes. She was able to do this while the board was busy discussing other matters. She surmised that everything was in place, even the low cost yet effective marketing strategies that assured profit for her father and their partners.

"Alex, is there anything you want to suggest or ask from the board?" Her father suddenly asked that made everybody's attention turned to her. Alex looked at her dad then to the board of directors. She placed the iPad on the table and took a breath before she started speaking.

"First, thank you for the warm welcome. As for the files presented, apparently none. The budget was quite huge but reasonable, the low cost yet effective marketing strategies were impressive. I'm foreseeing profit by the second or third quarter of next year from the data provided," she said with credence that seemed to impress the board.

The meeting continued until a certain idea came to her mind.

"Mom, I wanna go to dad's office," she whispered to her mother. Deep inside, she wanted to run away from the conference. Although she did not show her malaise to anybody in the room, but she felt restrained.

"Won't you stay and wait for the voting?" Her mother tried to stop Alex from leaving, "so, you can observe and listen to the process."

"Mom, please, I already know that and how it will turn out," she said, though she had enough already and her mother would not be able to stop her. With a sigh, her mother gave her the access card.

"Pardon me, it was nice meeting all of you. However, I needed to check some files from dad's office. Please excuse me," she tried her best to be polite as she stood and excused herself from her parents and the board of directors then she looked at Ms. Smith.

"Thank you dear, for coming and you did a great job," Enrique whispered to Alex as she gave him a quick hug.

As she left, the pride and satisfaction in her father's eyes were evident then a quick small smile to hide what she truly felt. She quickly walked out of the conference with Ms. Smith leading the way.

Outside, Osmond heard the conference door opened. He turned his attention and saw the blonde woman who welcomed them earlier followed by Alex. Osmond and Alex's eyes met, only that Alex annoyingly raised an eyebrow towards him. Osmond ignored Alex's gesture and proceeded to follow them, until Ms. Smith saw a particular woman and greeted her follwed by introducing Alex.

"Ms. Wilson, this is Ms. Margarette Alexandria de Ayala, the daughter of our CEO, you may call her Ms. Alex," Ms. Smith said, "Ms. Alex, this is Lorrie Wilson, your dad's secretary."

"Ms. Alex, it's an honour to meet you," the secretary said, and smiling at them.

"Same here, Ms. Wilson," then she saw her stared at Osmond for a few seconds which she felt an unexplainable annoyance towards the secretary.

"By the way, Ms. Wilson, the power lunch will start in half an hour. Please make sure everything is in order, including the high-afternoon tea," Ms. Smith disrupted Alex's thoughts and the secretary's ogling over Osmond.

"Yes, Ms. Smith," answered by the secretary then smiled but not without stealing another glance at the man behind the two women, who she surmised would be Ms. Alex's bodyguard, hence the lack of introduction.

"Thanks, Ms. Wilson. Anyway, I'll have to show Ms. Alex to her dad's office," Ms. Smith said, smiling at the secretary.

"Ms. Alex, this is your dad's office. If you need something just give me a call or Ms. Wilson."

"Thanks, Ms. Smith," Alex said, then Ms. Smith returned to the conference room across the hall. Alex swiped the access card to open the door and quickly entered disregarding Osmond who stood vigilant beside the door.

Osmond didn't bother himself on how Alex treated him. He focused on his duty. Even if they were inside the de Ayala's main office, his senses were still heightened. He knew that danger was everywhere and any odd or suspicious behaviour from anyone, even an office staff, he wouldn't hesitate to incapacitate the suspect. He even remember from behind his aviator how the secretary kept on glancing and smiling at him. He maintained his composure and ignored the woman. He never pays attention to any lady if he's on duty, unless she's a client.

Meanwhile, inside Mr. de Ayala's office, Alex looked around. She then proceeded to the table and sat on the executive swivel chair and saw the photo facing her. She smiled and carefully took it and caressed the picture, she remembered when this was taken, that was during her teenage days, she was between her parents who were hugging her.

After reminiscing, she returned the photo and looked around the office again. This will be her future as her father's successor. She stood up and turned around to walk towards the floor to ceiling glass window and stared through it, overlooking several high-rise buildings and other establishments within the central business district.

She suddenly remembered Osmond, his alluring physique hiding underneath his black suit, his arrogant personality that made him sexier, his dark eyes hidden behind his dark aviator that seemed to bore into her soul every time he looked at her, and how she hated him. She forced herself to stop thinking of him and walked back towards the swivel chair. She busied herself with the file she opened and read. After reviewing several files, she was once again staring at their family photo when the telephone on the desk rang.

"Yes?" She answered.

"I am sorry for disturbing you Ms. Alex, but your dad wants you to come into the break room for the power lunch," the secretary said on the other line. Very convenient timing, she was getting starving.

"Okay. I'm coming in a sec," Alex said as she returned the phone on the receiver and walked out of the office. Outside, Ms. Wilson was waiting for her, while Osmond was next to the secretary.

"Ms. Alex, if you please follow me to the breakroom," the secretary said and then Alex felt once again the irritation for the woman how she glanced towards Osmond.

Inside the breakroom, she didn't bother herself to join the conversation her parents were having with their colleagues. Though her father invited her, she declined his request and went straight towards the farthest table from them, to be alone.

She was enjoying her meal, a healthy tuna salad with sweet potato and quinoa, as she was returning to her table after getting a bottle of sparkling water, she saw from her peripheral vision Osmond standing not far from her. He was intently observing the people in the breakroom, then Osmond looked at her walking back to her table. Alex was grateful she didn't look at him, which would lead her being caught looking at him if ever she did.

After a while, she felt like going to the toilet. She stood and glanced around to find the toilet's sign. She immediately found it at the corner and felt Osmond's presence behind her as she walked towards the toilet. She was about to enter when Osmond suddenly spoke.

"Ms. Alex, I'm going to check inside first."

She just nodded as an approval as Osmond instantaneously knocked to warn anyone inside that he was about to enter the ladies' toilet.

"Anyone here? For security purposes, I'm going inside," he said in an authoritative and firm tone. Since no one replied, Osmond decided to come in to check every cubicle. He even inspected the ceiling then he went out to inform Alex.

"Ms. Alex, you can safely use the toilet now," he politely said as he opened the door for her and gave way.

"Okay," she replied entering the toilet without thanking him. Osmond brushed it off and closed the door and situated himself directly in front of the toilet door to stand guard.

After a couple of minutes, Osmond saw Alex's parents with three securities approaching him. He became extra cautious as he looked behind him at the toilet's door then to Mr. de Ayala who was now within an arm's reach.

"Mr. de Ayala, is everything fine?" He curiously asked, looking back and forth at the de Ayala couple.

There was an obvious distress and anxiety on the couple as Mr. de Ayala showed Osmond his iPad. He quickly looked at what Mr. de Ayala wanted to show him.

"Between the hours of night and dawn, the transition from certainty to uncertainty unfolds after eleven. The paradox on the table presents it-

self alongside the word "at," signifying the midway point of thirty, and its significance extends to all living beings."

Osmond sighed deeply and was trying to evaluate the phrase. He knew from the second email that whoever was behind it was a powerful and formidable person. He looked back at the couple and returned the iPad to Mr. de Ayala.

"Agent Gomez, the email before was asking about my daughter but this time I'm baffled about this kind email. I already commanded my team in this building to trace it," Mr. de Ayala said worriedly, "I have also informed the General, so he can also try to track it on his side." Osmond nodded at the gentleman as he was also alarmed. He then remembered someone and asked the patriarch of the de Ayala family for his iPad. He made a phone call and after several rings, the receiver answered.

"Agent McKain, this is a matter of utmost urgency. Among my associates, you are reputed for deciphering puzzles. Please listen attentively and seek the solution," he said as he glanced at the message displayed on the iPad. Moments later, the agent on the other line responded.

"I can't decipher the riddle, my apologies. The letters and numbers are all complicated and seem to have no connection, as if it is only a piece of a big puzzle that needed more pieces. So, I can't really point out the exact answer," Osmond heard from the other line.

"It is fine Agent McKain, then a draconian last resort is my choice. Thanks," he mentioned softly and firmly, and he ended the call and gave back the device to Mr. Enrique.

"But while we are trying to hunt down the people behind this, I made a decision which was suggested by the person that I really trust," Mr. de Ayala said with frustration as he looked at the toilet's door behind Osmond and knocked, "and I need to discuss it with my daughter."

Alex was washing her hands in the lavatory, after using the toilet, when she heard a loud rushed knock on the door. She felt sudden irritation as she was so sure that it was her new bodyguard.

"For Pete's sake, Osmond! What the hell is your problem?!" She annoyingly said as she was drying her hands under the machine. She hastily opened the toilet's door and was ready to shout at Osmond for the intrusion. She didn't expect her parents waiting for her outside instead of the person she was annoyed with. They were with three securities, and she also saw the annoying person behind them. Thus, the supposed angry face she was so ready to give Osmond was quickly replaced with question and worry.

"Mom, dad? What's going on here? Why are there securities?" She curiously asked. She suddenly felt something odd and was concerned about her parents.

"My dear, let's all go to my office. We need to discuss something important," her dad replied as he led them towards it, which made Alex more anxious.

Nine

Queensland

Osmond was steadily standing by the executive door of main office, although his thoughts was preoccupied by the events that transpired. He glanced at the other security personnel with him outside of the executive office while the de Ayala family was still conferring.

Meanwhile inside the office, Alex felt something was not right. She kept looking back and forth her parents as if asking for enlightenment.

"Dad, I don't get it. Please just spill it out," she worriedly pleaded her father.

Her dad sighed, grabbed his iPad and handed it to her. She confusedly looked at her father and took hold of the iPad. It was as her face was drained of blood after reading the email. As it was a mysterious message.

"Dad, please tell me do you have an enemy? When did you start receiving this dreadful email?" She successively asked her father.

"Dear, it just happened today and I have no idea since I cannot recall anybody that I had problems with; but my team are doing our best to track the people behind this." Mr. de Ayala said trying to assure Alex, "but I made a decision with Osmond that we kept from you." her father added.

"Wait dad! What do you mean kept from me? And why is that guy involved? I should go back to Spain if this is the case!" She replied while her father went to the door to summon the man that she hates.

"Agent Gomez," called by Mr. de Ayala gaining the attention of Osmond, "please come in."

"Yes, sir," replied by Osmond as he entered the office and closed the door behind him. He saw Ms. Alex looking at him then returned her glance at her father.

"My dear, you and your bodyguard will be leaving soon," announced Mr. de Ayala, "agent Gomez will take care of you for the meantime and that is to hide you away from us."

"But dad! Please tell me you're not serious about hiding me!" Alex complained as she was feeling an utmost frustration with what was happening.

"Alex, hard as it may seem for both your mother and me, this is for your own safety. Don't worry, you will be in good and trusted hands, my dear. I will do everything in my power to ensure the capture of the ones responsible as quick as possible. Once everything is resolved, we wouldn't need to hide you anymore," explained by her father whom she saw sadness and worry in his eyes.

After her father's decision, she looked at her mother for help.

"Mom, please. Talk to dad. I don't want to go, especially with him," she said giving Osmond a quick glance, "if you're worried about my safety, I can go back to Spain."

"Oh, my poor dear! But your father and I will be more assured if you're in the country." And her mother embraced her tightly.

"Alex, please. This decision is also heartbreaking for us; but please understand us why your mother and I came up with this," Mr. de Ayala said and hugged his wife and daughter.

Osmond was quietly observing what transpired inside with the de Ayala family. He was confident enough that he can succeed the mission to protect his client; however, the people behind the threat were dangerous enough to gave a mysterious and chilling message.

Subsequently, Alex softly nodded between her parents embrace agreeing with their plan and decision. She realised the price of living with affluence, she would be in constant threat. Hard as it may seem, she had to endure for the meantime. She knew her parents were worried too as she was but for now, she had to trust them.

"Agent Gomez, please take good care of our only daughter," Mr. de Ayala said after removing himself from the family hug to talk to Osmond.

"Do not fret, Mr. de Ayala, I will do everything in my capabilities to protect your daughter," Osmond said reassuring Alex's father.

"Thank you, agent Gomez. We will be forever grateful to you," said by Mr. de Ayala who wasn't able to contain himself and embraced Osmond also.

"Dad, where am I going?" Alex asked her father as it was her turn to disentangle herself from her mother's embrace. She wanted to know where she was going so if ever, she cannot stand Osmond anymore, she knows how to return to the mansion. She could care less if the situation was dire for as long as she could keep her distance to this man who kept on bothering her.

"Somewhere in Queensland, agent Gomez's hometown with his parents," Mr. de Ayala answered looking at Osmond who nodded for affirmation.

"I have already arranged your belongings, my dear. One of our house staff is on the way to the airport with it," Mrs. De Ayala interjected.

"Thank you, mom!" Alex said with gratitude towards her mom, "can I also take one of our house staff?" She added. Her mom was about to answer only to be interrupted by her dad.

"I'm sorry, dear, but we cannot do that for this kind of situation, as per agent Gomez and General's advise also. I can only trust your mom, Agent Gomez, and General," Mr. de Ayala explained, "nobody even knows where you are going, except for those I've mentioned. So don't also tell anyone."

She opted not to argue with her father anymore. She knew his decisions were always final, plus, it made sense. They do not know who was behind the creepy email.

A sudden thought occurred to Osmond from what Alex said earlier, but he kept it for himself for the meantime. Since, he knew the challenges he would encounter with Alex once they reach their destination. It would be a new, but temporary, environment for the sole heiress of Mr. de Ayala's empire. It must be a different, far from luxurious environment to avoid being traced.

Osmond thoughts were interrupted as Mr. de Ayala's phone rang. "Yes? Oh, okay. Thank you!" Mr. de Ayala said briefly over the phone and immediately ended the call after then proceeded to directly speak with Agent Gomez.

"Agent Gomez, Alex's belongings will be in the airport soon. Let's go to the carpark now," Mr. de Ayala said formally. Osmond led the way followed by the de Ayala family exiting the main office.

Once outside, Alex saw Osmond gave a signal to the other security personnel to leave and go back to their stations.

Using a well-secured lift, which only the CEO and few associates has access, they were able to reach the carpark. There were three vehicles on the floor and Osmond saw a black Range Rover Autobiography, which he assessed as the Sentinel edition. It could have been useful, but Osmond followed his own protocols. Ms. Alex would not use any assets, physical and financial, connected to her family. He discussed this with the patriarch the other day, which was affirmed by the latter.

Alex was about to approach the black Range Rover SUV Sentinel only to be stopped by Mr. de Ayala.

"Dear, sorry, but that's not the car that you and Agent Gomez will be using going to the airport."

"And why not, dad?" Alex asked cluelessly.

"All of our assets and properties from cars, private jet, and everything under our name can be easily traced," her dad explained.

"Whatever, dad," Alex agreed with a sigh, "so which car are we gonna use?"

"Someone is coming any minute to drop both of you at the airport," Mr. de Ayala said while checking the messages on his phone.

She just nodded and checked the time on her watch. It was already half past three in the afternoon, she sighed then looked at her mother and hugged her.

"I will miss you, mom," she said.

"I will miss you more, my sweet daughter. I am sorry if things changed so suddenly. Painful as it is, but we do not have a choice and accept the best way to keep you safe," her mother sadly said while brushing her hair softly.

"Oh, there he is," Mr. de Ayala said, interrupting the mother and daughter moment. They both disentangled themselves from the embrace to paid attention to the approaching black Volkswagen Tiguan. After it parked near them, a driver stepped out from the car.

Alex immediately noticed the cheerful disposition of the man, opposite of the first time she met Osmond, in all black suit who alighted the Volkswagen. The man was smiling that exposed a set of dimples on both his cheeks that seemed to radiate with his blond curly hair.

"Good afternoon, Mr. and Mrs. de Ayala," the man said holding out his hand to the couple who shook his hand. As he held his hand towards Alex, she just reciprocate the gesture casually, then saw Osmond was looking at them but she dismissed the glance.

"Oh, thank you for doing us a huge favour, Agent Mckain. By the way, this is my daughter, Alex," Mr. de Ayala replied then faced Alex, "Dear, this is agent Cedrick McKain. He will be the one to accompany you and agent Gomez to the airport."

"Dear, again sorry if we couldn't be able to go with you to the airport. It would be safer for all of us," Mr. de Ayala embraced Alex once more followed by Mrs. de Ayala for a quick farewell.

Alex couldn't help but let a tear fall and hugged her parents one more time.

"Mom, dad," whispered by Alex with her voice started to crack. She felt both of her parents' hands on her back to soothe her even for a bit.

Osmond and Cedrick were silent witnesses to the melancholic farewell of the family in front. Osmond then turned his gaze towards his colleague.

"Is everything set, agent McKain?"

"Yes, agent Gomez," Cedrick answered as he beelined towards the car he came in and sat in the driver's seat. He saw the family approaching the car with Osmond not far behind. Osmond opened the back door for Ms. Alex, who went in silently.

"Agent Gomez, we will keep in touch. Please do tolerate my daughter's behaviour once there," Mr. de Ayala softly bade his last request before allowing Osmond to close the car's back door, quickly glancing at their daughter.

"All good, Mr. de Ayala, no worries. We'll have to go now," Osmond replied and shook the de Ayala couple's hands before entering the car beside Cedrick, who started to drive towards the airport.

On the way to the airport, Alex saw how alert and attentive the two men in front of her then she couldn't help but stare outside the city, while she couldn't help but also to imagine the place she's heading to be hidden temporarily. Her temporary present and future, it seemed. Her thoughts were cut off as she saw they were entering Essendon Fields Airport.

The black SUV halted in front of a small sized private jet. Alex noticed several security personnel in the area, as Osmond opened the door for her. One of the securities approached agent McKain and handed the luggage to him.

"Shall we, Ms. Alex?" Osmond led the way, then she just nodded for affirmation as she started following Osmond toward the private jet's steps. Before entering, Alex gave a glance back as she realised Agent McKain was behind her with a laptop.

Ten

I Will Protect You

Alex sat on the brown leather seat of the private jet and opened a magazine to browse when she saw Cedrick and Osmond chatting by the jet's door. She paid no attention to them as she was certain it was about security protocols that would bore her and she just continued browsing through the magazine.

"Thank you, Agent McKain, for dropping us off and for lending me your laptop," Osmond said gratefully to Cedrick. Everything happened abruptly that he didn't have the chance to get his laptop at the hotel he was staying. He would just call the hotel to allow Cedrick to take care of his belongings there.

"No worries, Agent Gomez. If you need anything, just message me mate," Cedrick said with his bedimpled smile. Osmond caught Cedrick stealing a glimpse towards Ms. Alex which he disregarded, since he was occupied observing the tarmac's surrounding, alert for anything suspicious.

"Roger that agent McKain. Again, thanks!" Osmond said. He trusts Cedrick as they have been together several times with previous missions and he respects the man's capabilities as they succeeded in all of them together.

"Alright, agent Gomez, I will go now. Good luck on your mission," Cedrick replied and shook Osmond's hand. He descended the jet's steps and left while Osmond took a final look around the airport to assure everything was going well before approaching his seat across Alex.

Osmond glanced at her as the flight attendant closed the jet's door. He then put his previous thought before arriving at the airport into action. He placed the borrowed laptop on now fully opened varnished foldable wooden table and turned it on. He connected it to the jet's Wi-Fi and went directly to Australian Security Intelligence Organisation or ASIO's database. He entered his access code and went directly to the files of under surveillance for possible threat and espionage. He knew that whoever was behind the e-mail that Mr. de Ayala received was from a powerful person. As the private jet started it's push back, the pilot announced several details about their flight from Melbourne to Queensland. He took this as his time to review the profiles from the files to search for hints that would connect to his mission but to no avail. With a sigh, he decided to check the Australian Federal Police's database to inspect some files there. He evaluated the top ten notorious criminals who were wanted in the files. He also checked and verified several profiles of other renowned criminals. He memorised all the profiles he found just in case he sees them he could prevent untoward event against his mission. He closed the laptop once he felt the jet was taking off. He glimpsed at Alex once more then gazed outside the window to look the still bright sun was partially covered by thick clouds, recalling that daylight saving just started a few days ago.

Alex felt as if Osmond was looking at her. She put the magazine down to look at him but he seemed deep in thought while gazing outside the window. She wanted to confront him about it but decided not to bother him. She returned to browsing the magazine that started to bore her. She knew that it would take three hours until they reach Queensland, so she decided to rest a bit before they reach their destination. She thought of asking Osmond later his plans on once the jet landed since she was aware how massive Queensland was. Almost an hour passed as she started flipping another magazine, she felt Osmond stood from his place. She did not mind him as she didn't care where he was going.

Osmond headed in the mini-kitchen area of the private jet to check on the food choices. It was one of the responsibilities he accepted as requested from him by Mr. de Ayala, to also make sure Alex was healthily and well-fed. He first checked the mini-fridge and grabbed a Bee My Honey Fruit Dip, a bottle of water, and orange juice. He then grabbed the cereal snack mix and a couple of baked gluten-free apple cider doughnut from the bench top. Next, he examined the contains of the hotbox and got a couple of apple pies. He decided to gather a number of food so Alex would have a variety to choose from. He, then, arranged the plethora of food in the tray he grabbed nearby and headed towards Alex.

Alex felt Osmond's presence beside her. She put down the magazine she was holding and looked at him. She saw the tray he was holding towards her and regarded the cornucopia of food on it. She stared back at the man who was smiling at her, which was occasionally rare and took her by surprise that she tried her best to hide.

"Your snack, Ms. Alex," Osmond delightfully said. Alex again felt a strange sensation that made her speechless but she tried to regain her composure. She just realised that Osmond was arranging the various food on the foldable table in front of her. Although she was used to being served ever since she was born, she found it different when it was Osmond was the one serving her which she cannot really comprehend.

"Enjoy your food, Ms. Alex," Osmond finally said with a warm smile, reminding Alex how she found him really handsome, after serving her food.

"Thanks," Alex softly replied, still trying to regain her composure. Afraid to say more than she should if she had continued speaking to Osmond. There was something that awoken from deep within her from the first moment she laid eyes on him. However, she finally chose to ignore these unnecessary feelings and thoughts that might confuse her.

"You're welcome, Ms. Alex," Osmond said as he went back towards the mini-kitchen to return the tray and to get food for himself. After procuring his own food, he messaged his dad to fetch them once they landed at Innisfail Airport so they could directly proceed to their house. He then arranged his chosen snacks on the tray and brought it to his seat. He smiled inside when he saw Alex eating the food that he served to her until he remembered one certain thing.

While eating, Alex stole a glimpse of Osmond which she regretted as he was also looking at her. She quickly averted her gaze and continued eating.

"Ms. Alex?" Osmond asked her.

"Yes?" She replied but not bothering to look at him.

"Do you want to ask for something or need anything?"

Then she recalled the previous day's encounter when Osmond had asked her.

"Were you the man in the black suit with sunglasses yesterday?" She asked casually, not needing to specify further.

"Yes," Osmond replied immediately as they gazed into each other's eyes.

"I see," she responded quickly, pondering her best friend's reaction to her interaction with the mysterious man who had now become her personal bodyguard. A twist of fate.

"Ms. Alex. If you need anything, please don't hesitate again to let me know," Osmond told her to which she did not dare to answer anymore but continued to finish her snack. After eating, she decided to put on her AirPods and listen to her favourite soft music. She reclined her seat and put on the eye mask so she could take a nap.

Osmond sighed at how Alex reacted as he found her a bit of a brat. He thought that how she was being affluent and sole-heiress, thus, he won't take it personally. It was part of his responsibility since he accepted this mission.

Alex woke up after an hour and a half and felt that the private jet has already landed. She removed her eye mask and saw Osmond ending a call from his phone. She took off her AirPods and thought to ask him about their residence here in Queensland.

"Osmond, where and how far is your hometown from here?" She asked as she turned her eyes outside the window. Although it was kind of dark outside, she saw it was a rural area. She huffed a bit knowing that this would be the start of a strange new experience for her, well, for a while.

Before answering, Osmond checked the time on his phone. It was nearly half past seven in the evening and his dad would arrived anytime to fetch them.

"In Jubilee Heights. Around ten kilometres away from here," Osmond answered. Alex simply nodded as her quick response. She saw the man starting to grab her luggage and the laptop. Osmond descended the jet first as she grabbed her handbag to follow him. She was grateful that their final destination was near. She was exhausted physically and emotionally from this day. However, as she reached the tarmac, she saw Osmond just standing there and waiting for her.

"Uhm, where is the car?" She asked perplexed.

"Ms. Alex, my dad is already in the carpark waiting for us," Osmond replied.

"Okay, whatever," she wanted to complain for the car to be brought inside the tarmac, but decided to be quiet about it. Osmond started to walk and she lagged behind him.

"Ms. Alex?" Osmond noticed she was quite far behind, so he stopped and faced her.

"Osmond, please just go ahead, okay?" She answered in a serious and tired tone.

"I'm sorry but that won't do, Ms. Alex. I can't let you out of my sight as your personal bodyguard," Osmond calmly replied.

She loudly exhaled and started to walk towards the man she was annoyed the most now.

"Okay, fine, but don't get too close to me. Keep your distance!" She answered frustratedly as Osmond decided not to argue further and they started to walk beside each other.

Alex saw a man who seemed the same age as her father walking towards them as they exited the regional airport and stepping unto the car park area.

"Hi, dad!" She heard from Osmond who greeted his father with a hug.

"Son! Finally, after six months, you're back!" Said the older man. Alex silently observed the excited exchange between father and son. The older man took a look at her after the former disentangled himself from the embrace.

"My apologies, gorgeous young lady," the old man pertained towards her.

"A father just missed his son."

As a sign of respect, Alex smiled back at the father of her bodyguard.

"It's okay," she replied.

"Oh sorry. Dad, this is Ms. Alex, my client," Osmond introduced the two as he was suddenly concerned that Alex might felt out of place, "Ms. Alex, this is my dad, Martin Gomez."

"Nice to meet you, Ms. Alex," Mr. Gomez said holding her hand for a handshake, which Alex took and shook with a smile.

"Dad, shall we go now?" Osmond asked his father as they shouldn't stay there for too long as it was already dark and not safe for Alex.

"Ye-yes, son, sure," Martin replied as concern was seen on his son's face. They walked altogether towards the black Wrangler Jeep. Mr. Gomez went directly to the driver's seat as Osmond opened the back door for Alex before putting the luggage in the boot and walked towards the passenger seat beside his father.

"By the way, son, why the sudden visit? You usually inform us two days prior your arrival. Not that I'm not happy you're here, but it was kind of sudden," Mr. Gomez asked curiously while en route to their home.

"Sorry dad, let's discuss that at home," Osmond seriously answered his dad.

Mr. Gomez nodded to affirm his son's request, and he glimpsed at the lady behind from the rearview mirror. He saw her staring outside the car window and saw the sadness in her eyes that were occasionally illuminated by the street lamps they passed by.

Eleven

How It All Began

Osmond saw the concern in his father's eyes. He followed his father's gaze and glimpsed Alex from the rearview window. He, too, felt anxious from what he saw from her eyes that was soon interrupted as they approached the bridge over North Johnson River. It signalled that they were near their destination. It was the first idea that came into Osmond's thoughts when it came to Alex's safety. He knew that his hometown, specifically his home, was isolated from rest of Australia and, thus, was safe. Three hundred metres away, he saw their house's wooden fence.

"Ms. Alex, we are near," he said while glancing at her then Martin was attentively driving silently.

"Thank goodness. I wanna rest as soon as possible," Alex replied. She saw how houses were far apart from each other, even both sides of the road were surrounded by vast fields. She realised the reason her father and Osmond agreed that this place was safe for her to stay temporarily.

Few moments later, their vehicle entered a gated house. The bungalow type house itself was cozy looking with a simple tropical design, the fence that surrounds the place were made of wood and in the middle was a driveway made of grey bricks. It was then that the automatic outdoor censor light turned on in the porch area as the car parked in an opened garage. As usual, Osmond quickly stepped out of the vehicle to open Alex's side. He closed the door as soon as Alex alighted the vehicle, then he went to the boot to get her belongings.

"Thanks," Alex said in tired tone. She looked around to see the driveway between a Sir Walter DNA certified buffalo grass. Both corners of the front yard were a few palm trees and some tropical ornamental plants.

"You're welcome," Osmond replied as he carried their luggage. He saw his father closed the wooden gate and was now walking to them.

"Nana, come! Uncle Osmond is here!" A young boy suddenly said aloud.

The three turned towards the boy. Osmond smiled when he saw his seven-year-old nephew named Andrew, son of his older sister, Cathy. The boy flung his robot toy away to run towards Osmond. He welcomed his nephew with open hands and carried him on his arms. They hugged as Osmond gave the boy a peck on his cheek then ruffled his hair. He was laughing as he put the boy down. He remembered that it was Friday evening, as Andrew was usually dropped and left there to spend the weekend at their parents' house so he can bond with his grandparents.

Alex was quietly admiring the scene between uncle and nephew in front of her. She saw main door opened and there a kind-looking lady came out and she surmised the woman was the same age as her mother. She also speculated she was Osmond's mother as her eyes were as soft and alert as Osmond.

"Hi mom," Osmond suddenly said from behind Alex. He passed Alex and went straight to his mother in a warm embrace and quick peck on the lady's cheek.

"Welcome back, my boy, my dear son!" Said the old lady as yearning was obvious from her eyes.

Again, Alex was quite astounded how Osmond's family were very open with showing their emotions. She got distracted, though, when she noticed two small almond eyes were staring at her. She gave the little boy a small smile in return.

"Hello," she gleefully said to the little boy, "what's your name?"

"Hi! My name is Andrew," the little boy said, and picked his toy robot then hugged it tightly, as if it would protect him from Alex. He then ran behind his grandfather.

Alex then felt Osmond looking at her. As she glanced towards him, Osmond began to introduce to her to his mother.

"Ms. Alex, meet my mom, Celine Gomez. Mom, this is my client, Ms. Alex," Osmond said. Alex then shook Celine's warm hands.

"Pleasure to meet you, young lady. Such a lovely one at that," Celine warmly said and although she was smiling, curiosity was also evident in her eyes. The same curiosity she saw from Martin Gomez earlier.

"Oh, thank you!" Alex was already desperate to lay her body in bed, however, she composed herself as she was a guest.

"I'm sure you are already tired from the flight and drive," Celine said with a warm tone that Alex found it soothing, "let's all go inside and get you comfy, shall we?"

Osmond grabbed her luggage as they went inside led by his parents, followed by the little boy then Alex with him behind. As they enter, Alex felt that the house was not only cozy to look from the outside as it was also warm and homely on the inside. It may not be as big and elegant as their mansion, but there was more soothing feel here. It was well-organised and clean. From the foyer, Alex saw a dark brown leather couch and a medium-sized flat screen TV attached on the wall.

"Ms. Alex, I would lead you to your room," Osmond said still carrying her luggage.

"Yes, please," Alex replied, "Mr. and Mrs. Gomez, my apologies, but I had a very long tiring day. Please excuse me."

She immediately followed Osmond after the she bade goodnight to Osmond's parents. The two of them reached the last door on the hallway. Osmond opened the door on their right. A snug and pleasant room welcomed Alex. There was a queen-sized bed covered with a coral-coloured bedsheet and big white pillows. The walls were painted cream and the curtains were in peach. A soft light was coming from the carnation pink lampshade then Alex sat on bed as she was tired.

"Ms. Alex, this will be your room." Osmond mentioned and gently placed her luggage on the floor beside the bedside table.

"Thanks," she replied as she sat on the bed and started to remove her stilettos.

"I'll go ahead and let you take your rest. If you need anything at any time, don't hesitate to let me know. My room is next yours and the toilet is across your door," Osmond said and left. Alex didn't bother to look at him anymore but heard the door closing.

She sighed and grabbed her phone from her bag then lay on the bed. She saw there was at least one bar of signal on her phone. She tried calling her mom but was discombobulated that she couldn't reach her. She also tried her dad but with the same result. Tears started to fall. She gently placed her phone on the bedside table. She wanted to ask Osmond about it but decided to rest for a bit then take a shower.

Meanwhile, back in the living room, Osmond returned to see his mom waiting for him. Celine offered him and Alex a dinner but Osmond refused as he knew that Alex would be tired and would not eat. He knew that she would prefer to rest.

"Is everything alright, son?" Celine asked, "it's uncommon for you bring your client here, not that she's not welcome. She's more than welcome to stay. It's just that you have not done this."

They were sitting in the couch as Martin came with two cans of beer on his right hand and a bowl of chips on his left. The older Gomez set the bowl on the table and gave one can to Osmond. Although he removed his coat, he wasn't able to change clothes and was still wearing his white long sleeves.

"Thanks, dad!" He said then opened the can to take a sip. He looked at his parents before deciding that it was the proper time to answer their queries, since Andrew was also busy playing with his toy robot in the foyer. He took a deep breath before answering his mother.

"Mom, Dad. Please listen carefully to what I am about to divulge. This is a very confidential case," Osmond started in an almost hushed tone, "the woman I'm with is the sole heiress of the richest entrepreneur in the country. She is the only daughter of the de Ayala. It so happens that Mr. de Ayala received threats involving his daughter, Ms. Alex. So, Mr. de Ayala and General asked me to bring her since it's much safer here compared to Melbourne," he added while his parents were intently listening.

"Seems a really serious matter, son. Aren't you worried about your safety with this new mission assigned to you?" Celine asked with concern apparent in her tone.

"My guess was correct after all. She is Margarette Alexandria, which is why she looked familiar despite the blurred photos I've seen on the news since she's not a typical gorgeous woman as I've seen her initially at the airport," Martin said who was deep in thought as he sipped beer before continuing, "my concern, however, is our safety."

"Dad, I am Australia's finest top-secret agent. So, don't worry," Osmond replied trying to reassure his parents as he also reached out for their hands to hold within his hand, "I have already anticipated every side of this mission before accepting it. When General asked me, our hometown was the first that came to my mind. We know everyone here and every stranger that comes in and out of our town and I know every path and possible escape routes," he continued, "besides, Mr. de Ayala and General purposely stayed in Melbourne so nobody would know where Ms. Alex is and they are doing their best to track and to capture whoever the culprit back there."

Osmond's parents looked at each other before returning their gaze to him.

"Alright, son. Let's just all be extra careful while your boss is here. I'll also ask our friends and neighbours to wary of strangers and suspicious individuals," Martin said assuring confidentiality and reassuring the safety of his family then held his wife's hand.

"That would be a great help, dad. Just don't mention who really Ms. Alex is. Thank you so much!" Osmond replied and continued to finish his beer.

Alex was about to open the door to go across the toilet to take a shower when she heard a soft knock on it. Osmond stood in front of her when she opened the door, he was holding a bottle of water.

"Ms. Alex, I thought you might be thirsty and brought you water," Osmond offered. Alex held back on getting the bottle of water as she caught herself staring at him.

"Are you feeling fine, Ms. Alex?" Osmond asked with concern but he saw a sudden change on Alex's eyes, the usual fire he sees in them.

"OMG, Osmond, seriously? It's obvious, right? Well, I'm not!" Alex said trying to control her tone so she would not shout and let Osmond's parents hear her.

"Why can't I contact my parents?" She continued her rant cutting off Osmond who was about to say something.

Osmond drew a breath before answering her. He already anticipated being questioned about it once they reached Queensland.

"I am sorry, Ms. Alex. But to avoid being tracked and wire-tapping, I asked your parents to block your number temporarily. You may still contact them using my phone as it is equipped with a ghost VPN by our agency," Osmond calmly replied trying to soothe Alex's frustration which was effective as he saw her anger dissipate only to be replaced with her sarcastic eye roll.

"Psh, whatever. I get it," Alex said trying to dismiss Osmond. She went hurriedly entered the bathroom to take a shower leaving Osmond behind without glancing at him.

Osmond shook his head and kept calm. Since Alex's bedroom door was open, he entered and left the bottle of water he was holding on the nightstand before leaving and closing the door.

It was already ten in the evening when Osmond checked the time on his phone. He was on the porch drinking his second can of beer. He already had a shower and was now wearing a white fitted shirt and gray track pants. The night was calm and the crickets could be heard. He finished checking the CCTV cameras surrounding their property. He was now walking around the house for a final check when he realised he was in front of Alex's bedroom window and only the lampshade light illuminated it. It was almost two metres from where he was standing. He was in that state and place when he heard a sound coming from somewhere around the vicinity. He was suddenly alert and his senses heightened. After a few seconds, he heard the rustling noise again. He quickly retrieved his .45 caliber pistol. It was then he caught a movement in the shrubs by the fence, and carefully approached the source of the sound and movement.

Twelve

Seeing The Real Thing

Osmond's gun was pointing at the thick and tall shrubs as he carefully approached the source of the strange noises. He was taken aback as two jolted possums came out and ran away when they felt his presence. He felt relieved with only the two animals as he put away his gun on its holster. He walked towards the front yard after double checking the surroundings yet again to make sure nothing was out of the ordinary. He went inside straight to the kitchen to have a glass of water then ensured all the locks of the doors and windows in both the kitchen and living area were locked before walking towards his bedroom. Prior to entering his room, he looked at a particular door, and he thought Alex was now sleeping before he entered his room, and removed his trackpants, leaving his black boxer shorts and white shirt on. After being comfortable, he layed on his bed and turned off the night lamp. He slowly closed his eyes and fell into a light sleep after a while.

The first thing Alex saw after she woke up was the cream-coloured ceiling. She glanced to her side to see the analogue wall clock that signaled that it was eight thirty in the morning, but she doesn't want to get up yet. She turned the night lamp off on the bed-stand, and turned unto her stomach and closed her eyes for more some sleep, however, the previous occurrences came flooding her thoughts. She remembered two days ago she just arrived in the country, then a sudden change of bodyguard, the creepy email, and now, she was here in

Queensland temporarily for her safety. It took her half an hour before she felt she won't be able to sleep again and decided by standing up away from her bed. She went to the closet, which she recalled she had the time last night to organise, to grab a white robe to cover her body as she was only wearing her light silk pink nighties. After putting on her robe, she walked towards the window and parted the curtains. As she looked out, she was mesmerised by the view of the back yard that welcomed her. The sun warmed the garden, colourful flowers bloomed early to allow the bees and butterflies to flutter, it was a perfect weather for a little boy to play with his red ball that caught Alex's attention. The boy felt a pair of eyes observing him to make him stop playing and looked back at her.

"Hi little boy. Good morning!" Alex greeted with a warm smile as the rays of sun was on him, she always feels good and giddy every time she encounters a kid. She has been longing for a sibling ever since, with regret that her mom had complications that made it impossible for her to get pregnant when she was nine years-old.

"Uhm, hello. Morning," replied the boy who suddenly felt embarrassed having an audience and Alex suddenly was curious about him, and she thought about who were the parents of the boy, but he definitely called Mrs. Gomez nana last night, thus, his grandmother. If so, Alex thought if it was possible that the boy was Osmond's son and, now, she was wondering where was his mother. Although, she recalled Osmond not wearing a wedding ring, thus the young boy called him "Uncle Osmond" last night. She sought to dismiss her thoughts right after she heard Mrs. Gomez calling Andrew.

"Honey, come back inside now, please! Finish your breakfast," Mrs. Gomez called. Alex saw her approached the boy and reached for his right hand. However, Andrew shyly pointed his left index finger at her. The grandmother followed where her grandson pointing at, and saw Alex on the nook then smiled.

"Oh, you are awake now, lovely lady. Good morning!" Mrs. Gomez amicably greeted her.

"Good morning, Mrs. Gomez!" Alex replied returning the smile.

"Oh, stop! You make me feel old, just call me Celine," Osmond's mother replied warmly.

"Okay, Celine," Alex felt the sincerity and warmth from Osmond's mother.

"Anyway, my son is preparing your breakfast and is about to be done," Celine said then returning her attention to the little boy patiently waiting, "c'mon honey, let's get inside and finish your breakfast then we will visit your pops in the farm.

"Sorry dear, I need to attend to Andrew. Just head to the kitchen when you're ready," Celine said towards Alex.

"It's alright," Alex replied waving to Andrew and saw them entering the backdoor few metres away from her room and once again she allowed herself to enjoy the view of a well-taken garden. After several minutes, she decided to complete her morning ritual using the products she brought with her in the bathroom across her room. She, then, settled on wearing a white cotton shirt and blue-denim shorts. She went to the kitchen, planning of talking to Osmond to ask if she can call her parents back in Melbourne.

Osmond was preparing breakfast on the oak table. His nephew just finished his breakfast and his mom was about to finish putting the dishes on the dishwasher when he heard footsteps approaching and saw Alex entered the kitchen.

"Good morning. Ms. Alex. Breakfast will be ready soon," Osmond said while arranging the food he prepared for Alex. Mr. de Ayala made sure his daughter's needs was met while she was staying there by giving Osmond a special account which was more than enough for her needs and even unforeseen emergencies.

"Mornin'," Alex casually said to Osmond. She saw Celine glanced her way and the ladies smiled at each other before the older lady returned to her house-chore. Alex realised that Osmond was not in his usual uniform. He was wearing a gray cotton shirt with black shorts. Alex thought he look more appealing and felt comfortable and certain level of ardour towards Osmond. She tried her utmost best to disregard the thought and went straight to the breakfast table. She pulled a chair made of oak with soft upholstery and checked on Osmond again. She was amused as another thought came into mind that she wanted to ask Osmond but decided to forego with it. She saw the assortment of breakfast he prepared for her: avocado toast, vegan chocolate chip pumpkin pancakes, dairy yogurt parfait with slices of strawberries, banana, and blueberries. Across her, Andrew glimpsed shyly at her before resuming on playing with his empty plate with his blue plastic spoon. She returned the glimpsed and smiled at the little boy when she felt Osmond looking at her.

"How would you like your coffee?" Osmond asked her.

"Black coffee please with one teaspoon of sugar. Thanks!" She replied while they were looking at each other. She suddenly caught herself smiling at him that she couldn't explain but tried to compose herself.

"Sure, hold on," Osmond replied then went to the benchtop where the coffeemaker was to prepare the requested drink. He decided to get himself an orange juice and as he turned towards the breakfast table, he saw Alex pouring one on Andrew's empty plastic cup. The little boy was initially hesitant but she genially smiled at him which made Andrew drink at last.

"Thank you," Andrew said almost in a whisper.

"You're welcome, little man," Alex replied still smiling at him. After a few moments, she saw Osmond nearing the table with her coffee which he placed in front of her.

"Thanks Osmond," she said as Osmond replied with a cordial smile. She once again caught herself staring at the man as he was also staring down on her as he was standing in front of her. She reprimanded herself to calm down by taking a sip of coffee. It was perfect. Her kind of black coffee for a perfect late morning breakfast.

Osmond reveled on the amiable morning while Alex was having her coffee. For the first time, he saw a different side of Alex. She was smiling more and he felt good. He saw her make an effort to get close to Andrew as he saw her earlier serving the little boy his orange juice. He also admired how she manage to stay gorgeous with a simple outfit this morning. He heeded the thought quickly as it's not supposed to be. She is a client and he was her personal bodyguard.

"Son, Andrew and I will have to leave you with Alex. We will head out to your dad at the farm," Celine interjected between the thoughts of the two while preparing the meal preo insulated bag, "Don't wait for us as we will have lunch there with Martin."

"Alright, mom. No worries. Take care," Osmond said and returned his gaze on Alex. He just diverted his look as Celine and Andrew were leaving.

"Anyway, Osmond?" Alex edged in.

"Yes, Ms. Alex," he asked as their gazes met.

"I wanna talk to my parents once I'm done with my breakfast," Alex replied.

"Sure, Ms. Alex," he answered and Alex even asked him to join her breakfast while he curtly declined, "I am fine, Ms. Alex, thanks. I already had my breakfast with dad earlier." To which Alex just kept to herself and continued eating.

After Alex finished her breakfast, she excused herself to refreshen up in her room. Osmond was left in the kitchen to clean up. After wrapping up the chores in the kitchen, Osmond went to the living room and sat on the leather couch which gave him a view of the hallway with Alex's and his adjacent bedroom doors. Few moments passed and he saw Alex exit her room. He stood up.

"Please follow me to the porch, Ms. Alex. The signal inside is erratic and better there," Osmond explained as he walked towards the main door and felt Alex followed him. Once out on the porch, he scouted the area for any indication of danger. After securing the surrounding, he grabbed his phone out off his pocket and used his passcode to unlock it. He dialed Mr. de Ayala's number and handed it to Alex.

"Thanks!" Alex said before she put the phone on her ear and listened for the ringing on the other line. Osmond gave her a certain level of privacy by walking towards the front yard garden, as usual, the wide array of plants exhibited how well they were taken care of by his parents.

"Hello, dad? How are you and mom? I wanna go home now. I missed you both so much," Alex said misty-eyed. It was evident that she really missed her parents even though she parted ways with them just yesterday.

"Dear, Alex, we miss you too! How was the flight and how are you there?" asked Mr. de Ayala.

"The flight was smooth and I am fine here," Alex replied trying to hold back her tears, "They are very hospitable here.

"Dear, don't worry. General's staff and I are doing our best to track and capture whoever is behind those dreadful emails," Mr. de Ayala said with concern and sadness in his voice, "We, too, miss you so much. Your mom and I wanted you to be with us, specially, you just arrived in the country recently."

"Dad, where's mom?" She inquired.

"Your mom isn't available at the moment. She is in the bathroom. Don't worry you can talk to her next time you call. But do limit your calls, we don't want them to be able to trace you," Mr. de Ayala responded unknowingly that Alex wasn't able to hold back the tears flowing on her cheeks now, "My dear, I'm sorry to cut our call for now. I'm in a middle of a meeting with General's staff about solving the case about the emails."

"A-alright, dad. Please tell mom I miss her," Alex said almost whimpering due to hiding the break on her voice.

"Of course, dear, I will. We love you and take care there, okay?"

"Okay dad. You, too, and mom, please take care. I love you both!" Alex silently said and listened to the dead air from the other line as her father ended the call. She collected herself and wiped her tears away. She walked towards Osmond smelling the Aussie Box to return his phone. She, then, turned away from him and went to her room hurriedly without a word.

Osmond sympathized for Alex as he saw the sadness on her. He thought of ideas of how to preoccupy her, but then again, it would be difficult as she had already built a barrier between them. He sighed then went inside their home.

Meanwhile somewhere in Perth, a man in his mid-forties was sitting on his executive black swivel chair. In his hand was an almost empty glass of whiskey. He was facing a floor to ceiling glass window inside his office in his mega-mansion. Behind him and in front of his black wooden executive table were two men in all-black suits with eyes hidden by the dark sunglasses.

"So, any update?" he asked in a tone full of power and authority.

"As you clearly instructed," respectfully uttered by the right-hand man of the boss, "it was verified that the target was indeed in Melbourne, then our informant lost track about information of her yesterday."

"Hmm. Interesting," said the man, "it is alright, though. I've anticipated that and this is about game with pleasure," he added and finished his drink, a 1961 Macallan Single Malt Scotch whisky, then fiendishly smiled..

Thirteen

Duty with Patience

Osmond was on the couch watching an Ultimate Fighting Championship (UFC) on the tube. It has been an hour since Alex had called her dad using his phone. He alerted as he saw her came out of her bedroom in her white sneakers and sunnies. He had an idea what she was planning. He was reminded of his thoughts about her building a barrier between them, but this was the chance for him to pursue his plans about his charge.

"Can we go to your dad's farm?" She asked. "Sure," he replied then stood from the couch to prepare, "let's then have lunch with them there," he added.

He thought that her idea was alright, since it was also safe in their farm. He then went to his room to get his firearm.

They both proceeded to the kitchen to gather additional food and drinks to bring. He made sure the main door was locked before leading her towards the backdoor. There was a small gate in the backyard that leads to a two hundred metres beaten path towards the farm.

She noticed the various tropical trees and even bananas on each side of the trail. The pebbles and dried leaves crunched underneath her sneakers. The soft breeze eased the scorching noon sun while a parakeet chirped from somewhere. Several bees buzzed to her right as she found several wild flowers of violet and yellow petals and the trodden path reminded her of his parents' hospitality, warm and bright. She couldn't help but smile.

After several minutes, he saw their small cottage. It was where his father would usually rest after working on the farm.

"We're almost there," he motioned to her who smiled at him.

Osmond saw his mom busy preparing lunch on the table beside the cottage and under a big oak tree. Celine realised them coming and turned her head towards and smiled.

Alex took sight of the location of the cottage. It was small and cozy, the walls were made of local woods, the roof had brick shingles, the window frames were painted bright red. The cottage itself were surrounded by trees acting as its fence. There was garden of blooming flowers on all sides and a trail of white pebbles from where she was standing leading to the cottage then forked towards the other side where Alex thought might be the farm itself. She saw Osmond approached and helped Celine with the food they also brought.

"Oh, it's good thing the two of you decided to join us for lunch here in the farm," Celine said, "Alex might also feel bored there with just the two of you."

"This is a very nice place, Celine," Alex complimented.

"Why, thank you!" Celine said, "we usually spend our time here during the weekend, especially if Andrew's around so he can bond with his Pops," she added. Alex asked Celine and Osmond that she would just stretch a bit and walk around the cottage and take a closer look then left after Osmond allowed her.

"Where's Andrew?" Osmond asked his mom after sitting on the wooden chair.

"He's with his Pops at the vegetable fields," Celine answered but not looking at him. Osmond followed his mom's gaze and saw Ms. Alex casually walking by the birds of paradise and hyacinths.

"Mom?" Osmond curiously asked. He knew when his mother was in deep thought. Celine turned her gaze to him.

"Do you still remember Isabelle and how she was abducted fourteen years ago?" Celine asked with a certain seriousness in her tone.

"Of course, mom. Don't worry, whatever you're thinking, it happened years ago. Besides, Murray is far from us now," Osmond said pertaining to their former residence and assuring his mother as he felt the uneasiness of his mother's question.

"I'm sorry, dear. I just can't help but think about the similarities between Isabelle and Ms. Alex. The only difference is that Isabelle's parents blamed you for what happened, while Ms. Alex's parents entrusted their daughter to you," Celine sadly said and turned again towards Alex who was now looking up the flowering pink crepe myrtle tree.

"Don't fret, mom. Nobody expected for that to happen. I wasn't even ready then. But unlike fourteen years ago, I am now more prepared and ready," he calmly replied as he held his mother's right hand to reassure her.

"Alright, son. I believe in your capabilities as the finest agent," Celine said and gave Osmond a warm smile at last.

"Thanks, mom," he said then stood up to approach his father with Andrew coming from behind the cottage. Martin was carrying a basket filled with assorted vegetables like tomatoes, carrots, lettuce, and capsicums, while Andrew shyly ran towards Ms. Alex by the myrtle tree. The two giggled at something Andrew said to Ms. Alex that Osmond couldn't hear from where was. But Osmond smiled inside seeing the two become comfortable with each other.

Celine finally called Ms. Alex and Andrew towards the table to start their lunch, which was both pleasurable and overwhelming for Alex. Overwhelming as this was her first time to eat with this many people. Pleasurable as she enjoyed the interactions with them which made her feel as part of the Gomez family instantly.

It was four in the afternoon as Alex went out of her room. She saw Osmond on the couch of the living area. She had already showered and rested after coming from the farm earlier.

Osmond saw her coming out from her room. He had an idea as to what she wanted to do as she was again wearing her sunnies but now with her bag.

"Let's go to the supermarket. I need to buy some personal items," she said affirming his guess.

"Okay. Hold on a minute," he replied and turned the TV off as he stood and went to his room to grab his gun again and wore his runner shoes. He also took a brown snapback before exiting his room. He went towards the kitchen where his parents with his nephew were so he can inform them that he was going out with her and to ask his father that he was using the Jeep, then on the way out he grabbed the keys by the hallway keyholder.

"Please wear this," he said and gave the snapback to her so she could conceal her face as they both went out of the main door. She took the cap and wore it with no complaints. He couldn't help but admire how she was still beautiful even with her simple outfit. She was wearing a white cotton top, dark blue denims, and white sneakers she wore earlier. It seemed to him that whatever she wore, she would still be beautiful. He caught himself and disregarded the thought.

"Thanks," she said which he answered with a smile. He led her towards the Jeep and opened the door for her. She once again thanked him after wearing her seatbelt and before he closed the door. He beelined towards the gate and opened it before he entered the driver's seat and drove off.

While on the way towards the supermarket, she was silent in the back seat. He glanced at her by the rearview mirror, she seemed deep in her thoughts that he let her be. He returned his focus on the road before them.

They arrived at the nearest market after several minutes. He parked the car and quickly opened the door for her. She thanked him for the third time that afternoon. They walked together towards the main entrance of the market.

It was crowded than usual as it was a Saturday and while they walking side by side, she noticed him more alert and wary with every person they passed and encountered on every aisle they went or turn. His concern towards her safety deepened what she was feeling for him, although, he was not the first bodyguard she had. This time was different.

"Dear self, please do not misinterpret his concern for you and him being caring. He's just doing his job," she reminded and thought to herself.

She got everything she personally needed on the shopping cart he was carrying for her. She even offered for him to gather things for the house to at least reciprocate his parent's hospitality to which he graciously declined.

"Okay, these are all I need so far," she said pertaining to her stuff in the cart.

He and she were silent as they patiently waited in the queue. She can feel on her right shoulder his warmth permeating from his black shirt to her white blouse. It made her uneasy yet comfortable. He caught a whiff of her perfume. It made him stir from the inside.

She chose to just wait in the queue they were instead of lining in the self-checkout section as it was longer, which proved pay off as it only took them few minutes before it was their turn for their items to be scanned by a pretty if not pimply-glasses-wearing-young-college looking cashier.

The cashier started scanning Alex's items. Osmond was about to get his wallet when Alex stopped him and brought out her American Express Black Centurion credit card. After the staff finished scanning the items, Alex tapped her card on the EFTPOS machine. The cashier frowned as she showed Alex the "DECLINED" message from the machine.

"Hold on. Please try this instead," Alex said to the girl while tapping another card on the machine. However, it gave the same message. Alex frustratedly sighed. She was confounded as it was the first time that her cards were declined which was almost impossible. She then remembered her father's reminder before Osmond brought her here in Queensland.

"All of our assets and properties from cars, private jet, and everything under our name can be easily traced."

She gave him an embarrassed glance, as if asking for help. He got the meaning of her glance at him. He took from his wallet out a card given to him by her father for her expenses. She just dumbfoundedly looked at him, who was carrying all the shopping bags, as they both walked out of the supermarket.

"Could you please inform me ahead of time about things like these next time? I was humiliated in front of the staff and it was the first time that this ever happened to me!" she gritted through her teeth as they head towards the exit.

"My apologies. I thought you forgot what your father told you about your cards but that's why I offered to pay for the items," he explained, "Just please inform me if you will be spending in the future."

"Whatever! Let's just go back to your house," she said sarcastically with a sudden realisation that her plan to attempt and escape would be impossible because he and her dad thought of everything well before she was brought here.

They were both walking towards the parking area when a sudden rain shower burst. They instinctively ran to avoid getting drenched; but as they were close to the Jeep, she was caught off guard by an already forming puddle. She slipped and fell on her bottom.

"Fuck!" She painfully screamed.

He was, too, caught off guard by her shriek. He discarded the shopping bags on the wet ground and quickly ran to her side.

"Are you okay?" He asked her as he aided her to stand.

"Do I look okay? I can't believe this!" She wailed as she was already drenched, then she remembered her Hermes Himalayan Kelly bag which also got wet. She brushed off his hand holding her left arm.

"I don't need your help! Go away!" Her patience finally snapped. First, she was humiliated by the counter and she fell and got drenched by the rain, then, one of her favourite handbags was now wet and probably scratched from the fall.

He decided to keep silent and let her be. He felt pity with what happened to her. He grabbed the shopping bags on the wet ground, put them in the back seat of the car, and opened the front passenger door for her.

"Please come in the car. You'd get more drenched there," he said. She followed though obviously fumingly mad at the tough luck she experienced.

He offered his handkerchief so she could at least dry herself a bit. He saw her face fuming mad while inspecting her bag.

"Damn!" She seethed as she saw scratches on her bag. It wasn't easy to replace or get a new one since it was collector's edition and it was even customised for her. It took her almost a year of waiting for it to be delivered from France.

"We can buy another one online if you want to replace it," he said trying to comfort and appease her anger even for a little bit.

She smiled sarcastically at him.

"No! You can't simply buy this bag online! This is a collector's item! So don't tell me that we could just buy a replacement online! If I were you, I'll just shut up! You don't know anything. Besides, you are just my bodyguard. So don't freely offer any of your 'wise' suggestions!" She furiously shouted as if it would lessen her anger. She threw his handkerchief back at him only to realise it was too late for her to retract the harsh words she burst out.

He stared deeply at her. He was hurt. Not from the handkerchief thrown at him but at her words.

"Are you done? If not, come on. Say and do anything to me until you're appeased if you want," he monotonously said. They glared at each other. Her with anger in her eyes. Him with frustration and disappointment. He was getting emotional but he reminded himself to be professional and composed.

"You can easily replace me as a bodyguard; but please, can you at least try to give me respect? Might not be as a bodyguard, but as a human being," he firmly said. He never thought that she could be this unreasonable and harsh when angry. He then saw her smile sarcastically at him.

"Are you done? Oh please, cut the drama. It's not my fault I was born wealthy. And besides, you don't know how I feel," she retaliated. She then avoided his stare and looked outside. She pondered on the water trails on the car window created by the pouring rain outside. She knew that her anger and frustration greatly affected her harsh and disrespectful words.

She heard him sighed. He chose to let it go and focused on his driving. Then there was a deafening silence. Only the howling wind and pattering rain was heard. It did not help that the road was wet. He drove slower and more carefully than usual. Making the atmosphere inside unbearable for him and suffocating for her.

There was still an uneasy hush between him and her after they arrived at his house. Immediately after he parked the Jeep, she instantly alighted the vehicle without waiting for him to open the door for her. She quickly beelined towards her room without even giving him a glance. Meanwhile, he grabbed the shopping bags from behind and entered the house. As he made into the foyer, he saw the brown cap he lent her earlier on the small table. He sat disappointed on the chair by the table. He shook his head as he recalled the events that transpired. It was just this morning when she was happy eating lunch with them that quickly turn around just because of unforeseen circumstances with her card and her bag for her to even utter harsh and hurtful words. But he remembered the promise he had given to her father that he will be patient and tolerant with protecting her.

Fourteen

The Memory

It has been an hour after Alex and Osmond's confrontation. Alex had already taken a shower after she arrived at Gomez's house and changed into a more comfortable clothing. The rain turned into a soft drizzle outside the back yard. She watched it softly pattered on the grass and on the glass window. She heard a soft knock on her bedroom door.

"Come in," she said in reply to the knock, still staring outside the gloomy weather. The dark clouds were still overcast the already setting afternoon sun.

She heard the door opened and looked who came in. Osmond was carrying the stuff she bought earlier and gently placed them near her. She returned her gaze outside on the lazily rolling dark clouds.

"I may not be in your situation right now, but I understand how you feel. I was hoping we could get along as we are in this situation together. I know it's hard for you to be in this dilemma but we can't do anything about it for now. What I do know is that your dad, the General and his team are doing their best to solve this circumstance. So, I will do everything just to keep you safe as we patiently wait for them to figure this mess out," he first spoke to explain himself in soft tone that was almost a whisper but she heard it all clearly over the soft pitapat of the drizzle outside.

It was the first time for her to hear him say so much as if it was coming from deep within him and she was greatly affected. It was different but it as not supposed to happen. She realised certain things that she needed to disregard. She knew her true self was hiding within her, her good nature and nurtured by the love of her parents. However, she deliberately created her reticent personality. She needed to build an impenetrable and an invisible wall to avoid being abused or used by people around her, especially those she doubted their sincerity towards her. But then again, he was different. She felt the sincerity of his words.

She let out a breath before facing him. Their gaze met. She was hesitant if she really needed to voice out her thoughts and explain herself as he did because if she would, the walls around her would crumble. She might get attached to person in front of her and fall for him. But she remembered what she said to him earlier was way harsh even for him. She saw in his eyes that he was patiently waiting as if he knew she was uncertain on how to react. However, she made up her mind to break at least half of her wall to correct her actions before. She knew it was the right thing to do. She mustered enough courage to let him in partially and say her piece.

"I am so sorry. To set the record straight, I think we just got off the wrong foot since we've met and it got worse with time and that exploded this afternoon. I apologise for my rude and crass behaviour," she seriously said.

"I understand. I'm certain anyone in your situation will feel the same way," he said after recovering from what he heard from her. He was taken aback as it was the first time that he felt sincerity coming from her.

She was relieved from what he said. She thought that it would not make her less a woman if she would get along with him. She gave a smile a sign of gratitude to his acceptance to her apology. He smiled back. She saw the sincerity on his expressive eyes. She once again felt the strange sensation he alone can trigger within her. She slightly turned her gaze away from him to hide her eyes from him and looked at the door behind him instead.

"Anyway, I will go ahead for now to help mom prepare our dinner. Just follow us there once you're ready," he replied before leaving her in the room.

She felt ease and solace as soon as he left. She made amends to her action and words earlier due to frustration. She returned her gaze to the window. The clouds completely dissipated. The sun showed its temporary farewell as the sky glowed pink, orange, and gold inviting the star-filled night on it's place.

Alex decided to go out and join dinner with the Gomezes. She sat between Andrew and Celine. She even helped Andrew with his food.

After dinner, Osmond decided to go to bed early after his inspection of the surroundings outside. He recalled the events that transpired earlier at dinner while waiting for sleep to come.

"Oh, please stop that Ms. Alex. He already can eat on his own. He might get used to you feeding him and miss it once you go back to Melbourne," Celine said smiling at Alex who was still holding Andrew's spoon.

"I'm sorry, Celine. It's just that whenever I'm with a kid, I can't help myself but get attached to them. Being an only child, I didn't experience how it is growing with a sibling," Alex explained reminiscently while one hand was with Andrew's spoon and the other caressing the little boy's back who was comfortably allowing Alex to spoil him.

"Oh, I remember now! I completely understand. I appreciate your gesture towards our grandson, just don't spoil him too much," Celine answered with a giggle.

"I'm sure Ms. Alex knows what she's doing. Don't worry hon, Andrew won't get easily spoiled. Right, buddy?" Martin interjected while laughing as Andrew just gave him a wide grin, which made the two ladies giggle more. They continued eating dinner happily and laughing. Osmond silently observe them and was smiling at the sight he had beheld. Alex briefly glanced at him and gave him a small smile which he returned likewise.

Osmond felt a warmth and certainty at that moment in his bed reminiscing the events during lunch and, importantly, during dinner. He slowly succumbed to the sandman beckoning him to sleep.

The following day, as per his usual routine, Osmond checked the surveillance footages of the prior night. He was double-checking nothing untoward or unusual transpired. He was reviewing Cam 3 when he felt a presence behind him. He found his father with a cup of coffee for him. He reached for it and thanked the older Gomez then took a sip. Martin curiously eyed the monitor in front of his son.

"How is it going?" He asked Osmond.

"So far, so good. Nothing unusual. It's still too early to tell as Ms. Alex had only been here for two nights," Osmond explained.

"Seemed you had a good night's rest, unlike yesterday after you came back from supermarket," enquired by Martin. Although, Osmond was certain not to divulge anything to his family about yesterday's incident with Alex as it was trivial for him.

"Oh, nothing to worry about. I was just preoccupied thinking of improving our security system," he lied, "and I'm just glad that Ms. Alex seemed at home here and easy to get along with, especially with Andrew."

"Alright, son. If you need anything you can always count on me," Martin said tapping Osmond on his shoulder.

"Thanks, dad," Osmond replied and smiled while returning his eyes to the monitor. Their parents have always been like that, fair and kind, since he and other two siblings were young. Even now that he had to travel away from them several times; even his older brother, Larry, permanently lived in Cairns with his wife; and even when Cathy, their second, got married and lived with her husband, their parents were still supportive.

He was able to finish discerning the footages quickly. It was then he and his father went to the kitchen. They found Celine busy preparing breakfast for the family.

"Mornin' mom! Need help?" Osmond offered his mother who was busy frying bacon on the stove. He glanced at the table where other food was already set. There were poached eggs, sausages, slices of grilled tomatoes, toast, and much more to feed them all heartily. He thought of cooking another dish for Alex.

"Good morning, son! Thanks, but I'm almost done here," Celine answered, "by the way, your sister texted me last night before I went to bed. She and her husband will fetch Andrew later and have lunch with us."

"That would be great! It will be a livelier lunch later," Osmond happily said. He saw his father arranging his tools to use later at the farm. Osmond just decided to help him instead. As soon as Celine finished cooking, they saw Andrew came in the kitchen yawning with his unruly bed hair. Osmond smiled at him and ruffled Andrew's hair more as the couple laughed at the antics of the two.

Meanwhile, Alex just finished changing from her PJs to her white sundress with sunflowers print. As she was about to go to the kitchen, she thought of suggesting to Osmond if they can have lunch at the farm like yesterday.

The Gomezes were about to finish setting the table when Alex entered the kitchen. Osmond saw how she glowed. He felt an uneasy fluttering in his stomach. He tried his best to hide from the everyone in the kitchen. He found it was hard not to admire the beauty in front of him ever since they met.

"Good morning, everyone!" Alex gleefully greeted them. Osmond met her gaze and quickly turned away and tried to pretend to be getting additional forks from the kitchen drawer. The Gomez couple returned Alex's greetings with a warm smile.

"Hi there little boy!" Alex said also ruffling Andrew's hair which the boy grunted and made the elder couple laughed.

They started a cozy breakfast and Osmond was about to stand to get Alex coffee but she stopped him midway.

"Osmond, just stay there. I can manage. Thanks," Alex said and went to the benchtop to prepare her drink.

"Oh okay. Sure," he replied. But instead of remaining in his seat he stood and prepare Alex's plate with avocado toast, eggless pancake, and jam. Alex was warmly surprised that her plate was full as she settled in her seat with her coffee.

"Thanks!"

"You're welcome," Osmond replied with a smile that was reciprocated.

"I was thinking, let's have lunch again later," Alex suggested that made the couple and Andrew smile.

"Sure, it's okay," Osmond replied to Andrew's delight.

After breakfast, Osmond started to collect the used plates, cups and cutleries.

"I'll go ahead. See you all later at lunch time," Martin said as he collected his materials and went straight the back door towards the farm as Celine watch him by the door.

"Nana, I wanna watch Thomas and Friends!" Andrew said to his grandma.

"Sure honey!" Celine replied to Andrew and turned her attention to Osmond, "Son, I'll leave you here to take care of the dishes. And don't let Ms. Alex wash them!" She added and laughed as she eyed Alex smiling at her and sipping her coffee at the table.

"Okay mom," Osmond said as Celine and Andrew left the kitchen towards the living room. He returned to his task of putting the used plates in the dishwasher and put the pots used for cooking on the sink to wash by hand.

Alex just finished her breakfast. She was thinking of following Andrew in the living room. She stood to put her used plates and utensils on the sink. Osmond just finished wiping the countertop. He thought of checking if she was finished with her breakfast, so he can wash them himself and he turned around. To their surprise, they both collided with each other. Her, with a plate and a cup on separate hands.

Him, with a washcloth and a sponge. Body to body. Torso to torso. Wide-eyed looking at each other. He couldn't move immediately, as if all his reflexes decided to leave his body. She was too stunned to move away holding the dishes tightly, afraid she would drop them. He smelled her fresh vanilla and strawberry scent from her hair. She caught a whiff of his musky scent that sent tingles to her body. It was then she was afraid he would feel her trembling, she was the first to step back.

"I'm sorry!" They both said in unison.

He saw her cheeks blushed but she quickly turned away.

She felt her blood rushed to her cheeks but she quickly turned around to hide it from him.

She breathed deeply to calm herself but she suddenly felt his hands on hers.

He reached out for her but decided to gather the plate and cup on her hands.

She muttered a quick thanks. She tried to move her foot and was thankful it cooperated. She dashed towards her room. Without waiting for his reply or knowing his reaction. Without remembering her initial plan of joining the little boy and his grandmother on the living room. She rushed inside her room and quickly bolted the door. She leaned her entire body against the door. She looked up the ceiling and closed her eyes. She was certain that she was now uncertain. She wished that he wasn't her bodyguard. She wished it was another, so she wouldn't be confounded as she was. She was unsure if she could stop herself from continuously falling for him.

It was nearing lunch and the Gomez family, excluding Martin as he was already in the farm, including Alex were on their way there. On the way, Alex was holding little Andrew's hand as the boy tends to wonder and run after all bees and butterflies he saw. Hence, Andrew just gleefully pointed every insect and birds he saw on the trail to Alex who was more than happy to comply to the child's whims. It made her preoccupied with the little boy and avoid direct contact or conversation with Osmond. It was awkward enough, after the situation that occurred during breakfast, that Alex almost decided not go if not for the puppy-eyed request of the child.

Behind them was Celine and Osmond who were carrying the food and drinks they would need later. Osmond was in deep thought as he observed his nephew happily talking and playing with Alex.

"Son, are you okay?" Celine curiously asked Osmond as they near the cottage. It was then Osmond realized that he has been pondering the events earlier since they left home.

"Sorry mom. Don't worry, I'm okay. I was just preoccupied about reinforcing our house's security," he said as a harmless untruth to reassure her mom and smiled at her.

Upon arriving at the cottage, Celine and Osmond put the baskets on the table. Celine informed them that she would go to Martin to tell him that the food is there and for him to get ready. As soon as she left, Osmond sat on one of the Adirondack Chairs by the garden table. He spotted Alex with Andrew by the myrtle tree. The boy picked a pink flower from the lowest branch and put it on Alex's right ears. He was more bewildered by what he saw as his client's beauty bloomed with the flower.

Osmond had to stop and remind himself that he should be more professional around his "client" who was entrusted to him by Mr. de Ayala. He was on that thought when he saw Andrew pulling Alex and pointing somewhere. The boy was leading her somewhere. Osmond already knew that Andrew was leading Alex to the little boy's favorite place here in the farm, the stream. He stood from his chair as he, once again, reminded himself that his "client" should not leave his sight for her safety.

Fifteen

Insatiable Experience

There was an excitement within Alex as she was following Andrew. The little boy told enthusiastically of an enchanting place with a stream. It has been ages since she has been in one, her cousin brought her and their friends to one in Spain when they were all in high school. Her retrospection was cut as she felt a presence behind her. She gathered all her courage to check if her guess was correct and glanced back, only to realize that Osmond was staring at her and steadily walked behind them. It reminded her of the events that occurred earlier in the kitchen. She suddenly deflected her gaze back to a skipping Andrew in front of her. She hurriedly caught up with Andrew and took the little boy's hand to get far away as possible from Osmond's presence.

"We are getting closer," little Andrew said while holding her hand and disrupting her ruminations.

"Oh, I am so excited now!" Smiling at the boy dragging her, as she tried to hide her flushed cheeks from the man behind them.

"Come! Hurry!" The boy exclaimed running and pulling her. They both skipped happily towards the banks.

Osmond stopped and rested by a tree stump not far but within reach from where his nephew and Alex was. Alex was in awe with the wonder of the place while Osmond took the view in a different yet similar perspective.

She felt the cool afternoon breeze swaying the leaves allowing slivers of sunlight pass them.

He felt the cool afternoon breeze swaying his hair and dress softly.

She saw the sparkle of the running water so clear one can see the colorful myriad of pebbles.

He saw the sparkle of her eyes reflected by the shimmers of the clear running water.

She heard the burbling of the stream as a mellow laughter escaped her lips.

He heard her laugh amidst the trickling of the stream that a small smile escaped his lips.

It was then that Osmond thoughts went the other way. A distant past was trying to worm its way to surface from his thoughts. There was a reason Osmond avoided to be near any body of water. They reminded him of someone, Isabelle. His childhood best friend. They reminded him of how she was abducted and how he was still blaming his weakness. Yet, the current feeling, scene, and sound were somehow blurring the memory. For Osmond, it was like the uncertain present was trying to erase the dim past by a certain illumination he does not know the source. He forcefully snapped himself out of his sentiments as doubt began to creep within him. He preferred himself focused at the task at hand.

He stood from the tree stump and went nearer the river bank where he saw Alex and Andrew playing in the middle of the knee-deep water. He heard both of them laughing and was splashing water at each other. He found himself sitting on a huge rock under a Pandamus tree, smiling at them.

"Uncle Osmond, come here!" The little boy shouted at him joyfully as he was starting to get drenched by Alex.

"I'm fine here," Osmond smiled at his nephew then scanned the surroundings to make sure nothing untoward was in the area and returned his gaze at them.

Alex didn't mind if her sundress was starting to get wet. She was laughing and playing with Andrew. Osmond tried to warn the little boy about it.

"Hey, Andrew! Please stop. Ms. Alex's dress is starting to get soaked! You can still enjoy the water without splashing Ms. Alex," he then apologized to Alex, "I'm sorry about that!"

"Sorry," little Andrew said to Alex. He pouted his lips and bowed his head down.

"It's fine, Andrew. I am enjoying also," as she smiled and caressed the little boy's back, "don't worry about it, Osmond. I'm okay!" She shouted at the man on the rocks.

"Anyways, the food might be ready now. Let's head back!" Retorted Osmond as he saw Andrew laughed as Alex splashed him a little water as they started to walk out of the stream.

"Nana told me that mom is coming soon to the farm," said the little boy to Alex as he stopped to pick a pebble. He then threw it towards the water.

"Oh, that would be great! I'll get to meet your mom!" She excitedly answered Andrew, while Osmond got their attention again to tell them that they really should to go back for their very late lunch.

"Alright, we are coming! Come on, Andrew, we don't want your nana to get mad at us because we made her wait," Alex took the little boy's hand and they both allowed the warm sun and breeze to dry their clothes and walked towards Osmond who started to get up from his rock.

On the way back to the cottage, Osmond again felt a certain warmth looking at the pair in front of him. Alex was holding Andrew's right hand skipping together. Osmond realized that Alex truly has a heart for kids, that she would be a good mother to her future children. Until he noticed they were near the cottage already. He saw his mother setting the table with his sister, Cathy; while his father was busy talking and examining the baskets of freshly harvested vegetables with Cathy's husband, Andrei. It was then Andrew quickly ran to his dad.

"Daddy!" The boy shouted as Andrei welcomed his son with open arms.

"Hey, young man! How are you? Have you been good to Nana and Pops?" Andrei said as he ruffled Andrew's hair.

"Of course, daddy! I am always a good boy!" Andrew cheerfully said to his dad, "and I have a new friend!"

"Oh really? Who's that?" Andrei asked in curiosity.

"Ms. Alex! She is really nice and pretty!" As glee and pride was obvious in the boy's tone.

Osmond stood beside Alex while the father and son caught up with each other, as he saw how she admired the scene between Andrei and Andrew. A small smile appeared on Alex's lips. Osmond then noticed that the father and son duo were approaching them, with curiosity pasted on Andrei's face.

"Osmond! I am happy to see you again, mate! It has been a long time!" As his brother-in-law gave him a hug and few taps on his back which Osmond reciprocated.

"Thanks, mate! I am glad to see you again as well!" Osmond smiled as they separated. He glanced at Alex who was silently observing and he was about to introduce them when Andrew's small hand grabbed Alex's and pulled her into the small circle they've created.

"Daddy! This is Ms. Alex, the one I've told you about as my new friend! She's with Uncle Osmond when he arrived at Nana and Pop's house!" The little boy enthusiastically introduced her.

"Hi! Nice meeting you," Alex politely extended her hand for a hand shake, "and please, Alex will do," she added to which Osmond and Andrew smiled at each other realising a sudden familiarity and coziness from her.

"Oh hello, Alex! Nice meeting you! I am Andrei. Please pardon my son's behaviour. He tends to get excited having a new friend. And thank you for being his new friend," Andrei said accepting the handshake to alleviate the awkwardness as he felt intimidated by Alex's presence with a certain warmth, plus he knew how Andrew can turn in a shy little boy turn into a quokka with someone he has gotten close and like.

"It's okay Andrei, no worries. We've all been a kid once! Plus, this little boy has been well-behaved!" Defended Alex who hugged Andrew who giggled.

Osmond found himself smiling as he stood silently as the three conversed. He also noticed his dad watching and smiling them from the table. Osmond realized that it was alright to introduce Alex to his family as he trusts them. Although, he will make sure to be careful and to leave certain information as he cannot be assured about who his family interacts with outside their circle. It was at that moment that Celine called them at the table.

"Alright guys, mom is calling us for lunch," Osmond intervened with a smile to the three. They all walked towards the table at the side of the cottage, noticed how Alex was still wearing the flower, which little Andrew gave, on her ear. It was then Osmond accepted his admiration towards his client; but he vowed to himself never to cross the line and stay professional as possible. As they approached the table, Osmond saw his sister, Cathy, looking at their direction specifically at him with a mischievous grin.

"Hey there, little brother! I am so surprised to see you here! It has been that long!" Cathy said while giving a small chuckle and a hug to her brother.

"I am happy to see you to again, too!" Reciprocating the hug and jest from his sister, whom he saw stole a quick look at Alex.

"Oh, I am happy! And when mom mentioned last night that you are home, finally, after six months, I decided to come with Andrei to fetch Andrew so we can catch up with each other," Cathy retorted with a wink and maintained her mischievous grin which didn't escape Osmond looks. She then leaned closer to his ear to whisper, "so, spill the tea! Who's that gorgeous lady with you that my son seemed so fond of?"

Osmond knew instantly what Cathy was trying to imply, as she was the unruly and defiant one among the siblings. Their family was even happy when Cathy decided to settle down with a husband and a son hoping it would somehow tone her down. So, he knew he has to immediately interfere with her playful thoughts by introducing the two ladies. He assisted Alex from her seat, who was cheerfully talking to Andrew beside her, and have her face his sister.

"Ms. Alex, I mean Alex, this is my sister, Cathy. Cathy, this is my client and your son's new friend, Alex," Osmond said waiting for another of the unorthodox reaction from his sister.

"It's nice meeting you, Cathy," Alex politely extending her hand to the other woman. Almost everybody near the table was surprised, except Osmond and Celine who knew Cathy so well, how Cathy replied.

"OMG! You're so pretty!" Cathy almost shouted and ignored Alex's extended hand, instead went in to give her a big tight embrace, "Oh! It is nice to meet you too! Ha ha ha! How are you? I hope you are enjoying your stay here and that my little Andrew didn't give any headache! Although, he is so much like his well-mannered father, he sometimes inherited my naughtiness! It very unusual, in fact, you're the first client my brother brought home! So, where are you from? Oh, and I love your dress, it is so cheerful! And I am talking so much now! I'm gonna shut up now!" She added.

Osmond realised his sister was faster than him for him to prevent her to embrace Alex. He decided his sister was harmless for Alex and let her be. He slowly shook his head smiling as Alex hugged Cathy back and gave her a big smile while the rest of the family were laughing at Cathy's antics.

"Oh, I am just fine! I am from Melbourne. Andrew was such a little gentleman and a nice friend. Thank you about my dress and..."

Alex dutifully answered Cathy's inquiries but stopped mid-sentence and looked at Osmond. Osmond got what Alex was trying to tell him.

"And I took her here for safety reasons due to certain sensitive occurrences that her family is currently working on," Osmond interjected, finishing Alex's thoughts.

"Wait, why have I never thought of this after I realised a particular thing related to your profession? Osmond, don't tell me she is the controversial-"

Osmond quickly nodded in response to his sister's conclusion.

"I see! Okay, whatever those sensitive matters are, I hope you do feel at home here. Mom's apple turnover and strawberry shortcake are to die for! So, enjoy your stay here while your family is working whatever they are working on!" Cathy loudly replied then turned again to Osmond, "Have you shown her our state's beautiful destinations?"

"I've shown her my stream, mom!" little Andrew answered for Osmond, "we played there and she loved it!" He added.

"Good job, son!" Cathy said and teased Osmond, "unlike your uncle, I'm sure, who is less hospitable!"

"I will, big sis! But maybe someday, when things aren't as complicated as it is!" Retorted Osmond.

"Alright, that's enough teasing Cathy. Continue your interrogation as we eat. The food is getting cold," Celine intervened as she pushed Cathy to her seat while Osmond assisted Alex to her seat.

"Yeah! I'm starting to get hungry! We should eat now. I brought your favourite seafood! Fresh huge lobsters and baked salmon!" Cathy said as she got busy trying to put everything on everybody's plate from salads to breads, assorted fruits to seafood.

Osmond can't help but smile as they all started to eat. Osmond saw how down-to-earth and caring this heiress can be as she tried to use the lobster cracker and shared whatever she got to the little boy beside her. He saw how she smiled and laughed at Cathy's amusing behaviour and antics with her husband constantly apologizing yet teasing Cathy as well, how his parents made sure she has enough food on her plate, how happily engrossed Andrew was talking to her and grateful with the food she was giving him.

He suddenly realized that this was what Alex needed. A time and place away from her past and from what endanger her. To forget her worries. To be who she really is. To smile a genuine smile. To laugh.

Meanwhile, back in Melbourne, a man was deep in his thoughts in his dimly lit office. He was currently in front of his laptop and a goblet of red wine. His thoughts were of games he wanted to play against a certain person he wanted to eradicate. Games of great things to make that person kneel before him. He smiled as he finished his plans and even back up plans. He called in his most trusted right-hand man. It was as if they were whispering to each other as they discussed pertinent and important details of his games. The right-hand man left him after their accord. The man silently took a sip from the goblet and puffed his cigar. In the dimly lit office, the man observed the trail of smoke he exhaled, once again, deep in his thoughts about the games he cannot wait to play.

Sixteen

Mystery of Surprises

Several days passed after Alex had lunch with the Gomezes and had met Cathy and her husband. It was a delightful experience Alex would remember even after Cathy's family left with Andrei. As she would really miss the little boy, she knows they would see each other soon.

It was now a Tuesday morning and the Gomez family with Alex had just finished breakfast. As Alex was about to put her finished cup of coffee in the sink, the ray of sunlight coming from the kitchen window made her muse on how Osmond held her hand few days ago during lunch with Osmond's family. She smiled. An undeniable twinkle in her eye was reflected by the bright morning sun.

She started to return to her room as she saw Celine in the living room carrying the large box and seemed to be heading outside. Alex was about to approach Celine to help her carrying the box when Celine accidentally dropped it, spilling various ephemeras.

"Oh, are you alright?" Alex asked worriedly.

"I'm okay darling. I was cleaning the attic and was about to rid of these clutters," Celine replied as she started to go down on her knees and began putting the old photos, tattered magazines, and crumbly newspapers back in the box. Alex didn't hesitate to kneel beside her and helped Celine. The two women were about to finish tidying up when Alex picked an old photo. It's age was apparent with the state of it. Tattered, torn. It's edges started to wither. Its colour started to fade.

But the Alex can still clearly see the subject, rather subjects, of the old photo. Two young teens under a tree in a seemingly setting afternoon sun. It was apparent they were on a hill overlooking the golden valley below. The teenage boy dearly looked at the teenage girl as she was facing the lens. Genuine happiness was apparent in their faces as they both held each other's hands. It was then Alex recognized the young boy as Osmond holding the hand of a beautiful young blond girl.

"Ladies, everything okay in here?" The two women didn't even notice Osmond entered the living room. Osmond immediately saw Alex holding a familiar old photograph.

"Yeah, I was just helping Celine clean up," Alex replied while Celine seemed to notice that her son was looking at the photo Alex was holding.

Alex was about to put the photo in the box when Osmond reached out for it. After Alex gave the photo to Osmond, she and Celine stood. Celine put the box with various things on the side table sensing heaviness in the room.

Osmond stared intently at the photograph. It was the last joyful memory he had with Isabelle before her abduction. He felt the women looking at him, Celine with sympathy and Alex with curiosity.

"She's Isabelle," Osmond indirectly answered Alex's questioning gaze while he was still looking at the photo, "We were inseparable when we were young, until an ill-fated day..."

"She was abducted fourteen years ago," Celine explained, sensing her son's guilt to continue amidst the necessity to let it out. She knew that he needed to hear, if not say himself, what happened before to somehow alleviate the remorse her son was feeling, "please, Osmond, don't keep on blaming yourself. You were still young back then."

"But I was the one with her, mom," Osmond's voice started to crack, "I was useless and young, it was all my fault!"

"It was such a long time ago, dear," Celine tried soothing her bereft son, "nobody wanted for that to happen. Besides, a body has yet to be found. You what that means, right?"

"Yes, mom," his mother's words held a certain truth, "I also feel she's alive somewhere out there. Waiting to be reunited with her family and with us," as he hurriedly left the living room with Alex stunned.

"I'm sorry you have to witness that," Celine said to Alex who she noticed was seemingly quiet.

"It's okay, Celine. I might not understand what happened, but I understand that she was important to him," Alex replied. They both started to carry the box outside and resumed their unfinished task.

Meanwhile, Osmond found himself in the open garage trying to fruitlessly fix anything he could find there. He knew he was still affected by what transpired fourteen years ago, but he also knew this was not the right time to be unprofessional. He took a deep breath and regain control of his self. He needed to remind himself that he was on a mission and his client was still with him in his parent's house. He needed to apologize to Alex. He remembered Cathy's suggestion from their previous family lunch with Alex. It might even help him to be preoccupied and forget the pain of remembering Isabelle.

So, that afternoon Osmond decided take Alex to a famous spot in their state.

"Miss Alex?" He called from the other side of her room. She opened the door and was somewhat concerned for him after what happened earlier.

"Is there anything I can help you with?" She asked.

"Get ready. We are going somewhere," he replied.

"Where are we going?"

"Somewhere nice. You might get cabin fever staying here constantly. Plus, a little bit of sunshine and scenery will be good for you!"

"Okay, sure. Hold on, I'll just get ready."

Osmond smile widened as he left Alex to get ready in her room and him to prepare in his. He made sure he had everything he needed for her to enjoy the rest of the day and still be able to protect her.

He didn't need to change his clothes, wearing white tees and a brown chino with white sneakers.

As they were on their way, Osmond's phone rang. It registered Mr. de Ayala's number. He put on his hands-free earpiece to answer the call.

"Hello, Mr. de Ayala," Osmond greeted, "is there any emergency or anything I can help you with?" Alex glanced at Osmond hearing her father's name.

"Good afternoon, Agent Gomez," the patriarch of the de Ayala replied, "my wife and I would just want to talk to Alex. We are going on a business trip and would want to inform her that we will be overseas for quite some time."

"Of course, Mr. de Ayala. I'm on my way to her room now. Please don't make the call long to avoid detection or tracing. Don't also mention any specific location and details just to be safe," Osmond warned.

"Sure. And thank you for taking care of my daughter."

Osmond gave the earpiece to Alex so she can speak with her parents. Alex reached for it and nodded him thanks before speaking.

"Hello," she said to the other line.

"Dear!" it was now Mrs. de Ayala on the other line, "we miss you greatly!"

"I miss you both too, mom. Is dad there?"

"Yes, but we can't talk long as Agent Gomez reminded us it might be dangerous and this call might be traced. Anyways, your father and I just want to tell you we miss you and we are going to Singapore for a business meeting. So don't worry about us."

"Sure, mom. How many days will you be gone?"

"We will only be there for two to three days to sort some things. Don't worry, we will be back as soon as possible to continue the investigation with the General," Mrs. de Ayala said with concern on her voice, "for meantime, do take care of yourself and follow Agent Gomez's instruction for your safety, okay?"

"Yes, mom. I love you and please tell dad I love him too."

"Of course, dear. We both love you! Bye!"

Alex heard the end tone from the other line. She returned Osmond's earpiece to him.

"My parents are going to Singapore for business for two or three days. They said they'll hurry back to continue the investigation," she looked outside glumly.

"I'm sure they will be fine. I'm sure that the General assigned them agents to protect them," Osmond trying to assure Alex after sensing concern from her. He was more certain that this trip would be good for her to take away any of her worries and even his.

"Yeah, I guess," she replied trying to sound fine. She didn't need to worry Osmond any further. She felt he was also undergoing something after her discovery about his past earlier. She didn't want to add more on his plate. She opened her side of the window and allowed the wind to blow away all her troubles away. Even for a short while. To forget all her worries temporarily and just be with Osmond.

Osmond sensed what Alex was trying to do. He did the same. He opened his side of the window and allowed the breeze blow away his troubles, his past. Even for a short while.

They glanced at each other and smiled. Osmond returned his gaze on the road ahead. Alex returned her look outside.

Alex suddenly felt a change in the wind. It smelled warmly and salty. Even the sound changed. She then heard rushing of waves. Even the view changed, the Wattle, Acacia, Oak trees were replaced by Palm and Coconut trees. Everything she felt, heard, and saw invigorated her.

As the Jeep stopped. Alex was amazed. In front of her were stretch of sand, overlapping waves, salty breeze, warm afternoon sun. Osmond decided to bring her here in an isolated area in Wanjuru away from the busy Flying Fish Point area. As he also stepped out of the Jeep, he saw Alex genuinely smiling and soaking everything she was feeling, hearing, and seeing. He couldn't help but smile himself.

"Thank you!" Alex said to Osmond and walked closer to the shore after removing her sandals to feel the sea touch her feet. She took a deep breath and fill her lungs with fresh salty air. Being in a beach, with the sand between her toes, the sea on her feet, the wind on her skin were her happy place, her home in nature.

Osmond serenely followed her, after removing his sneakers, to where the sea kisses the sand. Until the water also touched his feet. Alex looked back at him and once again, smiled genuinely.

"Again, thank you for bringing me here," Alex gratefully said to Osmond. She knew that he didn't have any idea how she loved the sea, however, he brought her here. And for that she was glad.

"You're welcome, Miss Alex," Osmond felt happy too. He saw Alex sat on the sand not minding the splash of waves drenching her white skirt. He saw her picking and playing with the shells around her. He saw her allowing the waves to kiss her soft hands as well. So, he did the same. He sat an arm's length away from her and played, too, with the shells and waves.

Alex let out a soft giggle that made Osmond laugh as she splashed him with water. He returned the favour laughing. After playing for a while, they both stopped as they are getting drenched already. They sat silently on the sand, allowing the breeze envelop them, watching the sun setting, and touching the waves crashing at their feet.

"Osmond, what is your greatest desire in life?" Alex suddenly asked out of the blue. She was as surprised as Osmond by her question and her asking him that. She didn't even know what took over her to ask that question. She guessed it was a spur of the moment that she wouldn't take against Osmond if he decided not to answer.

The silence lingered, except for the sound of crashing waves on the sand. Silence that Osmond broke, "To protect everyone I love."

His answer was contrite but for Alex, it was full of meaning. She understood that for a man of few words, his answer meant greatly. Thus, she didn't push the subject further only for the favour to be returned to her.

"With almost having every woman's wishes, what's yours, Miss Alex?" Osmond asked Alex while still gazing at the sea and the setting sun.

Alex took a quick glance at Osmond, making sure she heard him right before answering with conviction, "to travel and explore the wonders of the world with someone I really love for the rest of our lives."

"That person would be so…" Osmond stopped mid-sentence as he sensed another presence in the area that he cannot see. He was certain someone was stalking them from afar. Alex worriedly looked at him but he only signed to be quiet, putting his pointer finger to his lips.

"We should head back. Someone's watching us."

Alex saw and sense the urgency on Osmond's face and voice. She tried not to panic amidst the impending danger. It has started to grow dark as the night creeped in following the already gone sun. Osmond grabbed her right hand and put her behind them as they hurriedly but carefully trod towards the Jeep. Once inside, Osmond checked if the Jeep was in any way compromised. Satisfied, he quickly started the vehicle and left the area.

They are now finished with their dinner and Alex and Osmond's parents decided to spend the rest of the night in their respective rooms. As for Osmond, he needed to double check the security and safety of their house and the surrounding yard. He made sure the surveillance cameras were active and working, before grabbing his handgun and going outside to examine their place.

On his patrol, he passed by Alex's room. He could see that only his night lamp was on. He presumed that she was preparing to call it a night and sleep.

He then felt an incoming object from his rear. He easily dodged a medium-sized stone and traced where it came from. He saw a silhouette coming from the bushes across the lawn. He grabbed his handgun and readied himself as he approached the area where the silhouette disappeared.

Upon reaching the bushes, a sudden kick from behind the tree disarmed Osmond and threw the gun several metres away from him and his unknown attacker who had his hood over his head. Osmond instantly realised that his assailant was trained in hand-to-hand combat. He knew that he needed to end the fight quickly. Time was of the essence for him to subdue his aggressor. He threw a right hook followed by a roundhouse kick only to be blocked by the stranger. The unknown man threw a left uppercut but Osmond was too agile and was able to evade it. Osmond then counterattacked with an elbow strike on his opponent's chest. True enough to Osmond's assessment, his enemy quickly recovered from his direct hit. The man started to tackle him but Osmond quickly stepped aside. The aggressor went down to give Osmond a low kick but to no avail as Osmond flipped backwards. Osmond saw an advantage. He knew his enemy mainly aims his head or lower limbs. He knew the fight was now on his favour. All he needed to do was to wait for an opening and target his assailant's thorax to wind him down. The man quickly stood up and Osmond was prepared for his countermoves.

"I concede, Agent Gomez!" The hooded man spoke which surprised Osmond who recognized the voice of the man.

"What the hell are you doing here, Agent McKain?" Osmond asked as he gave Cedrick a friendly punch on his stomach and ruffled his hair, "I was about to kill you mate!"

"I know! That's why I admitted defeat! I saw your stance ready to kill! Ha ha!"

"It's not a joke man! Jesus, mate!"

"I just wanted to see if my skills caught with yours. Apparently, I still need to train more! Ha ha!"

"Again, what are you doing here?" Osmond said as he started to retrieve his handgun from the ground.

"Oh, I have a mission here in Queensland," Cedrick said while trying to suppress his laughter.

"So, I decided to drop by and say hi!"

Osmond couldn't help but smirk at Cedrick's antics. He may look playful but Cedrick has the skills to wreak havoc. He was not even surprised if the man was able to locate them as he is a skilled tracker-agent.

"Anyway, I have to go. But be vigilant, I might drop again to play with you! Ha ha!" The younger agent joked. Osmond nodded at his direction before Cedrick skedaddled towards the fence and went over it.

"Typical of Agent McKain. He could have just used the gate!" Osmond said to himself laughing and went off to continue his inspection of their place.

Seventeen

Life and Death

Voices from opposite his bedroom door awakened Osmond. He felt the warmth of the sun's rays filtering his window on his eyelids with the chirping of early birds already busy with the start of day. He decided to finally open his eyes and got up. He grabbed a white fitted white shirt from his dresser and removed the black pyjama he wore the night before. As he was putting his shirt on, he caught a glance of the analog clock telling him it was past eight already. He hurriedly went out of his room realising he overslept.

Walking towards the living room, he was thinking of a reason or an excuse for him oversleeping. He cannot explain, but he had this urge to apologise to Alex. Stretching his still sleeping muscle, he saw his parents with Alex intently sitting on the couch across the television with the morning news on. Dumbfounded with both arms raised midway his stretch, curiosity got the better of him.

"...and luckily, the woman was able to save her two children, a five-year old boy and an eight-month baby girl, from the fire that started in the kitchen. She cannot specifically tell us the cause of the fire, however, the firefighters were able to extinguish the fire in the kitchen before it spread throughout the house," Osmond heard from the field reporter, "for now, that is the latest news from the fire incident since the mother is still in shock. This is Maddie, reporting to you live. Back to you Rebecca,"

"Thank you, Maddie. We would give an update, as soon as possible, once we gather more details from this incident," news anchor said before cutting into the commercial break.

"I feel so sorry for them! The kid and the baby must be so scared!" Alex worriedly exclaimed as her beautiful face showed distress.

"God have mercy on them! It's horrendous!" Celine said and looked to her husband. They didn't even notice Osmond's presence nearby who was suddenly focused on the screen, understanding what they were so upset about.

"O-Osmond... I want to help them in any way that I can," Alex suddenly felt her bodyguard's presence.

Almost two weeks in his parent's house, Osmond thought he had the slightest idea about the personality of the heiress of Mr. de Ayala. But, she kept on surprising him which he found endearing. He, then, remembered his intention of apologising for oversleeping.

"Miss Alex, my apology for waking up late. It will never again, it's just..."

"It's really no big issue, Osmond," Alex interrupted Osmond mid-sentence, "I already had a lovely breakfast with your parents," she added while tapping Celine's knee and giving Martin a smile.

Osmond couldn't help but smile and scratched his nape, turning his attention to his mother.

"Mom, I thought it was my turn to cook breakfast today?" He uttered while smiling sheepishly.

"It's no big deal, son. You have been working so hard and we decided you need more sleep. Right, honey?" Celine looked across Martin.

"True, plus, you don't have to count me out yet. Your old man is still strong as a bull," Martin chuckled while flexing biceps which made Celine and Alex snicker, "hey, you may have not noticed but I have been extra vigilant lately. I even know about the scuffle last night, son!"

"Wait, what scuffle? And why didn't you tell me?" Celine concernedly asked, while Alex went mum.

"Oh, that, haha!" Martin dismissed the worry of the two ladies in the room, "no need to worry, I surmised they were friends so I let the man go. Plus, I trust the abilities of my son so I let him handle it on his own. He is not a son of a marine for nothing. Haha!" Martin added with a hearty laugh.

Osmond knew he couldn't argue with his father regarding that. His father was in fact a retired marine. Although he was grateful that his father didn't interfere last night, else, Agent McKain was done for.

"You still have woken me up!" Celine reprimanded her husband.

"Oh, I don't want to disturb your beauty sleep for something our son can handle, honey," Martin tried to soothe his wife, knowing that if he did not, he would not hear the end of it. He also kissed Celine's cheek for additional assurance which he thought worked as Celine seemed to let it go.

"I'm sorry Martin to impose to you that you have to also be extra careful because of me," Alex said apologetically.

"No need to worry dear, my husband needed that extra action in his life," it was Celine's turn to reassure Alex, "I'm quite sure he's missing his glory days as a marine."

"Celine's right! You should have seen me in action during my younger years. I'm quite a hell of a lad compared to my son! Haha," Martin haughtily said. He tried to lighten the dreary mood from the news and the mention of last night's event. He was relieved when Celine playfully hit him on his nape with Alex giggling again.

Osmond was as relieved as his father and grateful to him for lightening the mood. He always admired his father's capability to protect his family and still make them happy. Something he wished he could do to his future family.

"That's it!" Alex suddenly stood from where she was sitting, surprising everyone, "I've decided to help the victims of the fire. Osmond, I need you to eat your breakfast. And after, you will help me finalise my plan."

"Sure Miss Alex. Mom, dad," Osmond nodded at the three to signal his leave.

He quickly reached the kitchen with food left and prepared for him by his mom. After he was finished, he immediately cleaned the plates and utensils he used. As he was eating and cleaning after the dishes, he couldn't be certain where the feeling of satisfaction and happiness was coming from but he welcomed it with a light heart.

As he returned to his room to prepare, he saw the three still watching the tube but was now laughing at the morning sitcom they were watching. Osmond was certain that it was his father's idea to change the channel to lessen the two ladies' worried minds.

Inside his room, he sat in front of his study table and turned on his laptop to conduct a quick survey regarding the victims of the recent fire. He needed to know that Alex would be safe with the people she would be helping. It was easy for him to retrieve information from the Australian Federal Police's database with the access given to him by The General. There was no grave criminal record on the father of the afflicted children. He was scheduled for a job interview, that's why he was not in his house; while the mother had just finished her shift as a cashier at a mom-and-pop convenience store. After reading further about the couple, he decided that it would be alright for Alex to help the family.

Osmond found Alex in the veranda on the hammock reading a book while his parents were busy tending over the garden. Alex was reading "Pride and Prejudice" when she felt a familiar presence coming out of the door. As their eyes met, an understanding became clear between them. He was ready to help her and she was grateful.

"Great read!" Osmond glanced towards the book she was reading.

"Yeah, it is!" She replied enthusiastically, "do you like reading books?"

"I do! Although, I much prefer a more political genre."

"Hey, Pride and Prejudice is somewhat political."

"Yes, it does. I've read that, too! But I'm more of a Scarlet Letter reader," He replied.

"Impressive. I do sometimes relate to Hester."

"You have a daughter I do not know?" He confoundedly asked.

"No, silly! Ha ha. I mean, being ostracised by society for being an heiress. They think I'm just another snob, spoiled brat from a family with money and power," she explained with Osmond intently staring at her, listening to her, assuring her she's not alone, "don't worry, though, I have outgrown them just like Hester. I realised that some people are just ashamed and guilty of their own sin so they look for a person to blame it on, just like the people of Boston. It so happens that I am famous and that they know me, so they immediately judge me."

"Don't misunderstand, Osmond, I realised who I am a long time ago and it doesn't matter what they say about me anymore. I am stronger and better now. I may not be as strong as you or your dad, haha, but I am within."

There was a moment of silence between the two of them as Alex turned towards the blue sky with a smile. Osmond couldn't help himself as he admired the woman more in front of him. He sympathised with what made her to be who she was right now, but at the same time he was feeling proud of what she had become. He then remembered her wish to help the victims of the fire from the news.

"Miss Alex, by the way, here are the details of the victims," he said after giving her the paper where he wrote what he found, "but we have to make sure that it would not be traced back to us."

"Oh, I was planning on meeting them in person. But of course, you are right. What do we do then?"

"We can send financial aid anonymously. I also found their joint account," he replied.

"That could work, can you please send them thirty thousand dollars?" She requested, "you can get the fund from the card that my dad gave to you without any trace, right?"

"I was about to suggest that."

"Thank you so much, Osmond. I knew I could count on you!" Alex excitedly said knowing that they would be able to help the victims of the fire.

"No problem, Miss Alex. I better go back to my room and start working on the transfer of funds, so you could also continue reading about Elizabeth Bennet," he said. As he was about to walk inside, he heard her calling him.

"Osmond?"

"Yes, Miss Alex? Is there anything more I could help you with?"

"Nothing. I-I just want to say thank you again," she replied so softly he almost didn't hear her. She then gave him a small smile as the rays of the nearing noon sun pierced through the clouds hitting her face that radiated a warm glow, emphasising her hazel eyes that enticed Osmond to gaze deep within.

"My pleasure, Miss Alex," he replied as softly as she did. Then, he headed toward his bedroom to work on Alex's request.

As unpredictable as the Australian weather, life is also. Unaware of the incoming danger, Alex was enjoying her mango yogurt after their lunch in the Gomez's farm while sitting in a white Adirondack chair under several trees in the windy afternoon. She was only a few metres away from Osmond who was preoccupied scanning the area for untoward signs while Osmond's parents were tending the farm behind the farmhouse.

"Hey, Osmond! When is Andrew visiting again?" Alex called him, "your nephew is so adorable and I miss him already."

Osmond stopped what he was doing and smiled. He was about to answer Alex's question, but as he spun to face her, his smile vanished. He saw an eastern brown snake resting on a branch just inches away from where Alex was finishing her mango yogurt. His brain processed the situation immediately and thought of a solution in a split second.

In a very soft and calm voice, Osmond commanded Alex, "Miss Alex, please don't make any sudden movements."

"Osmond? What is it?" She asked worriedly as she put down her almost finished yogurt with the spoon on the armrest. She was concerned by the sudden change of Osmond's demeanour.

"Just please listen to me. Take a slow breath and close your eyes," he replied, trying to keep his composure. He knew that if told her the truth there's a possibility that she would scream or panic and make unnecessary gestures that might provoke the resting venomous snake.

Alex was discombobulated by the situation and Osmond's commanding tone which he almost rarely used on her, nonetheless, she decided to follow him.

Alex was perplexed and about to ask more questions but she chose to obey her bodyguard's command.

"OK, you're doing just fine," Osmond said in almost a whisper. His focus now turned towards the serpent who was now looking at him, but was still stationary on the branch. The man and the snake glared at each other. Both intently watched and gaged the other's capability and ability. Osmond's adrenaline was now in full gear. His pupils dilated. Every inch of muscle in his body tensed, ready to jump in case the snake decided to attack. Sweat began forming on his forehead ever so slowly dripped down his chin. He still did not blink, enduring the sting caused by a stray strand of sweat that dripped his right eye. He was even ready to offer any of his limbs just to save Alex if the snake decided to assault forward.

"Osmond?" Alex whimpered ever so softly.

"Everything is going to be fine, but please stay still," he said trying to reassure her while raising his right hand towards Alex. It was as if the brown snake grew tired of their standpoint, it slithered away from the edge of the branch towards the trunk of the tree. Osmond was grateful for the sudden turn of events.

He saw the opportunity and began slowly advancing towards Alex while commanding her in a still soft and calm tone, "open your eyes, slowly stand. Walk. Don't run. Walk towards me. Look at me. Only me. Don't look behind you."

Alex slowly opened her eyes and saw Osmond inching towards her. She eventually stood and advanced towards him. Within arm's length, he grabbed her, enveloping her in an embrace as if shielding her from any form of harm. Her anxiety slowly dissipated as she felt a particular sense of warmth and safety in his arms that she would not want to let go. But he led her further away from her initial position.

"Osmond, what was it? You're making me worry," she finally got it out of her chest. Instead, the man holding her left wrist pointed towards a tree near the Adirondack chair.

She followed where he was pointing. She was left speechless by what she saw. With a gaped mouth and widened eyes, she recognised the venomous snake. Tears started to form as she hugged him gratefully.

With a ragged voice and realizing what Osmond did for her, she mustered enough energy to speak, "thank you! I would have freaked out if I had known there was a brown snake near me!"

"Everything's fine now. It darted back into the woods. You are safe," he whispered. He was initially uneasy as she was hugging him. Although, he understood why she did that and where she's coming from. She was scared. So, he raised his left hand to hug her back and his right hand to tap her shoulder to assure that everything was fine and will be fine. Because at the back of his mind, he reaffirmed his earnest sworn duty to protect her since the very first day of his mission.

Eighteen

The Force of Genuine Connection

Osmond got up around seven in the morning and glanced outside the window. Iridescent clouds resulted from the rising sun. It has been three days since the dreadful occurrence at the farm, yet he still was bothered by the memory of it. He was grateful that his reflexes worked to his advantage that day. Preoccupied with recalling the event, he did not notice his mother who was preparing breakfast watching him. He was intently staring outside the kitchen window.

"Breakfast is ready!" Celine called out to Osmond to help her set the table, but he was still staring outside. So, she called for him again with a motherly concern, "are you alright, son?" She asked, tapping his shoulder for assurance she was there for him.

"Oh mom, I'm sorry, you were saying something?" Osmond snapped back to reality, realizing where he was and who was with him.

"I said breakfast is ready and are you alright?"

"Got it! I'll help set up the table. I'm OK mom, I was just thinking about what happened a few days back at our farm involving Miss Alex," Osmond said, moving from the kitchen window towards the table to set it up.

Celine's motherly instinct kicked in, "you seemed to be worried about her. What's on your mind?" She asked as she put the freshly baked bagels on the table.

"Well, when we were at the farm three days ago, an eastern brown snake appeared on a branch only inches away from Miss Alex. You and dad were on the field and I had to act fast to save. Although I was able to save her, I can't bear to think that something bad could happen to her," Osmond explained as he sat down after setting up the plates.

"Jesus! Oh my, why didn't you tell us about it earlier?" Celine worriedly asked as she got fruits from the counter and put it on the table.

"Well, since nothing untowards happened, Miss Alex told me not to mention it to both of you. She doesn't want you to worry unnecessarily and she is that caring as she is."

Celine moved around the table to close the gap between her and Osmond. She put her hand on his shoulder reassuringly.

Osmond felt the warmth radiating from his mother's hand on his shoulder soothing the unknown growing anxiety within him. He looked at the kitchen window across the table to see that the wind picked up and swayed the trees violently as if empathically knowing how he felt. Clouds began to cover the bright morning sun, telling Osmond that although there will be a bright tomorrow, the storm was just approaching.

He broke the silence between them, "that was the first time I saw fear in her eyes. The same fear I saw in Isabelle's that day she was abducted. That's why I'm certain now that I would not let anything bad happen to Miss Alex," he said full of conviction as he returned his gaze on his mother beside him who was intently listening to him to let him know she was supporting him with whatever he decides to do like ever since.

"Oh, son. Stop blaming yourself for what happened in the past. You were young then, so how could you ever possibly defend yourself and Isabelle against three fully-grown up kidnappers? I sympathize with Isabelle's parents, but your father and I are grateful that nothing bad happened to you," Celine sincerely said while taking a seat beside Osmond and facing him so they can look at each other eye to eye, for him to see and feel that she was there for him, "And you know what? I personally believe that there is a reason you survived that ordeal. Maybe it was to protect and prevent what happened in the past to happen in the present. Maybe that is the reason you were assigned with Miss Alex's case, to protect like you did a few days ago."

"I guess you're right mom, you always are," Osmond said gratefully; and even though his mother didn't tell him, he surely felt her love with what she said.

"Of course, I am! You are my son and I know you are very emotional in defending people you care for. Remember Carlyle, your classmate in grade school? I remember how you fought two middle schoolers bullies just to protect him. You came home black and blue with bruises but was still wearing a proud smile. I was livid back then but your father was very proud of you," Celine said, slapping Osmond's right arm.

"Haha! Dad, even treated Cathy and I for ice cream that day! At least, those boys didn't bother Carlyle anymore after that," Osmond responded gratefully towards his mother for comforting him and reminding him of what he can do to protect those under his care; although, the anxiety for Alex was there it somehow diminished at the back of his mind.

Celine stood from where she was seated to give her son a hug to reassure him of her love, "luckily for you, he went out before the sun rose to do some errands. So, let's start breakfast. Your client might wake up soon and you need your energy to fulfill your duties for her. And yes, before you say anything, I have also prepared her breakfast," she added.

"Thank you, Mom," Osmond replied, giving his mother another quick hug. He also realized his anxieties finally dissipated because he knew his family was there to support him.

Meantime, Alex just entered the kitchen's entryway and saw Osmond with Celine with their backs turned to her. She surmised they were both having a crucial discussion with their solemn posture; she decided to let them have their mother and son moment. She returned to her bed to continue her reading as there were only a few more chapters left.

However, she seemed to focus on her book. The words were familiar but they were flying out the window. Alex was too distracted to continue reading. So, she stopped pretending, she closed her book and her eyes. Unmindful that she put it on top of her chest, but mindful of a memory that bothered her. A recent memory. Although she could remember the fear and anxiety she felt three days ago at the farm, she could also remember something special somewhere at the back of her mind. She recalled how Osmond's eyes were filled with care and concern for her, how her body seemed to be in perfect fit to his when he hugged and protected her. The warmth radiated from his body that seemed to calm her. His musk of mixed sweat and aftershave that seemed to mesmerize her. Seemed, since she was unsure of her emotions that day. It was nerve-wracking yet felt right. It pacified her and terrified her at the same time. She tried her hardest to calm the quick and loud beating of her heart for reasons beyond her mind. She breathed deeply and slowly until she felt she was ready to open her eyes and went to shower to wash all bewildering emotions and thoughts.

Few days had passed, both Osmond and Alex had moved on from the event at the farm realising that it was a natural occurrence for the snake to be there. They both missed the warmth and beauty of the nature surrounding the farm. However, Osmond would now be better prepared and extra vigilant for both natural and unnatural or planned events that could potentially harm Alex. So, he was currently at the veranda cleaning his .45 caliber gun that he would bring later at the farm for lunch.

As he was cleaning his gun, he peripherally saw Alex coming out of the door. He wondered what she could be asking or needing as she approached him but hid his curiosity. He finished putting small amounts of solvent to lubricate the moving parts and started to assemble them. He was wiping the gun with a luster cloth when Alex, who was several feet away from him for her safety, cleared her throat to make her presence known.

"Ahem, it looks shinier now," Alex smiled coyly.

"Good morning, Miss Alex," Osmond replied, acknowledging her, "yeah, it has been a while since I cleaned this one."

"I have never fired a gun before. I have always been fascinated by how it works since I was in college, but my parents weren't a huge fan of it," Alex coquettishly said that Osmond quickly realised where she was going through with this discussion, "Uhm, so, I was wondering if you could teach me how to use it?"

Osmond had just finished wiping the holster and put the gun back into it. He was still silent when he returned his look at her, assessing how he should answer.

"I mean, who could better teach me than you, right?" Alex continued after an awkward silence, hoping Osmond would agree, "I promise that I wouldn't tell my parents or anyone for that matter."

"Well, although I appreciate your candidness, Miss Alex. It's better if I think and assess your request. I haven't taught any of my clients before. So, please let me think about it," Osmond replied.

"OK, I hope you would see how it would be beneficial for me to learn how to use a gun," she answered gravely to assert her conviction, then smiled after a while, "I'll go back inside to help Celine with lunch. See you later."

The next day, the Gomezes and Alex decided to stay at the house for lunch. Although, no untoward event happened yesterday they opted to have lunch at the house since Martin and Celine had to leave for the town center for the groceries. Alex just finished taking her tea and entered the living room when she saw Osmond closing his black pistol case. She had the sudden urge to ask him regarding his decision about her request yesterday but stayed silent on the entryway.

"Oh, Miss Alex, there you are. I am just preparing the things we need for your training today," Osmond said as he noticed Alex by the door," And, yes, I am helping you with your request. If you're ready we can go to the field for your training."

Although surprised that her personal bodyguard agreed to teach her, Alex tried to hide her excitement from what she heard from Osmond, "Oh OK, I am ready!"

Osmond led Alex to an open field near the farm, where it would be far from any neighbours and safe to train.

"This is my training ground whenever I am here, "Osmond broke the silence as they entered an open field with various shrubs and trees surrounding the place. Magnolia trees by the east side where a couple of benches were situated if one decided to rest. He had bought the property two years ago.

"Nice place! It is very private," Alex voiced her appreciation of the place.

"Yes, thank you! It will be safe here so as to avoid any accidents," Osmond assured her.

She was now watching him prepare the area. He was about fifteen metres away from her, setting up what looked like a series of cans on top of a series of rocks with different heights.

He returned to where she was standing watching him. He got the clear eye shooting glasses for him and a yellow one for her. He also brought out a couple of earmuffs. After wearing his eye and ear protections, he assisted her to put on hers making sure they fit her perfectly.

She grew conscious as he got too close as he was putting on the protection and earmuffs on her. Although, she tried to hide it. She couldn't help but to take a whiff of his musk. She caught herself and decided to focus on what they will be doing.

"Are you ready?" He asked, catching her off-guard.

"Oh, yes, of course! I can't be more ready as it is!" She replied, knowing she failed to hide her enthusiasm.

"But before I let you hold the gun, I will have to familiarise you with several things about gun-safety," he warned her.

After he oriented the things she needed to know, he gave her the gun with the safety on. He stood behind her and made her do the weaver stance.

She was quite surprised by the weight of it, but she was also made aware of the weight of the responsibility of holding it by him. She was also flushed by him standing behind her as she felt his warmth on her back.

She couldn't turn to face him as she felt her cheeks blushing as she felt his pectoral muscles tensing and relaxing on her back. She smelled his minty breath instructing her what to do traveling to her left ear. She felt the hair on her nape stand, she was thankful that she did not styled it on a pony tail. She felt his biceps on her arms, guiding her gently. She tried her hardest to regain control of her own body and focus on the lesson.

"I am going to release the safety off now. Remember what I have told you earlier," he suddenly whispered between her left ear and the earmuff, sending chills to her abdomen, "Are you ready?"

"Yes, I am," she softly answered, trying so hard to ignore his closeness to hers and focusing on the can in front of her.

She felt his hand tensing on hers, giving her a signal to pull the trigger. BANG. She heard the loud noise even from the earmuffs she was wearing. Her body recoiled from the impact and she was grateful that he was behind her or else she could have been thrown off the ground she was standing on.

She saw the can flying off from the stone it was perched on. He gently stepped back away from her but not before switching the gun's safety on and putting it back on the holster.

He ran towards where the can fell and picked it up. He investigated where it was hit by the bullet and smiled towards her as she started to remove her earmuffs and eye protector.

"Wow, either that was beginner's luck or you have a good aim!" He shouted from where he was standing.

She relaxed her body as the cause of its trembling was now metres away from her and she was able to genuinely laugh at what he said from the distance, "of course, you were the one who was controlling the aim! Haha!"

"Haha! But you were the one holding it," he said as he ran towards her, "let's try it for a few more rounds, OK?"

He made her wear the earmuffs and eye protection again and allowed her to get a feel of the weapon on her hand more. He made sure she was aware of the responsibility of holding an object that could be either used for protection or for evil. She felt the gun's function depending on whoever wielded it. It made her realize that the gun was not supposed to control her but it was her that controlled it. She felt the revelation made her appreciate her life more. She was happy. He noticed her happiness.

The experience had brought them closer to each other that neither could deny.

Meanwhile in an undisclosed part of Australia, a well-dressed man in a black suit was sitting on his swivel chair. He was facing the clear huge glass window, deep in his own thoughts as a trail of smoke came out as he exhaled. His contemplation was disrupted when he heard a loud knock on the door.

"Come in," he said in his deep baritone voice, pivoting his chair to face the incoming visitor.

The door opened to reveal his right-hand man who rushed in with worry that made the man on the chair more curious. So, he motioned his minion to approach him which the other man obeyed submissively.

The man on the chair knew to trust his intuition was right and that something was off. His right-hand man whispered something in his left ear. He felt a burst of anger trying to erupt from his guts but he knew better and tried to control the raging monster from within him. He knew that someone, soon, would feel this monster's wrath as most people from his circle knew to avoid his anger and release the anger within him.

Once again, the wooden door opened and three new men barged in. The man on the chair glowered at the middle-aged man in the middle of the lot.

"The audacity..." he softly scowled at them.

Nineteen

His Affirmation

"Sir, please give me another chance! I have underestimated the situation and have not foreseen the consequences. Please allow me to prove my worth as one of your trusted men," the middle-aged man pleaded, tears forming in his eyes. He was on his knees in front of an emotionless man who was just staring at him blankly.

"Since you were foolish enough to act on your own, it means you are not afraid of death," the emotionless man spoke from the shadows as the room was dimly lit, only his silhouette was seen by the pleading minion. The man in the shadow's voice was enough to add more shivers down the spine of the man on his knees, as if the tiny sparks of hope were slowly waning from within him removing any sign of warmth.

The man in the shadows nodded to another minion in a black suit, who then proceeded to the cupboard in the corner of the room. The minion produced a small transparent jar. Inside the jar was black spider with a red-orange hourglass shape on it's abdomen.

The minion holding the jar with the black widow in the jar thought about the cruelty of their boss, but he knew better. It was a dog-eat-dog profession. He knew that sooner or later it was him or the man kneeling in front of the man in the shadows. He was apathetic of the man pleading for his life. Even between him and all the other followers of the man in the shadows, it was all about life and death, to kill or to be killed.

Meanwhile in Queensland, contrary to the dimly lit room where a silhouetted man hid and where a man's fate lies on a black widow, it was bright and sunny.

Alex felt the warmth of the sun on her skin and the droning of the busy bees and fluttering of colourful butterflies. The iridescent flowers which made her eyes glowed. She was picking a fresh batch to replace the wilting ones in the vase on the centre of the dining table while Celine was preparing breakfast.

"Oh, thanks dear! You really do have eyes for exquisite beauty," Celine exclaimed as Alex entered the dining area. Celine quickly glanced at the garland of flowers Alex was holding and gave her a quick hug. She was grateful when Alex offered to be the one to replace flowers this morning as she was preoccupied in preparing for a big breakfast, expecting some company.

"You're welcome, Celine! I just want to keep myself busy, plus, I enjoyed spending time in your garden," Alex replied as she immersed herself, once again, in the flowers in her hand. She admired how the sheaf produced such variegation, from pink to red, lavender to purple, blue to white. She also bathed her nostrils with the aroma that filled the room, closing her eyes in the moment and savouring the scent. She could also hear the dancing chirps of the birds from the trees outside.

Her enthralment was disrupted as she heard a vehicle turning in the driveway. She looked outside the window and saw a familiar red Honda Civic that entered. The backseat window rolled as the car finally halted and a familiar cute face came to her view, she saw Andrew.

"Aunt Alex! I'm back!" Andrew exclaimed loudly with a wide grin on his face, "I missed you!" He added. Alex was quite surprised as she didn't know that they would be visiting, nonetheless, a more than eager welcomed change to her routine for the day.

"Welcome back, little man!" Alex didn't hide the excitement in her voice, when she suddenly felt a presence behind her.

"Let me take care of those flowers, Miss Alex," Osmond politely spoke to let Alex know that he was behind her.

"Oh! Thanks, Osmond," she replied and quickly gave the garlands to him. She, then, hurriedly beelined towards the parked car and welcomed both father and son who had just arrived. As Andrei opened the child-locked backseat door, Andrew bolted towards Alex with arms wide open.

"Aunt Alex! I missed you!" said the little boy gleefully, bear-hugged the lady, while Andrei walked towards them after he brought out Andrew's backpack and stuff.

"Really? I missed you too, little man," Alex reciprocated, "hi, Andrei, thank you for visiting. Where's Cathy, by the way?"

"Actually, it was that little man there who demanded to visit you and his nana. Unfortunately, Cathy is busy with her duty at the hospital," Andrei answered while giving Osmond a wave of hello which the latter returned.

Osmond somewhat recalled how Alex and his nephew got so close and comfortable with each other even if the little kid was reluctant with their initial meeting.

"Uncle Alex, over here!" Shouted by Andrew when he noticed his uncle looking at them.

"I'm fine here," Osmond replied, planning activities that the two can enjoy, "come inside now you all, mom had already set breakfast. So, you can also both settle down, I know you had a long drive."

Later that evening, everybody was now settled and was enjoying the dinner prepared by Celine.

"I'm sorry if it took two weeks to visit and drop Andrew. We just arrived last night from Cairns," Andrei said in the middle of dinner speaking directly towards Alex and Osmond.

"I understand, but I surely missed this little man here," Alex replied while ruffling the boy's hair who was currently enjoying the one-pan chicken parmesan pasta that his nana prepared for him. There were also paella, sautéed asparagus and cherry tomatoes for everyone to enjoy and Celine made sure it was enough for them.

"Nana, I can't wait for our chocolate mousse dessert," Andrew said while playing with his spoon on an almost empty plate.

"Oh sure honey! Since you were well-behaved earlier and you ate all your food tonight, it will be your reward!" Celine exclaimed that ensued a boy jumping on his chair with joy.

"Yehey! Did you hear that dad? Nana will give me dessert! Thanks nana!"

"You're always welcome honey, as long as you promise to be a good boy," Celine answered with a smile while looking lovingly at her grandson.

Alex, who was now silent, was warmly observing the Gomezes around the table with her. She cannot help but feel nostalgic with the love and care that each member had shown not only to her but more so with each other.

"Who wants to visit the stream tomorrow morning?" Osmond blurted suddenly while exchanging his look at Alex and Andrew after wiping his mouth with the white table napkin.

"Me, uncle, me!" Andrew once again was jumping with glee on his chair.

"Not really surprised! Hahaha!" Osmond laughed heartily with everyone following suit. He returned his gaze to Alex who seemed deep in thought but was happy and was smiling. He felt happy for her to experience the love his family could share.

"Miss Alex, Celine mentioned that there was an unpleasant event that occurred last time in the farm when you were there and when Celine and I were at the market. I'm sorry about that," Martin's turn to speak apologetically before Alex cut him off.

"Oh no, no. Don't worry about it Martin. Osmond handled the situation very well and I will be more aware of my surroundings next time," Alex interjected.

"Yes, I am glad that he acted properly. Unlike when he was younger and acted impulsively," Martin laughed, which Celine tried to stop as he was trying to tease their son.

"Oh c'mon dad! Please stop! That was ages ago!" Osmond tried to hide his embarrassment but his flushed cheeks said otherwise.

"Uhm, why, what happened before? I mean Osmond being impulsive?" Andrei curiously asked while trying to stifle his laughter.

"Martin, cut it out!" Celine reprimanded her husband, although she was about to burst in laughter, too.

"OK, OK, I'm just trying to make them feel better," Martin defeatingly said as he raised both his hands as a sign of apology, "Anyway, don't worry Miss Alex, I have already planted marigolds, lemongrass, wormwoods, and pink agapanthus in the area. They are well known snake deterring plants! Not that I don't trust my own son to protect you, but it is also my responsibility to keep my farm safe."

And Osmond, know that your mother and I are proud of you for how you handled the situation. We always are," Martin sincerely said smiling and reached out to his better half's hand across the table who was also smiling.

"Thank you, dad! Twice. For the plants and for trusting me to do the right thing," Osmond gratefully said to his dad.

Alex felt at that moment that the remaining apprehensions and doubts she had with her bodyguard dissipated the longer she got the chance to know him and his family.

The next day, it was a most anticipated day for both Alex and Andrew. Together with Osmond who was behind the two, the three of them walked towards the stream. Alex was holding the little boy's hand who was pointing happily to everything he saw with the other. The different species of birds chirping in the area, the colourful butterflies playing on the field of flowers, the trees lush with leaves dancing whenever a gentle morning breeze swayed them.

As soon as they arrived, Andrew, with the permission of Osmond, rushed towards the stream to collect colourful stones. It was then Alex found her chance to ask Osmond regarding the update on the General's investigation as they were an earshot away from the child.

"Osmond, what's the latest update from the General and how are my parents?" she asked while still watching the boy by the stream playing.

"They still don't have a lead, as of the moment. They are extremely careful in investigating the threat to your safety," Osmond directly answered with gravity in his tone.

Alex could not help but sense the tense and alerted state that Osmond automatically put himself in after her question. She felt that it was not her intention to put him in that spot.

"I see, sometimes I can't help but wonder about the danger threatening me; but, also, it vanishes every time I see and feel the care and security you and your family gives me. Even if it's not their obligation," Alex quickly said to ease the sudden troubled man beside her, "I mean Martin didn't have to plant those snake-repelling plants and Celine didn't have to take care of me, but they did!" she added.

She even took the time to look at Osmond and made sure he looked back at her before giving him a cozy smile.

"Don't worry, because the time will come that you will surely be safe. But I'm happy and grateful with what you said," he meaningfully replied and beholden from what he heard. They were still gazing at each other when Andrew suddenly came running towards them and held Alex's right hand.

"I want to play hide and seek there!" Andrew said, pointing towards the bushes to their left where the stream turns. Alex was about to indulge the kid's request when Osmond interjected.

"I'm sorry little man, but you and your Aunt Alex can't play that game. Especially there."

The little kid frowned with a wrinkled forehead.

"But why, uncle?"

"Yes, why Osmond?" Alex asked instantaneously with Andrew.

Osmond approached and casually smiled to satiate the kid's curiosity. He knelt in front of him to meet the little kid eye to eye, then glanced towards Alex before returning to his nephew. He, then, put his hands to the kid's shoulders as a sign of the sincerity he was about to say to him.

"Listen, Andrew, there are some children's games that are not meant for adults because they are already grown up," Osmond prayed within himself that his nephew would leave it at that. Although he did not want to accept it, the reality of human threat on Alex's life and natural environmental dangers lurked in every corner.

Alex suddenly understood what Osmond meant. So to appease the curious child, she added, "don't worry little man, I will read a story for you at bedtime tonight! OK?"

She immediately held the boy's hand and led him back to the water to play and collect more colourful pebbles to avoid further scrutiny from his little innocent curious mind.

Though Osmond was smiling as he watched the two walk towards the stream, he couldn't help but feel a great amount of anxiety. Alex's question earlier had already created a gnawing feeling deep within him. Uncertainties that reminded him of his duties and responsibilities. He was still Alex's bodyguard. With a clenched fist, he vowed to never let his guard down. Whomever it was, whether a skilled mercenary or any threat or danger, he vowed to do everything in his skills and capabilities to protect the people he cared for, including Alex.

Twenty

Agent Cedrick McKain

"Let's get the ball rolling,"Agent Cedrick McKain said to himself as he checked his reflection on the rear view mirror of his dark blue Audi R8 which he parked on Pitt Street. He smoothed his fake thin mustache and checked the alignment of his brown colored contact lens, hiding his natural blue eyes. The stratus clouds, which were threatening earlier, were now producing soft drizzle on the pavement on this particular Tuesday afternoon of the second week of the month. It was an ordinary day for the rest of the people carrying assorted colored umbrellas; but it was an extraordinary day for Agent McKain as he alighted his vehicle.

As he entered the Le Petit Flot restaurant, his eyes spotted a lady in her early thirties talking on her phone wearing her black corporate ensemble. His target. He was led by the waiter to his reserved area. It was then that the lady stood up and gathered her clutch bag on her right arm with her phone on her right hand while her half-filled flute of white wine on her other hand. The lady in black was heading towards the powder room.

He saw his chance, standing up and heading towards the loo as well, carrying his highball glass of Tom Collins with him. He feigned an accidental collision with the lady in black.

"What the hell?" The lady exclaimed as her drink spilt on her blazer. She quickly put her clutch bag on the high-top table beside them to fix herself.

"My apologies, are you okay?" Cedrick asked the lady who was profusely wiping her blazer with her purple scarf. He quickly put his glass near the lady's clutch bag and gathered table napkins from the nearby dispenser.

"I am not okay, thanks but no thanks!" The woman annoyingly answered as she looked up the man she collided with. Her hostility suddenly faltered. She initially intended to give the bloke a mouthful, but her plan melted as she saw the face of the man. She found herself speechless as she examined the man in front of her, wearing a white polo shirt with his first two top buttons unclasped, khaki pants and a black top sider shoes. It was when she glanced at his face that she was in awe as he smiled at her. Gleaming white set of teeth and bed-impledd cheeks. His smile turned into a worry look as if asking if she was really alright.

"I am truly sorry I ruined your attire," Cedrick apologetically said. He caught the twinkle in her eyes and a small smile formed.

"Well, I guess it was an accident. I was also in a hurry and was on my phone. I think you understand, hectic and busy days," the lady sweetly answered as she finished wiping her blazer and was somewhat taken aback by the man's gentle demeanor.

"I definitely understand. But hey, I still owe you. May I treat you for a meal or a couple of drinks?" Cedrick casually offered. He saw the lady's smile turn into hesitance, "Please, don't fret. I am just trying to make it up for the accident," he quickly added and flashed his smile, displaying his deep set of dimples on both his cheeks again.

"How I wish I could say yes, but apparently, I have some colleagues who are on their way here for our lunch meeting," the woman seemed disappointed, "but I reckon, we should meet at a more suitable time?" She added as she fished out her calling card from her black Hermes Kelly bag.

Cedrick saw the name Nancy Fendley on the carnation pink, gold embroidered card. He knew that her acquaintances were coming, but it was all part of his plan. He also knew that she was associated with the controversial business mogul that would be soon tried guilty with the death of his assistant, but he casually feigned ignorance.

"Of course, Nancy" he answered as he put the card in his wallet, knowingly that the said date would not happen.

"Sorry, but I have to go now," Nancy said, fixing her hair sheepishly in front of a dashing man she'd ever met.

"Oh, sure, it was nice meeting you. Have a good one and take it easy on your lunch meeting. Anyways, I'm Gavin Celeste," Cedrick replied, intentionally disguising his identity.

"Thanks, Gavin. You too. I mean, enjoy your day too even if it's kinda gloomy outside," Nancy flustered.

He saw her walking towards the lady's room. He finished his drink from the table as he had finished his job before leaving the premises.

Meanwhile at an exclusive restaurant along Collins Street in Melbourne, Evangeline and Enrique de Ayala were about to finish their dinner as it was already half past eight in the evening. They had a dinner business meeting with some clients who immediately left after some business transactions. They were now the only patrons in the area as most had left early. A few staff were inconspicuously clearing the other tables. Soft jazz was being performed on the other side of the area, enough for the couple to talk.

"Enrique, we need to think of a better way to find the person behind the threat to our daughter," Evangeline said exasperatedly, "I miss our daughter and the longer she's not with us the more I am anxious about our situation. She has been away from us for too long. First, she had to go to college in Spain. Now that she has graduated, we have to be separated again because of that villainous person we still do not know!"

Enrique caringly looked at his wife. He gently placed his phone on the round table and took a sip of the red wine. The table was covered with white satin and on it were Angelique tulips as well as a golden candelabra with white candles softly burning. He cleared his throat and gently reached out to hold his wife's right hand with his left.

"Honey, you know we are doing this for her safety. Besides, I am always updating you with the reports from the agency and the agents we entrusted with our daughter's life," Enrique replied assuringly at Evangeline, "And all of us believe that the person behind this is powerful enough to keep his identity and location shrouded from our intels."

"I know, but I cannot help it. I'm worried about our daughter," Evangeline said, trying to hold back her tears, "I'm sorry to have brought this up, but I cannot even focus on our meeting earlier. I'm sorry honey."

"Hush there, love. I know and I understand. You are her mother, after all," he said, comforting his upset wife by squeezing her hand in his, "plus, I am confident about our daughter's safety under Agent Gomez's protection. I've known his capability and skills; besides, he was highly recommended by The General himself."

"Yes, I know that. But..." Evangeline caught herself before she continued, but she recalled their oath to each other not to keep any secrets between them. She took a deep breath and held her husband tightly before continuing, "but, I really wanted to contact Agent Gomez just to hear her voice."

She saw a mixture of disappointment, worry, and care in his eyes as he slowly let go of her hand. After twenty-four years of marriage, it was as if she could already read what he was thinking. Disappointment for her lack of control, worry for both her and their daughter, and care for he knew what she was going through. But she needed a semblance of assurance to at least alleviate the anxiety in her heart for their daughter.

He took a deep breath and averted his gaze towards the bussers, "excuse me, could you give us a moment please. Alone," he commanded with a tone that they can never say no to.

The bussers gave him a small nod of understanding before completely halting their clearing and leaving the premise. The last busgirl with a short blonde bob even closed the door to the area to give them privacy.

"My goodness, Evangeline! Please control yourself. You are aware how dangerous the situation is and one small mistake can lead to the demise of our daughter," he was flustered by his wife's revelation.

"I know and I am sorry. I am too anxious to think straight," she wiped a small tear that escaped her eyes. That was enough for her to hear a small sigh coming from the man she loves. She looked at him and he gave her a small nod of understanding. She felt his comforting warmth as he held her hand again.

"I am somewhat glad that you are still the Evangeline that I love after all these years. The caring and loving woman that I know," he said while directly looking at her eyes. He then shifted his posture to let his wife listen carefully, "but you know Agent Gomez's stern warning after our last two calls with her, right? He warned us that the enemy, as powerful as that person is, might have the capability to trace our calls."

"I understand," Evangeline answered defeatingly. She had to surrender for the meantime for the safety of their daughter. She realized that her husband, the father of their daughter, was also worried but had to endure not seeing and talking to their daughter as well. She also realized how selfish she had been not thinking of what Enrique has been feeling as well.

She moved closer to him and laid her head on his shoulder. She wrapped her arms around his left arm as if telling him how sorry she was and she understood his point. She felt relief when Enrique kissed her head and took a sip of his wine.

It was then she thought of her daughter's temperament, one of the things she got from her. She raised her head and looked at her husband.

"I wonder how Agent Gomez is holding up against our daughter's tantrums," she innocently asked, "I mean, you know how hard-headed

Alex can be. I suddenly sympathise with Agent Gomez dealing with her."

With that, Enrique let out a small laugh, "and from whom do you think she got that temperament of hers?"

Evangeline blushed knowing the answer and smacked her husband's arm.

"Oh don't worry about Agent Gomez," he said as the atmosphere between them lightened up, "he doesn't give up, come what may. He always does his job until the very last end," he added with a wink to reassure his wife.

"Fair enough. Perhaps, he really is our daughter's match when it comes to her temperament. It would be so nice if he can mellow down her tantrums when they return. That's something I will look up to after all this tribulation," she was grateful to her husband for consoling her worried heart.

It was then that Enrique kissed her and nodded to his classic black leather wristwatch, signaling her it was time for them to go home. She smiled and collected her black purse from the table before leaving the room.

Back in Sydney, Agent McKain was preparing for his latest mission after acquiring the access card from Nancy, the lady in black at the restaurant. As the darkness started to envelope the area, he made sure that his ensemble would perfectly camouflage his presence, from his black hoodie to his dark track pants, gloves, and ski-mask. He also made sure all his paraphernalias were complete. The last moment he checked the area was when the sun was setting as it was daylight saving time and it had been two hours ago when he had his reconnaissance of the area and disguised himself as a jogger. He just got back from his initial position and cars rarely passed by on the main road. The light coming from several lamp posts helped him to see better from where he was standing but enough to keep him hidden along with several tall gum trees, thick several wild pants, and wallaby grass swaying from the windy evening. As he waited for the perfect time to infiltrate the targeted mansion, he recalled his encounter with his colleague and friend, Agent Gomez, at Gomez's residence. He was confident with his skills and capability, as he was successful at most of his missions, but he also knew if there was an agent who could get the better of him, it was Agent Osmond Gomez. He had several chances to work with him in some of his missions and knew Agent Gomez's extra sensitive senses and intuition.

His senses went up as he got ready to walk towards the mansion, his ears heard the crickets and the rustling of the leaves, his eyes adjusted as thick clouds, his skin felt even the slightest breeze of the evening wind, and his intuition heightened. It was easier for him to blend in the dark. He walked casually along the main road, looking to his left and right, to avoid unnecessary suspicion. He even placed both his hands inside the pockets of his tack pants.

"This would be boring," Cedrick thought to himself as he missed all those actions but he recalled what his superior commanded him to do:

"This is a recovery mission. Your only task is to acquire the essential files and gun. Avoid unnecessary gun fights. Remember, in and out."

He just hoped he could get some action out of this mission, unknowingly that it would be one of these days. He was not a cold-blooded murderer, but he enjoys the thrill of adrenaline rush. He was almost fifty metres way from the whole facade of the mansion lined with several tall cypress trees next to the concrete fence accented by multiple round black steel in vertical position. It was all clear and quiet. The nearest residential house was about a hundred and fifty meters away. It was better for him since no innocent bystander could be involved if something awry happens.

He felt the wind picking up. He smiled as the sudden change of the weather was working towards his advantage. The job would be easier as the stronger wind could conceal any of his presence in and outside of the house.

Thus, he hurriedly continued his pace towards the success of his mission.

Twenty One

Assassins are like Shadows in the Dark

He was fortunate enough to manage to get in as soon as he could when no one was outside the mansion. After reaching the backdoor, it was clear, as was the auxiliary kitchen when he checked it. Then he slowly walked towards the lounge area, where he saw a shadow while the recessed dim lights were on. Cedrick was now thinking about how to finish his task as soon as possible. He quickly positioned himself in the dimly lit area of the lounge entrance, where a large black vase rested on a high console table, until he finally heard the conversation between the two men. He carefully glanced at them, noting they were both armed but it was not his concern but the advantage for him to finish the job effortlessly once he got the opportunity to incapacitate them, until the bigger lad started to speak.

"I was supposed to be catching up with my hookup tonight but it's not gonna happening and worst is, she even changed her mind to catch up next time for fun," the bulky man said frustratingly to his busy colleague on the phone, then he looked at him.

"C'mon man, stop that crap. We're supposed to be tightening our work until our boss finally comes back tomorrow," he said, after noticing the frustration on his colleague's face.

"Hey, remember, I shouldn't be on duty tonight, mate. I have my substitute, but he didn't make it," the first man replied.

"It's not a coincidence at all, man. Since you are here now, that means extra cash for you, as our boss mentioned that he would double the fee for our special duty now," the second man expressed his thoughts, then he put the mobile device in his pocket and shook his head.

"Well, fair enough. Anyway, I will make a long black coffee now. You want as well?" He asked.

"Yeah, since we need it, and no alcoholic drinks. As our boss clearly instructed before he left this afternoon."

"Exactly!" He exclaimed, then proceeded to the kitchen area without noticing the presence of someone wearing all-black attire as the man moved to the dark end of the dining hall close to the kitchen and started to collect things for making a hot drink before operating the coffee machine on the bench.

Cedrick smiled as he recalled the strongest sleeping pill he had in his pocket, which could make them fall asleep within half an hour. He just needed the right moment to spike their coffee. After waiting a few seconds, he saw the man heading to the nearby toilet after stirring the drink. Cedrick seized the opportunity to slip the pill into both cups after he heard the sound of the door as the man shut it. After a few moments of waiting, the man returned from the toilet, took the cups of coffee, and finally headed back to the lounge room. It was now time for Cedrick to do the task, and he set the timer on his digital wristwatch for thirty minutes. He was also hoping that the pills would take effect in less than half an hour. Within that time frame given by his superior, he had to successfully get the gun and files in five minutes once they finally become unconscious. This was his first solo mission, and for him, it was not challenging at all, but he was the one assigned to this task. He closed his eyes and took a deep breath after he looked at his digital wristwatch, and twenty five minutes to go but he was not really bothered by any incoming threat, since there were only two men guarding the two things he needed to retrieve, he was able to entertain himself by listening to the noise of the howling wind from outside. He was about to check the timer when the noise of voice from the lounge area caught his attention. He started to walk back to the spot where the large vase was to check them out until he saw one of them was already unconscious on the couch, while the other was starting to feel the effects and fell on the carpet.

"The wait is finally over," he said to himself while glancing at them. He quickly set the timer for five minutes then rushed upstairs, and when he reached the second floor, he looked for the server room to take control of the security system of the entire premises by shutting it down. He proceeded to the main target room, and got in by using the access card that he took from Nancy Fendley and went straight to the huge cabinet of walk-in closet. Opening it, he saw the black safety box at the bottom. He used the electronic device, and in less than a minute, Cedrick managed to take the gun and files he then quickly closed the box and the cabinet, carefully put the gun inside a zip-lock bag, opened his hoodie jacket to pin the folder to his waist, covered it with his jumper, and casually left the premises without leaving any traces.

As he walked, Cedrick noticed that the night breeze was settling down following his successful mission. However, he dismissed the thought when he arrived at the thick shrubs surrounded by several gum trees after crossing the main road. Throughout, he sensed something approaching him from ahead, and without hesitation or losing focus, he wasn't inclined to dodge. Instead, with a swift motion, his right hand seized the object—a short iron rod. Upon closer inspection, he saw a piece of paper held with a black rubber band attached to it, prompting him to remain vigilant and decide to speak.

"Who's there? And what do you intend by acting in such a way?" Cedrick casually asked while holding the iron stick. From that moment, he already knew that whoever was hiding somewhere in the dark was not an ordinary person. But rather someone with intentions far more sinister than he could have imagined. He never heard any kind of body movements to the surrounding. The plan was calculated precisely, which led Cedrick to anticipate an impending duel. If the purpose was the files and gun, then it would be a different matter. But silence remained, and when he was about to take his first step to search whoever it was, a sudden spinning back kick emerged from the left. He was almost struck by the attack, which led him to dropped the iron stick he held, but his reflexes were still on guard, and took the opportunity to reciprocate with a bodyguard combo followed by a couple of punches but failed to hit his target due to swift movements, and he couldn't determine if it was a male or female since the anonymous attacker was wearing an all black attire with a mask, but the good thing was, the hood of his jacket and ski-mask was an advantage for him to conceal his identity too while the gap between them was about less than ten metres.

Until he saw the hands of unknown attacker began to execute of rapid combo punch but he was already prepared and planned a certain thing while avoiding himself being punched, then all along the attacker stopped and to his surprised, a thick of white powder had thrown onto his face which caused irritation to his eyes and he started to rub them both. And felt relief that it was not lethal, but only a pure white powder. *"A distraction,"* he thought to himself, followed by curiosity about the identity of the unknown assailant. Then he felt it was starting to leave the place and never bothered himself to chase the unknown aggressor. But why? And what was the sole purpose of the attack without showing any interest for the things in his possession? Then he recalled the iron stick and was able to find what he was looking for after a few seconds by using the small flashlight from his pocket. Once he removed the rubber band, he quickly examined the paper, and Cedrick's curiosity deepened as he read the content.

"Assassins Are Like Shadows in the Dark."

It was written by hand and had a thought of urged to heighten his vigilance from now on after a recent life-threatening duel with a formidable adversary who adeptly countered his every move. He thoroughly scanned the surroundings for any signs of the attacker, but found nothing.

He was certain of two things: he had no enemies, and his mission that night was to retrieve essential items to use as evidence. He shook his head and folded the paper, knowing it would be useful when the time came to gather information. For now, he would keep this strange encounter to himself, but he would disclose this unusual event to his superior and to his most trusted companion Agent Gomez, when the moment was right. Then he casually walked towards where he parked his motorcycle and meticulously examined his bike if it was compromised or not, once satisfied, he started to left the area.

The next morning in Queensland, Alex woke up smiling as the early rays of the sun pierced through the windows. She stretched her arms and thought of her best friend, Elissandra, hoping she was doing well after their last encounter at the café. Alex was confident they would meet again soon, once the mysterious case was resolved. Glancing at the analog clock on the wall, she noted it was exactly seven o'clock. She remained in bed, listening to the chirping birds. There was another reason for her to smile that day: Osmond had mentioned after lunch at the farm yesterday that her dad would call tomorrow at one o'clock in the afternoon. She was looking forward to speaking with her parents, as it had been a while since their last conversation then she got up from bed then went to the bathroom.

Meanwhile, Osmond was in the kitchen, contemplating the latest news he had seen on TV with his parents, a business mogul and Nancy Fendley his business associate had been arrested at his residence. There was solid evidence implicating them as the prime suspects in the murder of well-known businessman's assistant. Then he was now thinking about someone who gathered the evidence against the two suspects, was it one of his colleagues? But he quickly disregarded the thought once he saw the breakfast that he was preparing were finally done, he smiled, and for sure Ms. Alex would definitely love them and he felt someone was approaching, it was his mother when he glanced at it.

"Oh, you're finally done," Celine said to her son.

"What time will you follow dad to the farm?" He casually asked while starting to wash some used kitchenware in the sink.

"Maybe in a while, since I've already finished my usual routine in the garden," his mother replied, looking at him. "But I'm worried about the news this morning. Even though it wasn't directly related to your client, I can't help but feel concerned," Celine finally expressed her thoughts about the headline news.

"Don't worry about that news, mom. I'm sure it has nothing to do with my client or her family," Osmond said calmly as he washed the last piece of kitchenware.

"Perhaps you're right. But I can't understand why those wealthy individuals or public figures are often involved in controversies. And I apologise for bringing this up since we all know what happened with Ms. Alex in Madrid. Still, I'm grateful we're not part of that world," Celine concluded her thoughts and began gathering the things she needed to take to the farm.

Osmond was caught off guard by the final thought of his mother. But he opted to express his honest opinion.

"You're right mom, but I think it only becomes controversial when people act in ways just to make a scene, and Ms. Alex was just a victim," he calmly replied then saw his mother nodded, then she spoke right after.

"I couldn't agree more, and we can't easily judge people," Celine answered with a smile while looking at her son. "Well, I love those choices of food that you prepared and surely, she would eat well," Celine said.

Osmond was about to say something to his mom when he saw Ms. Alex coming into the kitchen, thankful that she hadn't heard the conversation between him and his mother. As usual, he was mesmerised by what he saw: she was wearing a plain white shirt and black cotton shorts above her knees.

"Good morning!" Alex greeted the mother and son with a dazzling smile.

"Hey there! Such a lovely morning," Celine responded to Alex.

"Morning!"Osmond replied as he began making two cups of coffee.

"Anyway, I have to leave you two for now. And don't bother going to the farm just in case, since we will be having lunch here today. Enjoy your breakfast, Alex!" Celine exclaimed.

"Bye, Mom! And I'll prepare our lunch today and don't overwork yourself and say the same to dad," Osmond said, hugging his mother.

"I will for sure. Thanks son!"

"Thank you, Celine! Take care!"Alex smiled, before she pulled out a chair, sat down, and glanced at the array of food on the table, which brought a smile to her lips. From banana toasties, berry bircher muesli, pear pancakes to zucchini and corn fritters.

"Osmond," she said softly.

"Yes, Ms. Alex?"

"Thank you," she replied, smiling at her bodyguard as she picked up a plate to gather breakfast.

As he began to respond, Osmond felt an enormous joy at seeing her smile.

"You're always welcome, Ms. Alex," he said, approaching the table with two cups of coffee. "Would you like an orange juice or any fresh drink?" He asked after he carefully placed the cup of coffee in front of his client.

"Oh, I'm good, thank you," Alex softly answered after she took a bite of banana toasties.

"Alright, anyway, I have something to say, my sister and her husband will be here next week, also we don't need to go to farm after breakfast since my parents will be having lunch here,"

"That's great to hear! And also it's has been a while since the last time they visited us," she said, taking a sip of coffee. Then, after Alex grabbed a plate for Osmond.

"What do you want to eat?" She asked.

"Let me take care of that," Osmond said as he reached for the plate. Alex held onto it, refusing to let go while her left hand clasped his wrist.

"I said, what do you want to eat?" She asked again and getting a fork and entrée knife.

Osmond was reluctant to answer until he finally decided not to refuse Alex's offer, since he had only a couple of eggs benedict with coffee.

"Well, any of them. Thanks," he answered and smiled at her.

"No worries and enjoy, " Alex said while starting to select food for Osmond and once satisfied, she put the plate in front of him.

Osmond smiled at her after she put down the plate, and she smiled back at him. Then they ate together in silence but Osmond felt something that morning and maintained himself professionally, until Alex finally spoke.

"I think I should help you prepare lunch for today," Alex suggested.

"Are you sure with that?" Osmond asked her.

"Yeah, why not? Since I am done with the book I am currently reading,"

"Alright, so let me take care of these dishes for now and I would let you know once I sort everything out that we need to cook for lunch," Osmond said as he stood up from the chair.

"Of course, take all the time you need. I'll head back to my room for now. By the way, I really enjoyed having breakfast with you. Thanks again Osmond," Alex said with a warm smile as she rose from her seat.

"The pleasure was mine, Ms. Alex." Osmond replied, once again feeling a familiar warmth from her radiant smile.

Osmond opted to leave the dishes out of the dishwasher in order to prioritise securing the main door, the veranda, and finally, the lounge room windows, ensuring that the only access point would be the kitchen door for his parents just in case before he resumed from operating the dishwashing machine with a genuine smile playing on his lips.

Twenty Two

The First Kiss

It was nearly twelve in the afternoon when Osmond and Alex were both intently looking to the food on the table they prepared, from gut-healing salmon and cauliflower rice bowl, then muffin pan tomato tarts, to slices of fruit as their dessert while the centre table has a vase that filled with variety of flowers and their enchanting fragrance filling the kitchen.

"Thanks for helping me out even though you don't have to," Osmond responded to Alex while taking off his apron.

"Don't mention it, as I enjoyed what I did even it was only the basic ones. Oh, thank you as well for helping me picking those fresh flowers from the garden," Alex answered while she could not imagine how the man never allowed her to get near to him while he was cooking and saw how Osmond smiling at her.

"Well, there are two main reasons: you're my client and our guest," Osmond said as he began tidying the kitchen, glancing over to see Alex watching him.

"Okay, fair enough, and also I am running low of personal care. So, we need to go to supermarket later," she added, while her gaze following Osmond's movement.

"Sure, what time?" Osmond asked her Alex.

"When you're ready." Alex replied.

"Okay, so how about around four in the afternoon?"

"Yes sure." Alex answered Osmond.

"And I remember, I need to get mine as well," Osmond added while sorting out the rest of utensils from the drawer that they need for lunch just then he heard the door open and his dad walked in.

"Very timely dad! Lunch is ready," he mentioned as he started to prepare the table while seeing Alex getting glasses from the cabinet allowing her to continue helping.

"Oh thanks! And it seemed like Alex had helping you out to prepare," reply by his dad while looking at Alex.

"Yes Martin, and actually he just assigned me sorting out the veggies which I can't complain about it," Alex answered after she organised the glasses on the table.

"Glad to hear, and thanks for helping him."

"I was grateful for the opportunity to help him, as it saved me from having to find something to keep me occupied after finishing my latest book," she replied and turned her gaze to Osmond getting drinks from the fridge.

"Alright, I will leave you guys for now. I just need to change clothes."

When Martin left the kitchen, Celine entered, carrying a freshly picked selection of vegetables in a basket. She glanced at the dining table, and greeted Alex while sitting.

"Great harvest for today Celine and also our lunch is ready!" Alex exclaimed as she looking intently to the basket.

"Thanks Alex! And it seems like a well-prepared lunch," Celine replied to Alex as she noticed her son carrying the stack of four plates from the countertop.

"Yeah, mom, since you and dad were busy these fast days," Osmond explained to his mother, until he saw Alex was trying to get his attention.

"Yes Ms. Alex?" He swiftly asked.

"Can I suggest something?" Alex replied shortly to Osmond.

"Yes, sure, go ahead," he answered while walking towards the table with plates in his hand.

"Since that you mentioned that they need to rest for today, why don't we also buy the food the we need for next week when we go out to get the personal items we need?" Alex suggested politely, smiling at Osmond who was now setting up the plates on the table.

Osmond was about to express his approval of Alex's suggestion but was prevented when his mother started to speak and he looked at her.

"Thanks, Alex, I really appreciate your idea but actually his dad and I are about to get the essential things for the farm after lunch, so I should say we can get the things we need," Celine stated, refusing the offer as hoping that Alex would allow them.

"Celine don't worry about getting my personal need, as you and Martin might better to rest after lunch," Alex replied while maintaining the tone of her voice from Osmond's mother.

"She's right mom, and regarding the things that needed to the farm, we can manage to get those while you and dad taking a rest," Osmond added, becoming aware of how his mother had responded with refusal to Alex's suggestion but he quickly disregarded the sudden thought in his mind.

"Alright, thank you Alex," Celine said with a smile.

"You're welcome Celine," Alex said while smiling back at Osmond's mother. "Anyway, I have to go to the room, excuse me for a while."

Once Alex entered the room, she decided to leave the mother and son alone to avoid an awkward situation. She needed a moment to collect her thoughts. Taking a deep breath, she realised that Celine was genuinely trying to help her. Alex shook her head, composed herself, and moved on.

After witnessing the interaction between his mother and Ms. Alex, Osmond began to sense something unfamiliar. The presence of the sensation was unavoidable and left him puzzled. He then recalled the news from this morning, which his mother mentioned: "Even though it wasn't directly related to your client, I can't help but feel concerned," his thoughts were interrupted when he saw his father approaching them from the main bedroom.

"Hey son, remember this shirt?" Martin asked Osmond.

"Yes, of course, Dad! I chose that shirt when mom couldn't decide on a present for your birthday two years ago," he replied, gazing at his dad, who was wearing the plain royal blue Tommy Hilfiger shirt.

"Oh, I thought it was missing?" Celine asked to Martin as she placed the vegetables in a colander to dry.

"I just found it on top of the cabinet while I was taking something from there. I think I have an idea of how this shirt ended up there. I'll ask that little boy when he arrives," Martin said cheerfully. "Where's Alex?" He asked.

"She's in the room," replied by Osmond to his dad until he saw Alex was now heading back to the kitchen.

"Oh, there she is," Celine said. "My husband was looking for you and seemed like he can't start eating lunch without you," Celine answered who was now looking at Alex.

"Such a pleasant to hear Martin, and my apology if I am late for a bit," Alex said apologetically to Osmond's father.

"It's alright Ms. Alex, but it's true that the three of us here shouldn't start to eat without you," Martin replied to Alex and glanced at his wife and guess what, honey? Our son got some help while preparing our lunch earlier," Martin confessed while trying to suppress his laughter as he looked at his son.

"Oh really?" Celine's responded to her husband, then furrowed her eyebrows and turned her gaze to Osmond.

"Mom, don't worry, she volunteered to help me," Osmond assured his mother, trying to stifle his amusement at her reaction upon hearing about Alex's assistance.

"Don't worry, Celine. Your son didn't let me do much—just helped with the veggie prep," Alex reassured her with a smile, shifting her focus to Osmond, the man she initially disliked when she first encountered him in the cafeteria parking lot, but that was before.

"Glad to hear that, Alex! Otherwise, I would have had to reprimand my son for letting you do too much work," Celine replied to Alex as her attention shifted back to her husband.

"Alright, we shall eat now as this old lad really starving. But actually, I feel the same way when I arrived. Haha!" Celine exclaimed as they now walking towards the table for lunch.

As they began to eat, the smiles on their faces were overwhelming, while Osmond felt and saw how his mother tended to Alex's plate. From that gesture of his mother, the vague thought he had in his mind was completely dissipated. Alex couldn't have asked for more from that moment of experience, until finally, they heard Martin, who started to share funny old stories from the early days of his marriage to Celine, bringing more laughter to the kitchen of the Gomez residence.

After having lunch at the Chinese restaurant, Cedrick headed straight to his apartment to execute the plan for that day: to uncover information about his attacker from the previous night by scrutinising the piece of paper. Upon arriving, he gathered the necessary items, since he had already thought through the process: he mixed ninhydrin powder with acetone to create a ninhydrin solution, then dipped the paper into it, ensuring the surface where prints needed to be developed was thoroughly covered. He air-dried the surface completely to help the ninhydrin absorb onto the substrate. Afterward, he used a steam iron on low temperature to gently heat the treated paper to accelerate the development of fingerprints. As the paper heated, latent fingerprints would ideally appear in a purple colour. However, it was unsuccessful. Cedrick sighed, disappointed by the result which he had hoped for a positive outcome. Who was the assailant behind the mystery attack? Once he had the chance to encounter the shadowy figure again, having memorised the unknown attacker's tactics, Cedrick vowed to himself that he would use all his capabilities to capture the potential threat to his organisation, as he was certain that this enigmatic aggressor knew his real identity, and where he lived.

He concluded in his mind to look for another place, as he was living to this apartment for a few years. Without a second thought, he took his phone out from his pocket and dialled a particular number.

Back in Queensland, Alex was wearing a white shirt paired with black fitted jeans and a golden turban with sunglasses while walking through the aisle of the supermarket with Osmond beside her, pushing a cart with her personal needs that they had already gathered fifteen minutes ago. They first went to the store where they could buy farm products for Osmond's parents, and then they headed to the particular deli shop where they can purchased quality deli products.

Osmond stayed vigilant while he was pushing the cart, until he saw Alex refrained from her next step as she grabbed some items, which made him discombobulated, by seeing her to get those confectioneries, then he opted to ask her.

"Ms. Alex are those for Andrew?" He asked, as he looked at her.

"Yes, and why?" Alex replied, now having an idea of the man's question as they glanced at each other.

"Osmond, if you are trying to tell me that I should put them back, please don't," she warned Osmond in a playful tone, waving with packs of chocolates in her right hand and teasing him by grabbing lollies with her left hand, followed by a giggle.

Osmond shook his head while smiling then he carried out his plan and saw how Alex failed to swerve her hand away from him when he held her wrist to prevent Alex from putting the packs of sweets into the trolley, and it was too late for Osmond to process how the event turned out. He saw her smile was waning then gazed at his hand while still holding on it, then Osmond quickly thought of his duty as a bodyguard.

"My apologies, Ms. Alex. I never meant to do such a thing," he said, averting his gaze in a different direction. He took a deep breath, a sudden feeling of embarrassment about what he had done, and tried to compose himself, as his responsibilities should have been his top priority at all times, to keep her safe.

Osmond was not fortunate enough to see how Alex reacted to his actions. He let her unleash something unique at that time between them—a kind of smile that he had never seen since the first time they met.

"Alright Osmond, that was okay and I know what kind of man you are, and I believe that it was never your intention. Here is the deal, we would keep the rest away from him, or shall I say we will eat some of them?" Alex suggested to Osmond.

Osmond was confused if she was joking or not.

"Okay, I get what you're trying to imply. I like chocolates, but not all the time since I'm more into dark chocolates," she said, placing the variety of sweets into the trolley as she saw Osmond nod in approval.

"Let's take get your personal care now," Alex suggested to Osmond, who remained silent, still staring at her until she gently shook his shoulder.

"Mr. Gomez, are you alright?"

Alex reached; Osmond felt sensation that it was snapping him back to the conversation.

"I'm sorry, Ms. Alex, what did you say?" He asked earnestly.

"I was asking if we're ready to head over to the men's care section."

"Sure," he agreed, and they both began making their way to the area they wanted to visit.

"How are you feeling?" Alex inquired, showing her concern for him.

"Oh, I just got lost in thought. Thanks for asking," he replied, glancing at her before his attention returned to the cart he was pushing. With no further words from Alex, they continued their walk in silence.

Meanwhile, Alex smiled to herself, recalling certain events from the first day they arrived in the state of Queensland that brought a smile to her face. She shook her head; only someone brave and with genuine intentions would ever get her attention. Like this man, walking beside her while pushing the trolley. Agent Osmond Gomez, who really got her, to admire him after she finally discovered his true nature, and it stood the test of time. And remembered when there was an eastern brown snake near her and saw how calm the man was, just to ensure she would never be harmed.

Osmond was now attending to his personal needs while trying to remember what had happened a few moments ago. How had he never realised this particular thing? He had let himself be jailed by the dark memories from fourteen years ago. It was about time to let go of Isabelle and focus on what matters now: the present.

Meanwhile, Alex surprised when she saw how Osmond quickly gathered his things, which made her smile, knowing that he was finally alright.

She thought to herself, *"that's why I am falling for you."*

"I already got things for me" Osmond said to Alex and nodded at him while smiling and they were now walking to the cashier area and she noticed how the man became extra vigilant till they finally reached the counter and Osmond took his wallet out from his pocket while waiting for their turn, then something reminded him, then he smiled. He must surprise the very special to him, Margarette Alexandria.

While they were on their way home, Alex noticed when Osmond diverted into different direction and she asked him.

"Hey Osmond, where are we going?" But Alex never heard any from him.

Osmond looked at her, curiosity evident in her eyes. And he smiled, then Alex smiled back to him.

"It is a surprise, you must see this place after I brought you last time to the beach, this time it is a different one. But don't worry, it is closer to our home but we are taking the fastest route to get there."

"Alright, as you said, I can't wait to see that place," she replied after less than ten minutes, Alex saw a few hills in the distance. One hill, in particular, caught her attention rather, it was unlike any she had seen before. She couldn't determine its size in terms of width or height, but it was undeniably more beautiful than the rest and a smile escaped from her lips.

"Do you like it?" Osmond asked.

"God knows, how much I really appreciate the scenery," then she hugged Osmond, the man hugged her back, "thanks a lot Osmond!" She finally added.

"Your'e welcome. So, shall we?" Osmond asked her.

"Yes, let's go!" Alex replied joyfully then saw how Osmond quickly opened the driver's door and walked towards the passenger side to open the door for her.

"Thanks! So, are you willing to run to get to the top?" Alex asked Osmond when she got off from the Jeep and smiled at him while she knows that she can manage to run wearing sneakers.

Meanwhile, Osmond crumpled his eyebrows and he laughed instead of saying anything towards Alex, then he yelled afterwards.

"Alright! One, two, three, let's go!" Alex darted ahead, and he simply smiled and shook his head, letting her relish the moment. He chased after her, watching as the heiress ran freely, a rare glimpse of her carefree spirit. It was their first shared moment like this.

"Hey Osmond! Why are you still there?" She teased him and continued running.

Osmond's eyes were on Alex while still smiling. He wanted her to see seizing the moment.

Meanwhile, she refrained herself from running and glanced at him who was now getting closer to her. And she laughed by seeing Osmond that he was eager to get near her. And she took off her shoes to ensure she will be the first to reach the top. As she was getting closer to it, Alex felt Osmond was getting near to her as she were getting closer to their desired spot, a sudden urge for her to win just to tease Osmond.

"Alex!" Shouted by Osmond.

"Alex." The way he addressed her name was strange to her. First time she ever heard uttering from him. She felt something struck her senses, which made her a sudden stop from running. And when she turned her sight from her back, she saw Osmond was now almost a few inches away from her and holding a golden everlasting flower, while approaching to her, this time Osmond was not smiling while his eyes were on her, and her eyes were also on him.

The unexplainable silence replaced their laughters, while the gentle breeze of spring enveloped their senses, but it has changed when Osmond were finally in front of her and offered the flower that he was holding.

"For you," Osmond said in almost whisper way, still looking at her.

For a brief moment, Alex pondered the surprising change in events before accepting his offer.

"Thanks!" And an idea struck her mind, she ran quickly and shouted.

"We are not done yet! Haha!"

"That's not a problem!" Osmond responded, then he began to chase her. Deep down, he was certain that he and Alex would reach the top together, ensuring no one was left behind.

Eventually, they both succeeded.

Again, Alex was amazed how Osmond managed to made it, with her on top. And she recalled a particular event while she was holding the flower that Osmond gave her.

"You cheated!" She exclaimed, as laughter once more spilled from her lips. Then, she dashed away from Osmond.

Osmond didn't respond; instead, he joined in the laughter, embracing the joy of the moment.

As they sat entwined on the lush green grass still both laughing until Osmond restrained himself, wanting to savour the sound of her laughter. His heart soared with contentment, for he needed nothing more than the melody of her laughter ringing in his ears, as she holds the golden everlasting flower, its glow echoing the warmth of her smile, until the sun's aurulent rays softened into a symphony of orange and wistful hues. Until Osmond remembered a particular thing while he held her hand then their gaze met then turned his glance at the sky.

"Carbon element is such an interesting thing and it is better to forming a very complex and stable molecules than any other element. So, I concluded that love is vital to experience different feelings from sadness, pain and then happiness, as long as we always apply with love and passion to them so therefore; at the end of any situation or difficulties, we could finally see and feel the depth of life about great and beautiful things from tangible to intangible and that's how it works," then he looked quickly to the lady right next to him and their gaze met and saw her reaction. It was pure and genuine; the pair of her eyes were sparkling at that moment with exquisite smile and subsequently, for sure he left her in awe. He smiled at her then glanced to the early night sky. He was quite happy of how things going on now, unlike before everything was so unclear.

Alex giggled, followed by covering her mouth by right hand, she gave him a quick glanced then returned her attention to the beautiful sceneries in front of them and she slowly looked up at the sky then subsequently she realised the man was caring and sincere when it is necessary then now she is more getting fond of Osmond's humour and out of the blue, she realised that her personal bodyguard has this some sort of cheesy personality and she find it amusing and concluded to herself that Osmond was intelligent and has a wide and deep view of perspective in life then she remembered about heat and comet.

"Okay, I have these two thoughts about love. Osmond when it comes to heat, it is like love too and all of us usually rely on it for warmth to keep the relationship and the another thing, same as comets for me it is very rare and genuine like one of a kind love that we don't normally experience although it is imperfectly round when you look closely to it and it is dirty too, but that's part of it. So basically, it is extremely like once in a blue moon of our lifetime," she ended her statement while looking at the horizon with sparkling stars then she averts her gaze to her protector and he too was looking at the sky, the moment of silence was deafening between the two of them, until their gaze met again and instantaneously, they kissed passionately while their eyes were both closed.

Twenty Three

Their Emotions

In undisclosed exclusive suburb in the country of Australia, the man was smiling after his conclusion of his minor plans before the main event, it was satisfying and enjoying how things turned out and for sure the finale will be surprising for the person that he really hate for more than two decades, then he recalled the previous headline from the news when the business mogul and his associate were arrested. He shook his head while remembering how the business mogul set an appointment with him which he had accepted. But the event turned out well after declining the offer to have a partnership with him. He knew what kind of person he was, too impulsive to act such things, and brought him and his partner in jail.

"I was right, he's not worthy to be part of my world," he said to himself without gazing to his trusted man and raised his right hand to drink his favourite whisky, the twenty-five-year-old Yamazaki Whisk then after, he spoke, still without glancing to the man behind him.

"Can you see the paper on the table? Read my instructions." He said commanded and heard footsteps approaching towards his executive table and he knew the man was now reading his written order.

"Hold on, by sending a direct visible trap so we can lure them?" The man asked him after processing what was on the paper.

"Yes, since I am to each his own in a deeper sense of purpose," he replied in a deep tone of voice and now, turning his head towards him, then he walked outside from his library while his assistant following him.

"But I don't get it at all, it's quite confusing."

"Just do what I exactly said and the rest will follow," then a fiendishly smile formed on his lips when he turned his back while descending from the stairs without looking back to the man while the scent of his exquisite fragrance from mixture of sandalwood, sharper with spice were notably left behind until he gently caressed his shiny jet black hair, then he fixed the collar of his high-end brand black suit which was showing about his status symbol in the society. Things were now getting interesting, who have thought almost two decades ago he was just nobody and wanderer of every notorious suburb? Then he smiled and continued until he reached the state of the art and double high ceiling lounge room and commanded one of his staff to summon his driver since it is the date of every month that he need to visit a place and he vowed to fulfill the once a month to do to pay his respect.

The secluded residence was adorned by fence which was high enough as a fortress to cover the vicinity while inside were several tall pine trees and expensive ornamental plants then there was a statue of cherubin in the middle of fountain area across the vast garden. While the man after visiting a certain place, he was now standing in front of the garden and then he looked up to the shining moonlight bathed the quiet place in a peaceful glow then he began to speak.

"It may sound overused but there is no way that I could think as an alternative to this but in every fairytale story, making a wish from main character or regardless of the role is something that we should always consider and to look forward as well. But basically, there was a point in my life that I made a wish for myself while staring at starry night sky and that was a sole wish of mine that every human being shouldn't reach the adult stage," then he paused for a while and walked slowly towards the nearby oakwood table then grabbed a piece of smoke from silver case and saw his personal assistant took the lighter next to it and lit the cigarette for him.

"Thank you," he mentioned after his first puffed and the smoke was getting thinner until it completely dissipated in front of them.

Then the man just nodded and was still confused of what he heard but he was patiently waiting for his boss to continue about the profound thought, and he can't even look at him while looking at the high fortress of residence which was covered in well maintained vine until he realised his boss started to continue.

"When humans reach a certain stage in life, they evolve, beginning with a dramatic shift in perspective due to the intelligence they have acquired. Consequently, past and present experiences blend into one. The saddest truth, which we cannot deny, is that we might become ruthless to assert dominance over those we dislike, but I am not like that. For me, it is about vengeance, and I don't care about the material wealth, since it can be acquired by any skilled thinker and this, is about personal by destroying or even killing if necessary—to ease my grief. Since the fire requires oxygen to sustain it's presence," he concluded coldly, extinguishing his cigarette in the ashtray.

The trusted man was in shocked and awe at the same time, it took almost fifteen years of his service to hear the certain duration of how the boss expressed his thought. He was now thinking about the caused of his master's wrath, as the revelation was slowly unfolding as day goes by.

Osmond felt a mystifying happiness from within upon waking up earlier than six in the morning. Then he reached the switch button of lampshade to turn it off, and he got up from bed for some stretching before he walked towards the window then saw the dark grey sky still filled with stars until they were replaced by crepuscular rays when he looked at it again after he changed his clothes and he smiled genuinely as he remembered about the turning of events from yesterday that he never expected as he planned. For now, what really matters to him it brought genuine happiness that he felt that even words can never simply expressed.

As he got out from his room, Osmond quickly gaze to the particular room, and smiled upon realising of had happened last night when they got out. Even there was no usual thing, like a confirmation of exchanging words that they love each other. The experience was valid enough for him to conclude certain event.

"Morning son, you woke up too early," Celine mentioned to Osmond as she saw him walking to the kitchen.

"Morning! Yeah mom, and also to check some CCTV footage," Osmond responded while he was getting a cup to prepare his coffee. "Where is dad?" He asked.

"He went to our neighbour to help his mate when went here to ask his assistance, it seemed like a kind of emergency," Celine replied to her son.

"Okay," Osmond answered, suddenly recalling a recent conversation with his father about expanding the farm. "Oh, by the way, I transferred some funds to your account last night," he said.

"Why?" Celine inquired, her eyes reflecting her curiosity as she looked at her son.

"Dad mentioned a few days ago that he was considering expanding our farm, though he hadn't specified a timeline," Osmond explained while moving towards the table with his coffee.

"Why did you do that? As far as I know, the expansion is planned for next year, not this year," Celine replied.

"It's alright, Mom. At least the money will be ready if needed," he reassured her before taking a sip of his coffee.

"Okay, thank you, Osmond," Celine expressed her gratitude, reaching to hold her son's hand to show her appreciation for him.

Osmond smiled as he felt how he lucky he was, when his mind gathering all the events happened to him. He couldn't ask for more.

"You're always welcome mom. I did what is the right thing to do for my family," he answered.

"Alright, I'll leave you for now, since I need to sort things from the back," Celine said towards Osmond.

"Alright mom, as I am gonna start now to check the CCTV records," he answered to his mother, while he was about to stood up from his chair when he heard Alex's voice, calling his name and he walked towards her room.

"Morning Alex!" He greeted the woman that changed his life.

"Morning too Mr. Brave!" Alex said to Osmond.

Meanwhile, Osmond smiled as what Alex called him. Then, when he reached Alex hand to hold her, Alex started to speak.

"Would you mind to bring me breakfast here?" Alex requested.

"Of course, I am happy to do that," Osmond replied then he smiled at Alex, but his smile waned when he saw Alex bit her lower lip.

"Are you alright?" He asked, then Alex shook her head, looking at him.

"What happened?"

"My feet are sore," Alex replied.

Reflecting on the events of the night before, Osmond realised it was the reason why Alex was feeling under the weather today.

"I'm truly sorry for that, Alex," he said with a regret while still looking at her.

With a reassuring smile, Alex gently placed her right hand over Osmond's lips, preventing him from taking on the blame.

"Alright, stay here for the entire day, and I'll be back here with your food and pain reliever tablets for your faster recovery," then all along Alex kissed him on his lips, and he quickly gathered himself to reciprocate the kiss and hugged her dearly.

The morning went well, while Martin and Celine was worried about Alex, while his dad suggested to Osmond about calling his uncle who owns a chiropractic clinic but Alex refused when Osmond asked her.

It was now twelve past thirty, Osmond's and his parents were in the kitchen clearing the table after lunch, while Alex were in her room having a conversation with her father using Osmond's phone.

"Thanks, dad, for calling earlier," Alex said warmly as she chose clothes to wear for their upcoming trip to the supermarket. That morning, after her shower, she had noticed she was running low on personal essentials.

"Yes, since your mother and I have important matters to discuss with some business associates soon. So, I decided to call thirty minutes earlier," Enrique replied.

"So, how are things?" She asked.

"Same as usual but I can manage things. Anyway, I had a quick chat with your best friend Elissandra today since she was at the hotel with her parents, where we had our meeting this morning."

"Really? That's great to hear, dad! How is she?"

"She's doing well, and I was pleased that she was honest with me when I asked her about you," Enrique continued, his tone turning more serious.

"What do you mean, dad?" She asked, feeling a wave of confusion.

"She told me you've been so dedicated to finishing college and that you've never turned your attention to any man who showed interest in you. Thanks for never failing me," Enrique concluded with a simple, satisfied smile.

Her father's words, based on what he had heard from her best friend, rendered her speechless and uncomfortable, especially as she already felt certain feelings towards Osmond, and she was sure the man was the same to her. She bit her lower lip, then she decided quickly to change the subject; it was the reason of everything why she ended up in Queensland.

"Dad, any update from the General?"

"Still nothing, but we're doing the best we can since I'm also working on my own way to uncover the mystery," her dad replied.

"Whatever it is I'm happy to hear that dad since I can't wait any longer to be back there," she said. However, at the back of her mind, she felt differently.

"Your mom and I feel the same way, and I won't mind doing extra things at all just to make sure this case will be finally settled. Oh your mother is coming, it's her turn. Take care there and I love you."

"Alright dad, I love you too," she answered, until she heard her mother's voice from the other line.

"Hello honey!"

"Hi mom!" She greeted her mother.

"I am very happy to hear your voice."

"Same here mom," she replied.

"Anyway, I was so glad that your father mentioned to me that he did something to make sure this situation will be finally end, and we can't wait to have you back here," Evangeline told Alex.

"Yeah mom, I am glad as well that would be a big help," she answered, but the emotion was now starting to flood her mind.

"I am happy about what Elissandra told your dad, but I don't really mind at all if you are single or not," Evangeline said, "but I told your dad we must go for a vacation when this thing is over which he agreed," Evangeline finally added.

"That's great to hear mom!" She said, then she was about to say further when she heard a voice from the background that her mother was now needed for the meeting.

"I am sorry dear; I have to go now since this is matter and they need me there, take care there okay? I love you."

"It's okay mom, I love you too and keep safe," she mentioned before the line was cut and she put Osmond's phone on bedside table. She sighed, while recalling of what her dad's mentioned to her, and she disregarded the thought. She's an adult to make a decision for herself, until she realised one thing that she can't deny.

Her duty, as an heiress.

Twenty Four

Decision Behind the Truth

When Alex woke up at a quarter past eight in the morning, she was still in bed but was thinking about the decision she had finally made last night after mentioning to Osmond that her feet were now getting better. She gladly felt this improvement, a reason for her to take the first step to fulfill her responsibility. Even though it was painful for her now, it would surely be worse if they became an official couple. She rushed to get out of bed and left the bedroom. Before putting her plan into action, she scanned her surroundings. Upon reaching the living area, she looked at the porch and saw Osmond busy washing the Jeep outside. Then she headed to check the kitchen area, in case one of her bodyguard's parents was there. When the coast was clear, she walked back quietly to carry out her plan.

She cautiously opened the door, aware that it wasn't in her nature to invade someone's personal space like this. However, she felt compelled to search for something specific—a sum of money that could finance her trip back to Melbourne. As she surveyed the room, she noted the white-painted walls, a glass window draped with dark blue curtains, and a queen-sized bed also in white. To the right of the bed, a bright wooden study table held a closed laptop and several books. On the left stood a dark wooden coat rack where black track pants and brown shorts were hung. She quickly checked the pockets, hoping to find cash, but was disheartened to discover the track pants were empty. In the pocket of the brown shorts, she found something, but it was only five dollars and a few dollar coins. She suddenly felt annoyed, Osmond was such a cunning man. She looked around and saw the black wallet on the bedside table. She approached it and inspected what was inside that could be useful, but she sighed when she found out that it was empty except for a few cards. Even if she had the chance to get the ATM card that her dad gave to Osmond, it was useless; she didn't even know the password. Suddenly, she felt sadness and sighed. Hence, she opted to go out to avoid being caught. She didn't want that to happen since, for sure, Osmond would instantly know her plan. Thus, she went to the kitchen, and the first thing she noticed on the table was the white note next to the food that the bodyguard had prepared for her that morning.

She quickly grabbed the paper to read the note.

"Good morning, Miss Alex! Enjoy your breakfast, and please tell me if you are well now. We should prepare ourselves later in the afternoon, since I am going to take you to a place that I am certain will make you feel better."

And she slowly put the piece of paper back on the table, as she processed a well-planned at back of her mind when she started to eat her breakfast.

Outside the house, after Osmond finally washed the Jeep, he recalled an event he couldn't fully comprehend. He sighed as the memories flooded his mind.

It was supposed to be a normal walk in the woods for the both of them. He promised Isabelle that he would show her the waterfalls. He was carrying a picnic basket with all her favourite snacks; they could even hear the water falling even from where they were walking. The trek went smoothly, even after they alighted his bicycle which he left by the road. He wanted Isabelle to breath in the wonder and serenity of the trail towards the falls. Had he known it would end in tragedy, he wouldn't have pursued with picnic date.

It was already late in afternoon, the sky turned into different hues of orange and auburn when they decided to pack up and go home. They already left the trail and was nearing his bicycle by the road when the two men came out of a grey car parked on the other side of the road. He just thought they were planning on trek towards the falls. However, red flags went off his thoughts since it was almost dusk. But he was all too-late to realise what was happening, everything transpired within just minutes.

"No! Let me go! Please! No!" Isabelle's voice rang in his mind. If only he could do something that time to stop the two kidnappers, while the man in brown chino pants grabbed a red handkerchief from his pocket and aggressively placed on Isabelle's mouth and a few seconds, his poor childhood bestfriend passed out.

"Isabelle!" He screamed as loud as he can while trying to resist against the bulky guy from behind and he didn't expect the next thing. The guy behind him punched his stomach using a brute force and the pain he felt was so agonising, taking his breath.

"P-please, no! Let her go! " Osmond shouted again, and the ruthless man punched him again and again until he couldn't bear the pain as he slowly fell down on the ground while holding his breath. The two men walked away, with the man in brown chino pants carrying his precious bestfriend.

He closed his eyes in tears in the middle of the road after watching the grey car drove away with Isabelle. The sound of nature was unbearable. The water from the falls and the birds from trees were singing in pain and anger as they witnessed an awful and tragic event from two innocent teenagers as the image of vehicle slowly faded from his sight when he glanced at it again.

Osmond shook his head as he recalled the finality of the event, the last time he saw Isabelle. It was the reason that he was now a secret agent.

Just then, his phone beeped. He grabbed it to check the notification, and upon seeing what it was, Osmond was in disbelief, with disappointment on his face. Alex invaded his room, which was a big mistake, as he had installed a mini spy camera in the corner of his cabinet.

He walked inside their house and saw Alex putting the dishes in the dishwasher. He had a sudden thought about what had happened over the past two days. Was it real, or was she just trying to gain his trust to carry out her plan to escape?

"You don't have to do that," he said firmly, Alex had broken his trust, and remained himself calm as he was trying not to show about how he really feels in front of her.

"Oh, it's okay. I can manage since it is just a simple thing to do," Alex replied. "Anyway, thanks for the note and for the lovely breakfast. Actually, I can walk now, so we can go out later as you mentioned. What time we will leave?"

"That's great to hear, Alex! I will let you know once everything is settled," then he approached the woman and held her hand, he had already made a plan and looked at her as normally as he could, pretending that nothing had happened. Surely, at any time, the possibility of an unwanted event might become a potential risk for his duty. After she entered the room to carry out her plan, he was already prepared. When they arrived, he took all the dollar bills from his wallet and kept them in his safety box, keeping an eye on any potential source. She must have no access to any kind of useful way to break any protocols.

"I suggest that you should head to the room now as I have to continue my task," he politely requested, as he started to caress Alex's right hand softly while looking at it.

"I can help you with that if you want," Alex offered, then she smiled while thinking of what she had done earlier. She looked at him, her mind gathering thoughts about the conversation with her dad, which led her to decide to leave before things became complicated for them.

"It's alright. You must take some extra time to rest your feet, and we must be very sure that it will be okay when we leave this afternoon," he replied with confidence, making it clear that there was no reason for her to decline his request.

"Alright, Osmond, just in case you need assistance, just let me know," Alex replied, her eyes on him. Osmond's eyes were intently looking at her, without her knowing the reason behind his gaze.

After lunch, Celine spoke with Ms. Alex, informing her that she and her husband would be gone for two days using the Jeep, as Osmond had asked his parents for a favour. Someone's life could be in danger if they don't devise a plan to prevent Alex from escaping. He had already contacted the General, who agreed when he asked for backup and requested a certain colleague whom he could fully trust.

Cedrick McKain was inside the convenience store to buy something to eat and drink. He really wanted to take off his black bomber jacket but opted not to do so. Then he browsed the variety of drinks inside the chiller, and before he grabbed a soda, Cedrick glanced at his digital wristwatch and saw it was already half past eleven in the evening. It had taken him long hours to finish his job for the day even though it was not a mission. Nonetheless, it was about time for him to relax that night when he got home. He was thinking about what to watch on Netflix, until he noticed in his peripheral vision that two men were about to enter the convenience store. Both were wearing caps and jackets, and he initially felt something strange about the two. The impending danger was so unappealing to him that he opted to close the chiller's door and took a position in an aisle to hide himself so that he could carry out his plan. He was not a highly skilled secret agent for nothing; he knew the type of people with bad intentions and those who weren't, and he was right. One of the two men went back to the entrance to make sure there would be no one inside the convenience store except for the female cashier. The coincidence that he was there? Hell, that was a big mistake. It had been a couple of weeks since he had an interesting hand-to-hand combat scene, and it was with Agent Gomez. Until he had a mysterious encounter from recent event, the unknown attacker. And shifted his attention to the criminals, these two must be put in their place, and he carefully assessed the whole situation.

He stayed hidden until one of the men declared a robbery and pointed a gun at the cashier, who started to panic and scream. The man instructed her to shut up, which she immediately obeyed, while the other guy, the lookout, suddenly gave a right hook to an old man on the face who was about to enter the convenience store, rendering him unconscious. He dragged the poor old man inside. Cedrick looked at the man who knocked down the latter, who held a knife. He carried out a concrete plan, then took a can of Heinz beans from the shelf of canned goods and played with it by his right hand before he came out to reveal himself.

"Hey boys, what's up? You two are jobless at the moment and decided to commit a criminal act tonight?" He asked casually and simply smiled at them.

"Oi, I thought there was no one inside? There is one bloke here!" The man loudly said while holding the knife pointed at him.

Then the other man with the gun answered while still looking at him.

"Maybe he was just hiding! How dare you to show up? Trying to be a hero of the night?" The second man said boldly, his gun still pointed at the speechless cashier, who was about to scream again, but the man cut her off immediately.

"Don't you dare scream again! Or else, every piece of your brain will scatter on the floor in a split second!" Warned by man to the helpless lady, and she nodded.

Cedrick remained silent and composed, choosing not to react to what he saw and heard. He opted against using his gun, instead focusing on another plan. Holding the can, he needed intense concentration to aim at a specific part of the criminal and avoid causing harm to others. By his calculated movement, he threw the can of beans at the gunman's head. Caught off guard, the man failed to dodge the incoming can, resulted to knocked him unconsciously to the floor, while

Cedrick kicked the gun away to prevent the other man from retrieving it. He then moved rapidly towards the final threat: a man wielding a knife, who stared at him intently. Taking a deep breath, Cedrick cleared his throat and, with a determined smile, prepared to confront him. He was eager to conclude the ordeal, looking forward to finally relaxing in his bedroom.

"I am not scared of you!" The man yelled, attempting to stab him in the neck. Cedrick simply stepped back to avoid the blade, facing a rapid barrage of strikes aimed at various parts of his body. Remaining calm, Cedrick easily dodged the attacks; his reflexes were unparalleled. As far as he knew, only one person could best him in hand-to-hand combat: Osmond Gomez, but now two of them, *"The unknown aggressor."* Challenging him would be suicidal. Suddenly, he noticed the man pause briefly before launching another attack. Cedrick quickly devised a plan—a swift, concise dodge—before executing one of his signature moves: a powerful rear horse kick. It struck the man's stomach with enough force to blow as a devastating move ; the attacker clutched his chest, gazed at Cedrick in intense pain, struggled to breathe, and then collapsed unconsciously on the floor. Cedrick merely glanced at the last opponent, having defeated him effortlessly, and remained unfazed by the two attempted robberies.

"Amateur and silly robberies," he said to himself and looked at the stunned woman, who was literally in awe at witnessing an action scene usually can be seen only in movies.

"It's okay, you're finally safe from these culprits," he smiled at her, his dimples appearing on both cheeks. These special physical attributes were always his best asset, enhancing his facial attractiveness. He then casually walked back to the beverage section, grabbed a soda from the chiller and two sandwiches near the cashier area, and proceeded to the counter to pay for the items.

"Wow, that was unbelievable! You quickly knocked down those two criminals," the cashier exclaimed. He chose not to reply, instead

Cedrick instructed her to call the police to handle the incident. After tapping his card on the EFTPOS machine, he casually left. Once in his car, he recalled someone who made him smile and eagerly anticipated an event he had been waiting for, then his phone rang. He retrieved it from the pocket of his fitted black denim jeans and was surprised to see the caller's codename before answering.

"Hey, Agent Gomez! What can I do for you?" He asked cheerfully while fastening his seatbelt. He glanced at the streetlights lining the city road and heard the wailing of approaching police sirens. The two robbers were surely about to be arrested.

The caller hesitated for a moment before explaining the reason for the call. Suddenly, his heart pounded so hard that he struggled to comprehend.

"Agent McKain, this is urgent. I need your backup as soon as possible. Something came up earlier today, and you're the only one I can truly trust with this," Osmond said clearly on the other line.

"OK. Affirmative," he quickly replied.

"What's your ETA?"

"I'll be there tomorrow evening but expect a surprise," he said and ended the call. He smiled, realising that fate had provided him with an unexpected opportunity of what he truly desired.

"Finally," he thought with a mysterious satisfaction before he started the engine, its quad exhaust roaring, and his car disappeared into the night.

It was already half past ten in the evening, Osmond was getting some fresh air outside of wooden gate, and all along, he felt something and by trusting his gut, Osmond swiftly managed to dodge the incoming unknown object to him and until he saw a piece of marble on the ground.

He stayed calm while his senses were still heightened by anticipating the second attempt, and without words, he certainly knew where the object came from. And he walked towards to the darker side that filled with tropical trees, until someone spoke up.

"Agent Gomez, without any words you never fail to amaze me," Osmond smiled when he heard the particular voice before he speak.

"Thanks for coming Agent McKain, I know it was you then I am glad the General agreed when I requested you as my backup," he gratefully said and hugged Cedrick after they shook hands and saw a medium size of backpack as they now both walking towards the gate.

"Very timely, since I am just done with my latest mission and I have a maximum of thirty days off," Cedrick answered and saw Osmond nodded gently as a reply.

"Anyway, I want to eat a light snack," Cedrick mentioned playfully.

"Sure, I was thinking about that so let's eat together," Osmond said as he opened the gate and followed Cedrick inside.

"Anyway, if you don't mind asking, what was the reason?" Cedrick asked Osmond as he placed the plate with Cornish pasties.

"She invaded my room yesterday morning. And from that event, I knew her initial plan," Osmond answered as he opened the fridge and grabbed the two cans of beers.

Cedrick shook his head, before he laughed at Osmond.

"I know. She's Margarette Alexandria, she is capable of doing such thing despite of my ability, I sworn to her dad that I would always ensure her safety, no matter what. That's why I asked your help," Osmond ended his answer to Cedrick as he put the can of beer in front of him.

"Thanks mate!" Cedrick said, as he opened the can of beer.

"No worries! Cheers mate!" Osmond exclaimed.

And Cedrick remembered Ms. Alex and opted to ask Osmond about her.

"Anyway, how is she?"

"She is fine. Probably she's now sleeping," Osmond replied, as he recalled before he went out he checked her room from the backyard.

"Okay, does she know about this? I mean, having me here as her backup bodyguard?" He asked Osmond and took a piece of Cornish, the traditional snack inspired by the recipe brought to South Australia by Cornish miners then grab a bite.

Osmond sighed, then took a sip of beer.

"Actually, no," he answered. He was now thinking of his reason, why the sudden of having Cedrick as back up. Would he tell the truth that he knew her plan?

"So, that would be a huge question from her when she wakes up tomorrow seeing me here," Cedrick told Osmond.

"Don't fret mate, I can manage this," he answered Cedrick.

"Alright mate, I have no doubt about that," Cedrick said, as he took another sip of beer. And he remembered about what he had encountered previously. A deadly duel with shadowy aggressor.

While Osmond was observing, he noticed Cedrick retreating into deep contemplation. Given his familiarity with Cedrick's demeanour, Osmond was certain something serious was on his mind.

"Mate is there something wrong?" He asked while looking at him.

Cedrick took a deep breath while looking at his mate before he spoke.

"After completing my first solo mission with success, I faced a life-threatening encounter. An unknown assailant attacked, and if that shadowy figure had intended to end my life that night, I wouldn't be speaking to you now. What was thrown at me turned out to be a pure white powder, likely used to distract or possibly warn me," Cedrick revealed to Osmond, shaking his head.

Osmond was shocked by Cedrick's confession. Despite knowing the man's capabilities, the way Cedrick detailed the confrontation allowed Osmond to evaluate the situation. Suddenly, Alex came to mind, and Osmond's heart began to race.

"Cedrick?" He asked.

"Yes, mate?" Cedrick replied, bewildered by Osmond's worried expression, as if Osmond himself had faced the highly skilled attacker.

"Are you certain you weren't followed?" Osmond asked seriously.

"Absolutely sure. I arrived three hours before coming here," Cedrick reassured, though concern still lingered on Osmond's face as he looked at him.

"Alright, as you've said," Osmond replied and started to gather his thoughts about Cedrick's encounter with the mysterious, skilled attacker. Knowing his mate's capabilities and skills, he was now sure of one thing: the attacker planned it well, and having this kind of confidence to duel with Agent McKain was undeniable proof. But what was the purpose? He initially concluded that it could possibly be connected with his client, Ms. Alex, but he dismissed the thought since it was Cedrick's encounter after his mission. The possibility of his thought was only a way of ensuring Alex's safety. He inhaled deeply and slowly shook his head, until he remembered what he saw, trying to collect any hint of a reason for such an act. Yet he found nothing, as he had never seen anything suspicious about Alex's behaviour, and everything seemed normal unless she used tactics against him. He realised that sooner or later, Alex would change how she treated him, and he felt uneasy about making a decision, but he had to. That was his top priority at all times. He finally opted to become formal starting tomorrow so he could focus on her as his client, to show his duty even if it could cost him something valuable, which could possibly be taken from him and the fact once she discovered that Cedrick would be her second bodyguard, she could definitely assess that he knew her plan.

Twenty Five

The Good Samaritan

It was scorching hot afternoon and the summer season has just started a few weeks ago while the place was like a ghost town with one way road and several wild plants and gum trees to each side but the early effect of hot season was already visible on their leaves until a teenage boy in school uniform with backpack appeared from the corner of an empty street. However, there was an oddity in him the way he walked until he entirely stopped to scanned the area only to find that there was nobody to help him until he saw a good spot and sat down on pavement with shade followed by disentangling the school bag from his back and he touched a certain part of his abdomen by right hand and he initially closed his eyes and took a deep breath. It disappeared earlier when he left the school, but the pain was there again and made him realised about "survival" from the unkindness of summer's heat, he was totally alone while dealing with the ache in his stomach then he glanced again to his surrounding and everything was spinning due to dizziness.

"Please stop, not now," he softly said in agony, as two tiny drops of tears slowly fell from his eyes onto his cheeks and he promptly wiped them away to lessen his feelings of self-pity and tried to be tough to endure the pain and eventually, his mind processed the reality of the unwanted event, which could make his feelings even more painful.

"No, I am not gonna cry again," he bravely said while taking a short period of rest before he could resume his walkway back home. He slowly moved his right hand to grab the bottle of water from his bag to keep him hydrated and he felt a spark of relief when he was done drinking but the pain was still there which he tried to ignore and instantaneously, his attention was shifted when he heard the sound of incoming vehicle that caught his attention until the black sedan finally stopped in front of him then the driver alighted from the car followed by a man from the passenger side which wearing a decent attire from a white polo shirt, black jeans, and paired with black top sider then he and his companion had a quick glance before they approached the helpless young lad.

"Are you OK young man?" Asked by the latter while approaching and he did not hear any response to his query. Instead, the boy slowly shook his head while looking at him and bend down his head then he walked faster to help the young boy and followed by the boy's quick reaction of right hand from preventing his intention to him. Then the juvenile finally spoke "don't get near me! I don't know you!" The good samaritan stopped for a couple of seconds but not of what he heard but to asses the place, and no one was there to help the poor lad except from him and his trusted companion. And now he was wondering how long the boy got stuck in a terrible place while he was in pain, and he resumed from walking before uttered a calm but enough for him to convince about his pure intention to help.

"This place is not safe for you since you are not well and needs help so that's what I am doing now," he said as his skin felt the unfriendly dryness of wind from heat of summer until he saw the unexpected turn of event. The poor young one passed out. He swiftly moved to prevent the young lad from another misfortune as his two hands were lucky enough to rescue the boy.

"We must get to our place in the right time," he told to his companion while he was carrying the boy and walked towards the vehicle.

"Yes, sir, I'll do my best to get there," the driver responded as he opened the car's backseat. He watched as his employer gently positioned the young man comfortably and secured the seatbelt around him. In a rush, he closed the passenger door, and both he and his employer moved to the front of the car. The sound of the exhaust roared to life, then gradually faded as the driver sped off as fast as he could.

As he opened his eyes, the first thing he saw was a dirty white coloured ceiling and he slowly shifted his gaze to the left area of the room then there was a two huge windows with a white curtain and two brown tub chairs in the corner but in a split of second, a certain thing came up to his mind that he was in unfamiliar room but have seen an old portrait hanging in the wall which he instantly ignore and tried to recall what had happened and how he ended up in the strange room when he was having a terrible experience in an empty street until a few moments passed, his mind was unpliable enough to remember things. He sighed and was about to got up from the bed but it never happened when he heard a sound and saw the oakwood door opened followed by three strangers, an old woman in white uniform and two men in their mid- twenties in a decent attire but tried to control himself just to refrain from making a scene like panicking or shouting but out of the blue, he finally remembered perfectly about a certain person who tried to approach him and what exactly happened from the time they saw him sitting on the pavement until he collapsed.

"How do you feel now?" A question from unknown man while approaching him and finally stood in front of bed when he stopped while intently looking at him.

"I-am f-feeling okay now," he replied. "Thank you," and he gazed to the huge windows as he started to feel about being uncomfortable with unknown people in front of him while the blast of air conditioner intensified what he felt.

"You're welcome and glad to hear that you're totally fine now and the good thing was, just a tummy's normal pain as what the doctor's said."

He can't utter a single word to the person who rescued him while he was looking at them and saw how the man simply smiled to the old woman then nodded after but the way he ended his words made him to feel about being genuine and the ambiance in the room started to feel lighter unlike a few moments ago. Then he saw how they silently staring at him which he totally ignored since the feeling of a great admiration towards the man's gesture standing in front of him while the two of his companions were now both sitting in tub chairs but in a matter of seconds, he realised something and took courage for himself to say so.

"Can I go home now? I think it's getting late," he casually requested then removed the white blanket were covering half of his body, but the man suddenly stopped him.

"You haven't got a proper rest yet and don't be in hurry since we can drop you off to your house and explain to your parents what happened to you," the man calmly replied to him before turned the gaze to his trusted companion.

"Please bring his food here," he said casually.

"Absolutely sir," then the man stood up from the chair and started to walk until he completely out of the room.

Then the man returned his gaze to the young boy in bed then smiled at him and let several of seconds to passed for the boy by adjusting himself until he feels comfortable with everyone in the room.

"Don't worry you are safe and in good hands, put all your worries aside and I am sorry if I am not allowing you now to go home yet," he gently replied to him but also he made sure to himself the way how he executed his words was enough for the boy to stay with them.

"And why not?" The boy replied shortly to him with curiosity in his eyes while they were exchanging of glances but he took a short deep breath without taking his eyes off from him until he heard a particular sound from the boy's stomach and an amusing smile formed on his lips but he gradually gathered everything when he saw how the boy responded to nature's call. Hence, he managed himself that don't carry away with it by asking him. Instead, he let him freely on his own how to respond while his hands were both casually situated in his two pockets and in a matter of split second, he started to say things about the latter's question.

"Well, there are things that quite hard to say but at the same time easy to do as well. So, my apology if I couldn't answer your question since it might be one of the two could trigger something," he seriously replied to the likely young lad and followed by silence inside of the room and after a while, he saw in his peripheral vision that his trusted man was now walking back to the guest room from kitchen carrying the antique golden tray and he silently opted to approach his trusted employee.

"Let me handle that, please, since he is my guest," he politely requested. The man nodded, handed the tray to him, and their eyes met in silent acknowledgment. Offering his usual smile as a gesture of gratitude, he glanced at the tray while taking his time to carefully examine the variety of foods on it, ensuring everything he had instructed earlier was complete and well-prepared. From spiced chickpeas and oven-baked sweet potato fries to skewered melon balls, honey-roasted peaches with Greek yogurt and granola, and hummus with carrot sticks—everything was meticulously checked. Finally, he inspected a beverage in a blue cup with a silver lid and straw. He had personally selected the ingredients for the fruit smoothies: fresh blueberries, strawberries, frozen bananas, Greek yogurt, and a splash of milk, designed to refresh the teenage guest after a dreadful event. The selection of a healthy meal was more than adequate to satisfy his empty stomach.

Meanwhile, the juvenile was in awe when he saw the selection of food on tray in front of him as he was so starving. But in a matter of few seconds, his glance turned to the right side of the room and a particular thing caught his eyes again which was the old portrait painting in canvass, and he examined carefully what he was looking now for the second time until someone broke the silence inside of room.

"You must eat now to regain your strength pal," offered by man while still holding the tray and came over to the bed then he sat down then sighed but managed to smile at the boy who seemed shy to eat.

"Or maybe you wanted me to feed you like a baby?" He playfully asked and was about to do his playful antic, until the boy managed himself to reply quickly.

"I can eat on my own Mr."

Then he smiled while slowly putting the tray on the table next to bed.

"Sure, but if there is anything else you want just let me know," he casually offered while he was looking to the young man who's started from eating the oven-baked sweet potato fries and after a few bites he saw how the boy quickly grabbed the beverage as it seemed he was so thirsty then he heard the particular sound.

"*Slurp!*" But then it did not end there, and he heard the same sound again which made him smile by the young man's demeanor and it was a pleasant sight for him then he felt an urge about a quick glanced to the specific object on the wall but he dismissed his thought so it could not affect his job later after he drop off the young lad to his home.

"Thank you Mister," he heard and his gaze went to the young lad and saw how his eyes were grateful was for his aid.

"You're welcome. I did the rightful thing when I saw you," he replied gently. But suddenly, there was an urge from inside of him to say which was usual for everyone.

"A piece of advice for you as a student, keep it up and whatever dreams you have, as long it is your heart's desire then chase that. Perhaps, your own thing," and he ended his words firmly, while saw how the teenager nodded with a smile as an approval then he continued sipping his smoothies before he answered with salutation while smiling at the man in front of him.

"Yes sir! And I promise that!"

"Great to hear," he joyfully replied and approached with a smile, then he offered a fist bump, which the latter reciprocated. They started to talk about random things, and he sincerely shared his perspective on what he heard from the young lad. They both got along well, filled with laughter. Until they happily dropped off the teenage guy at his place, but he and his driver opted not to step out of the car. And it didn't end there; he discreetly did something he felt was the appropriate way to help without discussion when things were revealed. For sure, the life of a certain one would be changed forever once the young man discovered what he had put inside his backpack.

Twenty Six

Exclusive Preview of Book Two

Osmond was inside a restaurant, sitting in the corner at the end of Reine & La Rue, anticipating a meeting with someone that early evening. They had arranged to meet at six o'clock, and he arrived thirty minutes early. Despite having seen each other just the day before at his place—a heartfelt reunion that nearly brought him to tears—he clung to the promise she had made to meet again that evening. He glanced at his watch; it was ten minutes to six then he let his left hand rested in his jeans pocket, brimming with excitement, while his right hand lightly tapped his phone on the table. He kept his eyes on the entrance, watching as everyone turned their attention to a stunning blonde woman who entered the elegant restaurant. She wore a knee-length red dress with black high heels, and the golden strap of her classic black Chanel bag sparkled under the chandelier's light then a waitstaff member in corporate attire approached Isabelle politely, clearly about to ask the usual question and saw how she elegantly reciprocates the waiter's gesture, until their gaze met.

Osmond smiled when he saw Isabelle was now approaching together with busser and quickly stood up to hug her. Then he pulled out a chair for his childhood bestfriend.

"Thanks," Isabelle said casually, flipping her wavy blonde hair. "What time did you arrive?"

Osmond smiled at her question. Should he tell the truth or choose to lie?

"To be honest, I arrived at five-thirty," he confessed, unable to take his eyes off his childhood best friend. Isabelle was even more beautiful than the night before, her straight hair now styled in soft waves.

"You look wonderful tonight," he complimented with a smile, his gaze still on her.

"Oh, thanks! You also look handsome and stylish," Isabelle expressed her gratitude, then smiled as she silently appreciating Osmond's overall look tonight. He was wearing a long-sleeve white polo shirt rolled up at the elbows, black fitted denim jeans paired with black leather topsiders, and his hair styled in a classic manner using wax.

Her radiant smile made Osmond's heart flutter. It was always a joy seeing her since their teenage days then especially now, catching up after all the time they had spent apart.

"So, how have you been since yesterday?" He asked, a playful tone in his voice. "Since we last spoke, of course," he added.

Isabelle laughed softly after settling into her chair with elegance. "It's been a whirlwind, as always. Work is relentless, but it feels good to unwind and catch up with you. I've missed our chats," Isabelle replied, but deep down in her mind was a certain wish of courage; then she dismissed the emerging emotion.

Osmond nodded, feeling a warmth of familiarity and comfort between them.

"I know the feeling. Life's been quite the ride, but moments like these remind me what really matters," their conversation flowed easily, like they hadn't spent years apart, beautifully wrapped in the glow of the evening. Osmond cherished these moments, basking in the serendipity of life bringing them back together in a corner of a beautiful restaurant at the end of Reine & La Rue.

Meanwhile, along St. Kilda Road, Alex and Cedrick were on their way to the CBD while pop music played, and the SUV's window was halfway opened. As usual, Alex was wearing a yellow turban and sunglasses. One and a half months to go before summer starts, and the sun was still up due to daylight saving.

"Alex, where would you want to eat?" Cedrick happily asked his friend after they bonded and went on a long drive earlier. Since it was twenty-five degrees, he saw how wind gently blew Alex's hair on her temporal point area.

"Well, I'm not sure yet, but I'll have a look on my phone," Alex replied.

"Okay, when you see something, you like, just tell me and we'll be there," he said as he was driving and after a minute, Alex gently locked the screen of her phone, as it was only an eyeshot away from him.

"I remember this, since I never tried the Reine & La Rue along Collins Street, let us go there," Alex said to him.

"Sure," Cedrick responded with a nod since anyone who's aware of the stunning former stock exchange would definitely know where Reine & La Rue is. Then after few minutes, Cedrick turned left two blocks away from Flinders Street train station then he went to the nearest parking space and they walked for a less than five minutes to get in the upscale French restaurant.

When Alex and Cedrick greeted by the security staff at the main entry, Alex felt an inexplicable feeling when a wait staff approached and escort them to their table. Unbeknownst to her, Cedrick had already spotted Osmond in a corner. Despite Osmond's back being turned, Cedrick recognised him, Osmond was engaged in conversation with a beautiful woman. Who is she? Cedrick wondered in his mind, but he needed to act before things got complicated. He sensed something was off and had a bad feeling for that early night.

"Alex, can we go somewhere else? To be honest, I'm not a huge fan of French cuisine," Cedrick suggested, hoping to coax Alex away from the area.

"Cedrick, we're here now. I promise you'll like my favourite French dish. Excuse me for a moment; I need to use the restroom," then Alex stood up and smiled at the waiter stationed by their table.

"Wait, hold on," but it was too late. Cedrick couldn't prevent Alex from heading to the restroom, so he followed her, feeling even more anxious.

As Alex walked, she noticed a man with his back turned, speaking with gorgeous blonde woman, and she paused for a while and carefully gazing at them which was not normal for her to do such thing but there was an urge within her.

"Wait, is that Osmond?" She asks herself wondered and squinting at the woman then her face seemed vaguely familiar, though she couldn't recall where she had seen her before. Just then she turned and saw Cedrick walking towards her.

"Come on, Alex, let's eat somewhere else," Cedrick trying to conceal his reaction from Alex since she had possibly recognised the man behind her.

"Hold on, Cedrick, as I am trying to recall about something," as she spoke, the memory she had been grasping at clicked into place. The woman from the photograph, it was Isabelle!

She suddenly felt a surge of anger. How long had her boyfriend lying to her? Without hesitation, she moved toward where they were sitting, but Cedrick grabbed her wrist and started to speak.

"Alex please, don't," he pleaded as he looked into her eyes.

"Do not worry, Cedrick. I know what I'm doing, and I won't cause any trouble," Alex shrugged off Cedrick's hand, but it remained firmly.

"Cedrick, please let go of me," her voice was firm as she forcefully removed Cedrick's grip on her arm. Then she quickly slipped into the bathroom; after composing herself, she exited the restroom.

Osmond's attention was drawn to a woman approaching— it was Margarette Alexandria! He could see the sharp gaze in her eyes, which only made him anxious as she moved closer to where he and Isabelle were sitting.

As she neared their table, the fear on Osmond's face became clear. An idea sparked in Alex's mind, she was a decent woman and has a reputation to maintain after all; so, she would not make a scene.

When she reached the table, Alex smiled mischievously before she spoke up.

"Oh hi Osmond! Good evening and what a small world!" She said with apparent decency in her tone.

As Cedrick watching the unfolding scene, unsure of how to react.

Osmond found himself at a loss for words in that moment. Amidst the countless restaurants in the city of Melbourne, why was Alex here? and who was she with? Mustering his courage, he finally spoke up.

"I'm good, Alex and how about you?" He concealed his shock and anxiety from Isabelle, who sat opposite him before he answered, "I am okay, who are you with?" Osmond replied calmly, hoping to diminish his bewilderment.

"I am with Cedrick, we were just spending time together for a few hours," Alex answered exuding with confidence as she responded to Osmond. Whatever their business for that night was entirely fine but lying to her was a different story and she was determined to keep her own matters private, casting a meaningful glance at Osmond.

As Alex spoke, Osmond saw Cedrick in a few steps away, which apparent the visibility of uncertainty of how to react. He waved and smiled at him , which Cedrick quickly reciprocated. Turning back to Alex, Osmond smiled that only heightened the tension—one that seemed forced and masked a deeper frustration.

Cedrick stepped closer, hoping to ease the emitting tension between Osmond and Alex it was the only solution he could devise, or perhaps he could suggest moving to another place to eat.

"Alex let's head back to our table; the waiter is waiting, and this is getting awkward," Cedrick whispered without getting near her.

Alex glanced at Cedrick.

"Alright, Osmond we are now heading back to our table. Enjoy your dinner," when Alex and Cedrick were about to leave, then the woman in red interrupted them from leaving.

"Wait, why don't you just join us? Since you're friends with Osmond, right?" Isabelle finally spoke.

Alex halted and turned to acknowledge her, offering a smile.

"Sure, thanks," as she returned to the table, deliberately sitting next to Isabelle to keep an eye on Osmond's expression, she looked at Cedrick, who seemed hesitant to sit with them.

"Cedrick, come take a seat," she smiled at him then shifted his gaze to Isabelle.

"By the way, I'm Alex and you are?" She extended her hand towards her, a smile plastered on her face, as concealing her feeling and emotion. Osmond's childhood bestfriend exuding a blonde goddess of beauty and a sense of sophistication, evident in her graceful demeanour.

"I'm Isabelle, his childhood bestfriend," Isabelle gracefully replied, then looked at the man in front of her, then at Alex. Ms. Margarette Alexandria, to be exact. *The famous heiress.*

"Oh, my bodyguard's childhood bestfriend, nice meeting you Isabelle," Alex replied then she and Isabelle shook hands, her gaze shifted to Osmond and Cedrick were next to each other and both silent. Though she wanted to ask about anything to Osmond or Isabelle, she just stayed calm and not do such thing, she chose to make the scene between them formal for that night.

Meanwhile, Cedrick's mind was now finally forming a conclusion.

"My mate's childhood bestfriend, damn! This is big trouble!" He said to himself and took his cell phone from the pocket of his slacks to pretend that the situation was not on him, and he made himself busy with device.

"Have you guys taken your order?" And Alex took the menu cards and gave them one by one to her three companions at the table and she gazed at Osmond eyes for a few seconds then turned her eyes to the menu.

"Not yet," Isabelle answered, then Alex just nodded, and she looked again at premium quality menu card that she was holding.

Osmond watched as Isabelle and Alex chatted, while right next to him was Cedrick focused intently on his phone, Osmond wished he could vanish, as everything would have already unfolded. He would significantly face challenges the next day and beyond, uncertain about how to explain his meeting with Isabelle to Alex..

And before anything else, thank you and finally you are done for reading the first book! While I don't have any remarkable tales to share, but only one thing could really define myself, and that is embracing my perfectly imperfect nature. Please follow my official Instagram account: *thisismarcusdizon* for the latest updates on my second book. Thank you all!